Cadence was already soaking in the frothy warm water when Adam joined her, dressed in loose swimming shorts. She could not help but admire the perfect cut of his body. He was lean and toned, with sculpted slabs of muscles right down to the hair-sprinkled flesh of his lower abdomen. She knew right away that it wasn't the heat from the tub or the red wine that caused her temperature to rise several degrees.

Adam settled into the seat beside hers, then pulled her over into his lap while his arms wrapped loosely around her waist. Her hands settled on the tops of his thighs. They sat like that for several minutes, both enjoying the pressure of the jets, the view, and the feel of the touching skin. Eventually, outside was pitch black and the only light in the solarium came from a low-voltage lamp near the French doors.

"It feels like we're the only people on the earth," Cadence said in a lazy voice.

Adam responded by placing a feathery kiss on her temple and she let her head fall back onto the top of his shoulder. He pressed his lips to the exposed length of her neck, his tongue brushing the skin and his teeth nipping at the tight tendons. She stifled a groan and dug her fingers into his legs. Then he sucked hard on her flesh and she let out a deep gasp.

"I've wanted to do this all day," he whispered into her ear.

Also by Sophia Shaw

DEPTHS OF DESIRE

SHADES AND SHADOWS

MOMENT OF TRUTH

SOPHIA SHAW

Kensington Publishing Corp.
http://www.kensingtonbooks.com

DAFINA BOOKS are published by

Kensington Publishing Corp.
850 Third Avenue
New York, NY 10022

All Kensington Titles, Imprints, and Distributed Lines are
available at special quantity discounts for bulk purchases for
sales promotions, premiums, fund-raising, and educational
or institutional use. Special book excerpts or customized
printings can also be created to fit specific needs. For details,
write or phone the office of the Kensington special sales
manager: Kensington Publishing Corp., 850 Third Avenue,
New York, NY 10022, attn: Special Sales Department,
Phone: 1-800-221-2647.

Dafina and the Dafina logo Reg. U.S. Pat. & TM Off.

ISBN-13: 978-0-7582-2028-8
ISBN-10: 0-7582-2028-6

First mass market printing: July 2007

10 9 8 7 6 5 4 3 2 1

Printed in the United States of America

ACKNOWLEDGEMENTS

I would like to thank everyone that has contributed to the development and research of this story.

Deon Clements, my big sister—thank you for helping me with the accounting and industry content. Your knowledge and ideas became the central theme for the plot.

Roland Jackson, my big brother—thank you for providing information on the systems and technical aspects of the story. You helped it all come together.

Natasha Jackson, Beverley Drummond and Trina Warias—my constant supporters and contributors! Once again, thank you for being there and dedicating your time to the process.

Jonathan Shaw, my husband, publicist, marketing specialist, event planner and so much more—thank you for your time, dedication and support. I love you.

Chapter 1

Adam Jackson checked his watch for the third time in an hour. It was still only a few minutes after eight PM. He tried to hide his boredom as he looked around at the forty or so people mingling at the dinner party. Finally, his eyes found the back of his friend, Yvonne Grant, who was the host of the party. She seemed to be having a great time as she laughed with the group she stood with.

Adam had known Yvonne since high school, and they had become very good friends over the years. She and her husband, Calvin, lived in a spacious bungalow in a suburb of Orlando, Florida, and this party was a long-overdue housewarming. Yvonne would not hear of Adam missing it, and insisted it was time he started to go out and meet people instead of working all the time.

So, there he was, leaning against the wall at the back of the dining room with only a glass of Jamaican white rum on ice to keep him company. Adam shook his cup, causing the ice to tinkle. He took another drink just as Calvin approached him.

"Hey, Adam."

"Hey," Adam replied with a slight nod. "How are things going?"

"Good, so far," Calvin told him. "How about you? Do you want another drink?"

"No, I'm good."

"Well, why don't you come outside? We're about to set up a game of dominoes and we need another player."

Adam shrugged.

"Sure, why not?" he accepted, then downed the rest of his rum before setting the empty glass on the dinner table.

Both men walked from the dining room toward the back entrance of the house. They passed Yvonne on the way, and she gave them an approving smile. It was obviously she who had pushed Calvin into coaxing Adam out of his solitude.

The game table was set up on the covered patio just off the family room. Adam and Calvin joined two of Calvin's friends, who were already seated. After quick introductions, the domino game got under way. The next couple of hours sped by, and several more men gathered outside to watch and occasionally play after each round.

By ten-thirty, the group was loudly laughing and slamming down domino bones with every play. Adam had just lost a match and was being subbed out. He gave up his chair and smiled at the ribbing from the other players, but was enjoying himself more than he had in a long time.

It was easily over two years since Adam had spent an evening hanging out with a group of guys. He was often invited out, particularly by Yvonne or his other friend, Vince, but always found some excuse, usually work. Now, he wondered why he had resisted.

As the next game got started, Adam stepped back into the house to use the bathroom. Yvonne walked over to him as soon as she saw him.

"Having fun?" she asked.

"I'm doing all right," he responded with a hint of a smile.

Yvonne's eyes immediately brightened, and she took his hand and gave it a quick squeeze.

"Do you want something to eat? I just put out some dessert."

"No thanks, I'm just going to run to the bathroom," he replied.

"Okay," she said, and squeezed his hand again before letting go.

The doorbell rang just as Adam turned into the powder room near the front of the house.

Cadence Carter let out a deep, calming breath as she waited outside her neighbors' door. She had just moved into the house across the street three weeks before, and had met Yvonne and Calvin earlier that week. They seemed like a nice couple, so Cadence had felt obligated to accept the invitation to their party. She really wasn't in the mood to socialize with strangers, but was committed to at least making an appearance. Her plan was to make an appropriate excuse to leave after about an hour.

The front door opened while Cadence was shifting her grip on a bottle of South African merlot. The sounds of classic R&B music and conversation spilled out into the warm Florida night.

"You made it," Yvonne said with a warm smile.

She was a tall, slender woman with a red-brown complexion.

"Hi, Yvonne, sorry I'm late," Cadence replied as she stepped inside.

"No worries, no worries."

"This is for you," Cadence added, handing Yvonne the bottle of red wine.

"How sweet, thank you. Come, let's get you something to drink."

Cadence followed Yvonne through the house and smiled politely as she passed groups of people chatting together, or swaying to the music. A bar was set up on a table near the kitchen, and Yvonne added Cadence's bottle to the other wine there.

"What would you like?" asked Yvonne.

"A beer is fine."

"Okay, I'll grab one out of the fridge."

While she waited for Yvonne, Cadence looked around at the house, which was quite similar to hers. The layout was pretty much the same. All the houses in the immediate area were built around ten years ago. A few were two-stories, but most were bungalows, like Yvonne's and the one Cadence had recently bought.

The party was clearly in full swing, with well over sixty people mingling around the house, while eating from small dessert plates or sipping a variety of drinks. There were about another twenty people out on the enclosed patio, mostly men. She recognized Yvonne's husband, Calvin, as he stepped through the sliding doors from outside. He nodded when he saw her and she waved back. Calvin started walking toward her, but was interrupted when approached by another guy. Cadence was immediately struck by how different the two men were as they stood side by side.

While Calvin was fairly average looking, with an open face and stocky build, his friend was anything but. It wasn't something obvious like his size or clothing, though he was tall, probably just over six feet, on the slender side, and dressed in a conservative shirt and slacks. What struck Cadence was the character and details of his features.

The first thing she noticed was his lips. They were full and well sculpted, with a boyish tilt at the ends. He wore a moustache, but it was thin, well groomed, and made him seem older. The next thing she noticed was how serious he seemed. His shoulders were rigid, and his jaw was set in hard lines. Even the way he spoke to Calvin suggested restrained impatience and restlessness. Cadence was sure it had been a long time since he had truly laughed.

She turned away from the men when Yvonne returned.

"Here you go," Yvonne said as she handed Cadence a chilled bottle of Corona with the cap removed. "Do you want a glass?"

"No, this is okay, thanks."

"So, are you finished unpacking?"

"Almost," Cadence replied after taking a small sip of beer. "Thank God I don't own a lot of things; otherwise it would take me forever to get everything in the right place."

"I know. We've been here for almost a year, and I still have unopened boxes in the garage." There was a small pause before Yvonne continued. "Is it just you?"

Cadence knew exactly what Yvonne was asking. It was the same question she got from the real-estate agent, lawyer, and mortgage specialist she had dealt with during her house-hunt five months ago. It seemed unbelievable to everyone that she was able to buy a home on her own at twenty-eight years old.

Her appearance probably didn't help, either.

With her mass of thin dreadlocks hanging below her shoulders, and her penchant for jeans and flip-flops, Cadence knew that it was hard for business people to take her seriously. At five-foot, one inch, and 110 pounds, she also didn't look much older than eighteen.

"Yup, just me," Cadence responded simply.

Yvonne only nodded in a slow up-and-down motion. The additional questions were in her eyes but stayed discreetly behind her lips.

The tension was broken when Calvin approached them, followed closely by the guy he had been speaking to.

"Hi, Cadence. I'm glad you could come," Calvin said to her with a warm smile and his hand extended.

Cadence shifted her beer bottle to her left hand so she could shake his hand.

"Thanks again for the invite," she responded. Her own smile revealed the shallow dimples in her cheeks.

"Adam," Calvin said as he turned to the other man now standing between him and Yvonne, enclosing the four of them in a circle. "Cadence has just moved into the house across the street. Cadence, this is a good friend of ours, Adam Jackson."

"Hi," the two strangers said to each other.

There were a couple of minutes of polite chitchat about how nice the party was, and how many of the neighbors had attended. Then, Adam and Yvonne stepped away into the kitchen leaving Calvin and Cadence alone.

"So, how are the renovations coming?" Calvin asked Cadence.

"What a nightmare! My kitchen is a total mess,"

she replied. "I still can't believe that the contractor just disappeared."

Cadence had met Calvin the previous Tuesday when he spotted her struggling to bring in bags of supplies from her car. He had just parked in his garage, but jogged across the street when one of the bags broke, spilling its contents all over the driveway. After introductions, Calvin helped Cadence carry everything from the trunk of her car into her garage. One of those items was a new kitchen faucet.

Cadence met Yvonne the next day when she saw the couple outside and went over to thank Calvin again.

"Did you find anyone to finish the job?" he asked.

She shook her head. "No. One of my sister's friends was supposed to come by today, but of course he didn't show up. I'm going to have to find someone else this week."

"Maybe Adam can help. He's in construction," he suggested. "Adam?"

Adam raised his head when he heard his name, then came back over to them.

"Hey, maybe you can help Cadence out," Calvin started. "Her kitchen was being renovated, but the contractor took off."

"Okay," Adam replied, but his tone indicated he was still confused.

"What exactly do you still need done?" Calvin asked Cadence when she and Adam stood in silence.

"Um, it's not a lot. The sink and faucet need to be put in, and some caulking still needs to be done."

"That doesn't sound too bad. Do you have everything needed?" Adam asked.

He looked Cadence directly in the eyes for the first time, and she was momentarily frozen by the intensity reflected in them. She was also surprised at their color; a dark copper brown, several shades lighter than the cool chocolate of his skin.

"Yes," she stammered. "I think so."

Adam nodded, then glanced at Calvin, who only smiled back.

"Okay, I can probably stop by this week to have a look at it."

"That would be great! Thanks!" Her deep smile flashed the twin dimples. "I'll give you my phone number and you can call when you're available."

"There is a pen and a note pad in the kitchen," Calvin offered.

"I'll be right back," Cadence told them.

"What was that about?" Adam asked Calvin as soon as she was out of earshot.

"What?"

"Did Yvonne put you up to this?"

"Hey man, it's not that complicated. She needs some help, that's all."

Adam clearly didn't believe him, but held his tongue.

"Here it is," Cadence said when she returned and handed Adam the piece of paper. "I really appreciate your help."

"No trouble," Adam responded softly, then turned to Calvin. "I have to get going."

"So soon?" Yvonne asked as she approached him from behind.

"Yeah."

"Okay, I'll walk you out," offered Yvonne.

"Calvin, I'll speak to you soon," Adam stated as the men shook hands.

"You too, man. It was good to see you."

With a polite nod to Cadence, Adam left.

Chapter 2

Cadence ended up staying at the party a little longer than she expected. Once she began walking around, she met several other neighbors, including the couple in the house on her right, Erica and Nathan Clements. Everyone on the street seemed very nice, Erica in particular.

Cadence got home just after midnight. She headed straight to her bedroom to change out of the clothes she was wearing, and into comfortable track pants and a tank top. She then went into her bathroom to wash her face clean of makeup and brush her teeth. Back in the bedroom, she picked up an oversized cotton scarf, then headed to the kitchen, where she plugged in the electric kettle to make a cup of chai tea.

Cadence was not exaggerating when she told Yvonne she had moved with very little. The house was virtually empty except for her bed, which was really only a mattress and box spring resting on a metal frame, and an old television sitting on a box of books. There was also a dated kitchen table with two chairs. She hadn't gotten around to buying furniture for the other rooms, and was starting to feel guilty about it.

The kitchen had a few supplies, but most of it was still in boxes, since her new stove still had to be delivered. Cadence had never been much of a cooker, so the delay really didn't bother her. However, the mess and disorder left by the unfinished renovations drove her crazy.

While waiting for the kettle to boil, Cadence used the scarf to wrap up her locks and keep them out of the way. She then relaxed against the kitchen counter and tried to imagine what her house could look like filled with beautiful things. Her last place had been a cramped studio apartment near downtown Orlando. There hadn't been enough space for anything but the essentials. It seemed unreal to her that this generous-sized home was all hers.

The house was a three-bedroom bungalow with two bathrooms and a covered porch in the back. The living room, dining room, and kitchen ran down the right side of the space, while Cadence's bedroom and a cozy family room were at the very rear, facing the backyard. The two spare bedrooms were along the left side as was the garage. She planned to use one of the spare bedrooms as a guest room, but had converted the room closest to hers into the perfect place to work: her art studio.

Once the water was ready, Cadence made her tea in a foam cup, using a plastic spoon to stir. She then headed to the studio, the only other room with any furniture. She stepped into the room, turned on the light, and took a few seconds to look around.

Three of the four walls were lined with oil and acrylic paintings of all sizes. They were the accumulation of six years of hard work and focus. The subjects ranged from landscapes to portraits to semi-abstracts. Each piece was rich in color and texture, intricate in detail.

The closet in the room had been turned into a storage unit for paints, her prized brushes, and other supplies like blank canvases, rags, and paint remover. She also had a shelf with a collection of prints. These were copies of the seventeen originals she had sold over the past three years, some of which were now available as limited prints.

Cadence walked over to her easel, set up near the window, and put her cup on the table next to a padded stool. She sat down and assessed the canvas board in front of her. It had her next project sketched out with watery cream lines. After about ten minutes of inspection, she took a sip of her now-tepid drink, and started squeezing brown, orange, and red acrylic paint onto her palette.

Three hours later, she put down her brush and rolled her shoulders forward to relieve the tension. The very center of the 24x30-inch board now hinted at the picture she was bringing to life. Cadence yawned loudly and stood up. She stretched again, and stepped back to look at the painting with perspective. Satisfied, she headed to bed, stopping in her bathroom to wash her hands and drop her cup in the garbage.

Cadence slept deeply until her phone rang late Sunday morning. It took three rings before she woke up, and by the time she rolled over and picked up the receiver, she had missed the call. But she knew who it was even without checking the call display. After a few minutes of stubborn squirming to try to fall back asleep, she gave up and sat up.

Predictably, the phone rang again. It was her closest friend, Steve.

"Hey," Cadence said in a groggy, scratchy voice.

"Hey, are we still on for brunch?"

Cadence and Steve used to have a regular routine on Sunday afternoon to get something to eat and hang out for a few hours. But not for the last five weeks while Cadence was moving.

"Sure. What time is it?" she asked, still fuzzy-headed.

"Just after eleven-thirty."

"Okay."

"How is one o'clock? At Emma's on East Colonial?"

"Okay."

Cadence couldn't resist another thirty-five-minute snooze before she headed into the shower. By twenty minutes to one o'clock, she was dressed in comfortable bootleg black jeans and a snug white T-shirt. At the door to the garage, she stepped into rigid leather boots and took a heavy black and silver nylon jacket out of the coat closet. In the garage, she pressed the button for the automatic door opener. Florida sunlight spilled into the room, revealing a brand-new Yamaha V Star Custom motorcycle next to her ten-year-old Honda Civic.

With practiced ability, she rolled the black and chrome bike out onto the driveway before straddling it and gunning the engine. Cadence slipped on her full helmet and slowly rolled down to the street while the garage door closed behind her. Within a few minutes, she was heading west on Colonial Drive.

Cadence had been riding a motorcycle for over four years. Up until two months ago, she had a beat-up Honda almost as old as her Civic, a gift from the boyfriend who taught her how to ride. It was the same boyfriend who talked her into starting her dreads and getting a tattoo at the base of her lower back.

Carlos Perez had been a really great guy, but he had a problem with fidelity. When she broke up with him, he had bought her the old bike to try to win her back. Cadence still kicked him to the curb, but kept the bike.

When Cadence pulled up to the restaurant, she found a spot close to the front door. She dismounted, then immediately pulled off her helmet before she could start sweating in the mid-October warmth. Directly beside her, two men stood frozen and staring at her as they were about to get into their cars. Cadence smiled at them, then walked away as they stammered out a variety of compliments. She couldn't help but laugh to herself.

Steve was already seated on the restaurant patio and she spotted his broad shoulders and dark, shiny bald head right away. When Cadence got to his table, she sat in the chair in front of him and put her helmet on the seat beside her.

Cadence met Steve Hamilton when she had moved to Orlando from Fort Lauderdale nine years ago. He had interviewed her for her first position as an illustrator in a publishing company. Her raw talent and impressive portfolio got her the job without the required college diploma.

They had worked together for almost five years, and they had become very good friends, even though Steve was at least ten years older than she was. He was the first person to suggest that Cadence try painting professionally. He had also been very supportive once she decided to do freelance illustrations, and had offered her several contracts since she quit her full-time job four years ago.

"Hi Steve."

"Hey sweets, you look terrible," Steve commented, even before she removed her riding jacket and hung it over the back of her chair.

She wrinkled her nose at him and started reading the menu.

It wasn't possible for Cadence to look terrible. Her skin was as smooth as melted caramel, with contoured cheeks teased with shallow dimples when she smiled. Her lips were pink and pouty. The effects of too many late nights only showed around her deep-set eyes, making them appear even sultrier. They were the only element of her face that revealed her maturity.

"Where is Beverley?" she asked after a few minutes.

Beverley DeSouza was Steve's passionate and possessive girlfriend and the mother of his four-year-old daughter. It was very rare that she would let him hang out with Cadence alone and she usually tagged along for brunch.

"She dropped me off and went to Target."

Cadence nodded.

"How is Emily? Did she start soccer?"

"God, four going on fourteen! That little girl is going to be the death of me. She had her first practice on Wednesday and got into a shoving match with a little boy who was at least seven years old. You should have seen her; she was fearless. I just hope she doesn't get kicked off the team!"

Both were laughing and shaking their heads by the end of the story.

"Nah, I bet he provoked her."

"Yeah, that's what the coach said."

"See? I'm sure she'll be fine. When is her first game?"

"Next Saturday."

"Great, I'll be there," promised Cadence.

They spent the next hour or so eating and talking, mostly about people they knew in the publishing industry. When Beverley arrived, Cadence was talking about all the things she needed to do around the new house, and Steve was offering his time to help out. Beverley barely said hello before putting in her objections.

"Sweetheart, you know that my mother is coming up from Miami in a few weeks, and there is so much to do before then," she explained to Steve in a sweet but firm voice. "I'm sure Cadence has plenty of men to help her move into her little place."

Cadence had never seen a woman actually bat her eyes in an attempt to look innocent and beguiling like Beverley could. Particularly when she wanted to get her way. She was beautiful and voluptuous, and used all her assets to her advantage.

"Beverley is right," Cadence agreed. "You're way too busy, and I already have someone coming in to finish the kitchen."

"See, baby?" Beverley added, appeased for the moment. "Now, Cadence, how is your little gallery thing going?"

As always, Cadence chose to ignore the obvious attempt to diminish her accomplishments. Beverley's behavior was so childish and petty, it wasn't worth confronting, and it would only put Steve in an awkward position.

Cadence had done various gallery showings in the last three years, but mostly in Florida and a few other southern states. Her current showing was her first in New York City, and it had been a huge success. It was a collection of her latest paintings on display in a Manhattan gallery for the past two weeks. Cadence had been there for the opening weekend—her first trip to the Big Apple.

"It's going well. I sold a couple more pieces," she replied simply.

"Great stuff!" Steve exclaimed. "Soon, you'll be so rich you won't have to do any more commercial work. But I have to tell you, I'm getting a lot of requests for you from my writers."

Cadence laughed, but looked down at her fingers, modestly.

"I'm not giving up illustrations any time soon. I have a mortgage to pay! And I like doing it."

"Darling, we have to get going," Beverley interjected, looking at her watch as though she was bored.

"Oh, I have to go, too," Cadence agreed. "I can't put off shopping for furniture any longer."

They all stood up, and when they said good-bye, Steve squeezed her shoulder and Beverley gave her a fake two-cheek kiss in the air, and promised to talk soon. Cadence watched them walk away hand in hand while she shrugged on her jacket and picked up her helmet. Disdain was clearly written all over her face.

How could some women live like that? Losing themselves completely for their men, and desperately trying to hold on to them. Worse, how can a smart and successful man like Steve not see through her thinly veiled pettiness? Cadence knew so many women like Beverley, including her own mother. She had vowed a long time ago that she would never be like that. Her pride and love for herself was far more important than any man.

Cadence used the rest of the afternoon to stop at electronics, furniture, and department stores in the area. She saw a few things she liked, but just couldn't commit to any purchase. Where should she start? A new television? She would love one of those slim, flat screens. Family room furniture? A new bedroom set? It was not that she couldn't afford what she wanted. For the first time in her life, she actually had real money in the bank. It was more that it was so hard for her to stop being thrifty and stringent with her budget, and buying necessities only.

In the end, she found herself at Target, and

stocked up on a few toiletries that could fit in the
cargo compartment of her bike. When she got onto
her street, Erica Clements was outside with her two
boys, six and eight years old. The children were as
blond and pale as she was. The two women chatted
for a moment while the kids inspected her motorcycle with wide, delighted eyes.

Cadence was back in the house by a few minutes
to six o'clock. She put her purchases away in the
bathroom, then picked up her bedroom phone to
order her dinner from a local Italian restaurant
that delivered. The message indicator flashed, so
she dialed into her voice mailbox. The first was
from her sister, Monique, asking when the women
could get together and hang out.

The second was from Adam Jackson.

Chapter 3

Adam spent the first part of Sunday doing the ordinary things he made time for every weekend. He did his laundry, cleaned his apartment, and called his mother in Jamaica. His laundry was only two loads: whites, and darks for his work pants and shirts. The apartment was a small one-bedroom, and since Adam really only slept there, there wasn't much to clean. The long-distance call to his mother, on the other hand, lasted over an hour.

It was just after three o'clock in the afternoon when Adam showered and got dressed in clean work clothes—blue jeans and a dark blue golf shirt. Adam owned a building company that made custom homes in Orlando. It was a small operation with eight full-time employees, and they relied on contractors for the various skilled labor needed. As a licensed general contractor, Adam managed the developments himself and spent most of his time at the building sites. When deadlines were tight, which they almost always were, it included work on Sundays.

Adam got his first job in construction right after

high school, and while in business college, he spent summers either laying brick, installing drywall, or doing various types of flooring. Once he graduated, he decided to stay in the business and started doing renovations. Three years later, he had the opportunity to buy an old house on prime real estate. With several small investors, Adam gutted the existing structure and rebuilt the ultimate executive home. It sold for top dollar, and launched Iris Custom Homes, named after his mother. That was almost six years and over 250 homes ago.

When he was ready to leave his apartment, Adam stopped in the kitchen to get his car keys. He hesitated, then picked up the piece of paper he had tossed on the counter the night before.

Adam stared intently at the information written diagonally across it. The name *Cadence* was scripted in bold, loopy letters and the phone number underneath was underlined.

He sighed loudly. He was going to have to call her. It would be rude not to. He might as well get over it, because there was no doubt that Yvonne was going to bug him until he did.

He sighed again and sucked his teeth with annoyance.

Adam knew that the reason he was hesitant had nothing to do with this particular woman. She seemed nice enough, and very attractive, if he were into petite women with that natural look. It should not be a big deal for him to help her with whatever had to be fixed in her house, and then be on his way.

The real problem was that everyone, including Calvin and Yvonne, was insisting that he start dating again and he wasn't sure he was ready. Adam was now single for the first time since he was seventeen years old, and he just wasn't interested in the dating scene. And no one seemed to understand how he felt, particularly his male friends. They all just laughed their asses off, with envy in their eyes, and told him to go get laid and have fun.

He looked at the phone number again. The guys were probably right. After the strain of the past two years, he should just take things easy, enjoy himself. Keep things casual.

Adam dialed the written number into his cordless phone, and after three rings, her voice mail kicked in. Her voice was deeper and silkier than he remembered.

"Hi, this message is for Cadence. It's Adam Jackson. We met last night at Yvonne and Calvin's party. I was calling to set up a time to have a look at those renovations you needed finished," he explained briefly, then gave his cell phone number before he disconnected.

Once he put the handset back on the phone charge, Adam grabbed his keys and headed out of his apartment. He lived on the second floor of a complex of three-floor garden homes, so he jogged down the stairs that led to his outdoor parking spot. Once in his truck, he drove over to the shopping mall just a few blocks away.

The Mall at Millennia was Orlando's newer, upscale indoor shopping complex. It was the type of place that Adam normally avoided like the plague, but he needed to get a gift for his godson, Aaron, and didn't have enough time to be picky.

Aaron was turning six, and he was having his birthday party that afternoon at a bowling alley. Adam planned to run into the nearest athletic store that carried kids' sizes and be out in thirty minutes.

He would stay at the party for a little while, then head to his construction site.

Adam was about to enter a store when his cell phone rang. He stopped in the mall hallway where he knew the reception was better.

"Hello?"

"Hey, Adam."

"Vince, what's up?" Adam asked.

"Did Carol give you the address to the bowling alley?" his friend Vince asked.

Vince and Carol were Aaron's parents. The birthday party was scheduled to start in about fifteen minutes.

"Yeah, she sent me an e-mail on Friday. On Orange Blossom, right?" Adam asked.

"Oh, good. Yeah, East Orange Blossom, just down the street from Walgreen's."

"Okay. I'll be there by about four-thirty."

"Cool, man. See you then."

Adam ended the call, then hurried into the store to pick out a pair of basketball shoes and an Orlando Magic jersey. With ten minutes to spare, he went to the customer service desk and had the purchases gift wrapped. He was then back in his truck and on his way to the bowling alley.

Things were already underway when he got there, and children of various ages lined up for their turn on the alley. Aaron had just finished rolling a ball, and waved wildly when he saw his godfather.

"Hi Adam," Carol said when she approached him and took Aaron's gift out of his hands. He did not miss her curled lips when she noticed his casual clothes.

"Carol," he said with a cool nod, then shook his head with exasperation as she walked away.

For as long as he had known her, Carol could not see him as anything but a basic laborer, which, in her eyes, meant he wasn't worth her time. She and Vince had been together for about one year before Aaron was born, but they had broken up just before she had found out she was pregnant. Their relationship since then had been the quintessential example of how bad it could be if a man had a child with the wrong woman. They shared custody of Aaron. Vince had his son every other weekend and alternating holidays. Otherwise, they barely tolerated each other.

Adam could not care less about what Carol thought of him, and his opinion of her was even lower. But he hated to see his friend have to deal with her bitterness, greediness, and pettiness. It also bothered him that Aaron was always caught in the middle.

Adam swung around quickly when a heavy arm fell across his shoulder.

"Adam! What's up? Glad you could make it, man," Vince Martin stated with a wide smile.

Adam had known Vince since high school. He was average height, about a couple of inches shorter than Adam, but had the physique of a linebacker.

"Hey, Vince," he replied as the two men tapped fists.

"How was Yvonne's party?" Vince asked.

"It was pretty good."

"Yeah?" Vince replied with raised brows and wide grin. "I wish I could have made it. But I'm glad you went."

"It's no big deal," Adam said dismissively.

Vince just chuckled and punched Adam on the shoulder.

Back in the day, Vince, Yvonne, Adam, and Adam's girlfriend at the time, Rose, were part of a group of friends that did almost everything together. But once they got married, Adam and Rose abruptly stopped participating in most of the things the others did.

The group of friends had gotten smaller over the years as most people got married and started families, but several of them still got together every couple of months. Now, they mostly hung out over dinner or drinks to relax and talk, and they often invited Adam to join them.

Aaron ran up to his father and Adam, interrupting their discussion. His excitement was obvious as he spoke a mile a minute, and he told his godfather about every gift he had received so far. A few minutes later, Aaron was off again to play with his friends.

Adam stayed at the party for another hour, then headed north into the suburb of Altamonte Springs. He turned into the construction site, and maneuvered through dirt roads until he reached his houses, wrapped around a cul-de-sac. The site was being developed by seven different builders, and was a combination of upscale apartments, town houses, and detached homes. Adam had twenty-eight lots that were sold out, and the first of his buyers was closing in about two months. The next couple of weeks were going to be critical to keeping the houses on schedule.

An hour later, Adam's phone rang while he was in the middle of rechecking inventory.

"Hello?"

"Hi, um . . . can I speak with Adam Jackson, please?"

"This is Adam."

"Hi Adam, it's Cadence Carter. How are you?"

Adam let go of the tiles he had been counting as they leaned in piles against the wall, and they fell back against each other, causing a loud clang. He straightened from his crouched position.

"Hi, Cadence, I'm doing all right. How are you?"

"Great! I was surprised to get your message," Cadence told him in the low, sultry voice he now recognized from her voice-mail recording.

"Really? Why?"

"I thought you were just being polite by offering to help me with my kitchen."

Adam was taken aback by her direct statement and was unsure how to respond. She spoke before his pause became noticeable.

"I'm pretty flexible all week, so just let me know what works for you," she told him.

"Okay, I was thinking of Tuesday evening. Maybe around six-thirty?"

"Perfect. I'll be home."

"Okay," Adam said again. "I'll see you Tuesday, then," he reconfirmed.

They both hung up. Adam looked down at the phone and smiled. He was finding it hard to put together the voice on the phone with the petite waif from the night before. From what he remembered, Cadence Carter looked barely out of her teens, with slender hips and sweet dimples. But over the phone, she sounded like a grown woman with the curves to match.

Adam shook his head and smiled again. His friends were probably right; he did need to get laid.

Chapter 4

As usual, Cadence lost track of time while working and was now running late. She did not check her watch until the model she was sketching needed a stretch. By then, it was almost six-fifteen on Tuesday evening. Adam Jackson would be there in a few minutes, and the oversized cotton shirt she was wearing was covered with charcoal smears.

"Damn!" Cadence exclaimed as she hopped out of her chair. Malcolm, the owner of the body she was sketching, looked at her quizzically. He stood completely naked except for blue sport sandals on his feet. Apparently, he found the ceramic tiles in the studio cold.

"What's up?" he asked as he casually scratched his chiseled chest.

"I'm sorry, Malcolm; I've gone way over time again. We're going to need at least one more session. Maybe for another two hours?" Cadence estimated, her eyes were still fixed on her sketch pad.

"That's okay," Malcolm assured her. "I can't do

tomorrow, but how about Thursday? I should be fine for the whole afternoon."

Cadence swiftly added a few lines of shading to the drawing, then inspected it again. It was almost a full minute before she responded to him, and then it was with a furrowed brow and a wide-eyed stare. Malcolm knew immediately that she had not heard a word he said. He gave her a tolerant smile that, coupled with his gloriously nude body, would have given any other woman a spontaneous orgasm. She only glanced back at her sketch, her head cocked to the side and her eyes squinted.

"I said: how about Thursday afternoon?" he repeated.

She was nodding in agreement when the front doorbell rang.

"Oh, no . . . !" Cadence exclaimed, then glanced again at her watch. It was only twenty minutes after six o'clock. "He's early!"

She rushed out of the studio, but stopped short a couple of steps from the front door. Her fingers were dusted with black smudges from her charcoal pencil and Cadence wiped them off on her shirt, adding to the sooty streaks already there. With a frustrated grunt, she quickly stripped off the top before opening the door.

"Hi Adam, you're early," she said, breathless. "Come in. I'll be back in a second."

The last statement was made after she had turned away from the door and was almost halfway into the house. Adam was momentarily speechless as he watched Cadence disappear. Though she had only faced him for a moment, he was left with a clear image of her in a thin, white cotton camisole that revealed every dip and swell of the petite torso it was supposed to cover.

He stepped over the threshold and closed the front door behind him. Since it would have been rude to walk farther into her house without her there, he stood in the small front foyer patiently waiting for Cadence to come back out. Adam was casually looking around him when a big, muscular, half-dressed man walked into the empty room in front of the doorway.

"What's up?" the man said to Adam while zipping up the front of his jeans. Adam responded with an upward nod, and then watched the man pull on a short-sleeved button-down shirt.

Cadence was back several seconds later, now wearing a cotton tank top with the jogging pants she had on earlier. Adam looked down at his feet in an attempt to give the couple some privacy as they walked past him to the front door.

"So, Thursday at the same time, right?" Cadence said, while opening the door.

"Sounds good," the guy confirmed. "Oh, this is the invoice for the last two visits."

Though he could not hear their conversation Adam caught a glimpse of a white envelope as it was handed to Cadence. He then turned away as they said their final good-byes, and the door was closed.

"Sorry about that," Cadence said to him with an embarrassed smile. "I completely lost track of the time. One minute it's only twelve o'clock and I have the whole afternoon ahead, and the next minute I'm behind schedule. I swear I lost at least an hour somewhere."

Adam did not interrupt her rambling, but

followed her as she walked into the empty house and stopped in front of the unfinished kitchen. She casually tossed the envelope on the counter, then turned to face him.

"Thank you so much for offering to help with this. The whole thing has been so frustrating! Who would have thought changing a few things would turn into such a nightmare?"

Cadence stopped talking again, and they both looked at the cause of her troubles. Adam could see that someone had started the work, then abandoned the job. There was no sink, faucet, or stove. The built-in dishwasher had been pulled out and disconnected. There were also several stacks of tiles that he assumed were for a backsplash.

"So what happened?" he asked after a few minutes.

Cadence let out a deep breath.

"I just needed a new sink and faucet, and to have the dishwasher replaced. I had called up a plumber to do the work, but after he removed the old stuff and unhooked the dishwasher, he never came back. A friend of my sister promised to finish it, but he hasn't called me back in over a week."

"What about the tiling?" Adam asked.

"Oh, that was the plumber's idea, but I was going to try and do it myself. It didn't look that hard," she added defensively after Adam gave her a sideways glance.

"Okay. So what about the new fixtures?" he asked.

"They're all in the garage. Except for the stove. It's going to be delivered next week. "

Adam nodded, then walked into her kitchen area and looked around for about five minutes. Cadence watched him, while chewing on the tip of her thumb. She was resisting the urge to keep babbling on and on. What was wrong with her? She didn't usually chatter like that, but for whatever reason, Adam's silence was making her want to fill in the blanks.

He didn't turn to her again until he had fully inspected the disconnected dishwasher.

"Well, it seems pretty simple. I'll go ahead and put the sink and faucet in now. Where is your garage?"

"Through here," Cadence indicated, by leading the way past her two spare rooms and a small laundry room.

Once there, she showed him her collection of supplies, including the hardware, caulking, and a few other things the renovation store had told her to get. She then helped him carry everything back to the kitchen.

"Okay, I'm going to get a few things," Adam told her.

He was back quickly with a large toolbox and a couple of power tools. Cadence watched him lay the necessary items out on the counter. He then took off his button-down cotton shirt, leaving himself in a white undershirt and low-slung jeans. She had been right about her first assessment: Adam Jackson was slender, but every muscle of his arms and upper chest was cut and molded perfectly. When he got down on the floor and started unpacking her new double sink to prepare it for installation, it became very hard for her not to stare.

"Would you like something to drink?" Cadence asked him in a voice that was several tones deeper than normal. "I have some ice tea. Or maybe a beer?"

"I'll take some water if you have it," Adam replied, without pausing his actions.

She was grateful for the distraction of finding a plastic cup and filling it with ice and filtered water from the refrigerator. It had been a long time since the sight of male flesh did anything to her insides. Every male model she sketched had a beautiful face and perfect body, but she never really saw beyond their creative value. But Adam was different. His strong hands and sinewy muscles were not just for show; they knew how to do things, fix things, and make things. It was incredibly attractive to her.

"Here you go," she told him as she placed the glass of water on the counter near the sink. "Do you need me to do anything to help?"

"Thanks," Adam told her before he took a long drink of water. "It looks like everything is in order, so this shouldn't take too long."

"Are you hungry? I was going to order a pizza for dinner," Cadence told him.

"That's okay . . ."

"Come on, it's the least I can do. It's only seven o'clock and the Domino's down the road delivers pretty quickly," Cadence insisted. "What do you like on your pizza?"

The question was asked while she was walking toward her bedroom to get the phone. His answer was muffled to her, so she asked again when she was back in earshot.

"No, really," he protested. "You don't have to do that."

She was already dialing the restaurant when she replied. "Well, I'm ordering dinner either way, so you might as well stay and eat my leftovers . . . Hi, I'd like to place an order for delivery."

Adam shrugged in response, then went back to work on the sink.

Once she finished placing the order, Cadence decided to go back to the studio to finish off some work and clean up a bit. When she checked on Adam's progress about twenty minutes later, he was starting to install the faucet. Cadence stood around watching him for a bit, not wanting to interrupt him, but making sure he didn't need her for anything. She left again when he didn't pause to acknowledge her presence.

Not much of a talker, is he? she thought to herself with a little annoyance. Maybe she was being sensitive, but his quietness was now bordering on rudeness. Clearly, her first impression of his personality was pretty accurate. Adam Jackson was not a cheerful man. The rigid shoulders and clenched jaw must be permanent fixtures.

When Cadence sat in front of her easel again, she turned her sketch pad to a new page and stared at the blank whiteness for several long minutes. She then picked up a pencil and started drawing in light, airy strokes. The lips developed first and she didn't stop working until she captured their combination of masculine rigidity and vulnerable fullness. Next came the square chin and contour lines under his cheekbone.

Cadence stopped at that point and looked out the window without really seeing the limited view of her neighbor's brickwork. When she looked back at her sketch, she pushed the stool away from the easel. Though Cadence had drawn images from memory thousands of times, she was always still surprised at the ease with which the details came to her mind, then transferred to paper. The accuracy in her unfinished drawing of Adam Jackson was even more surprising. She abruptly put down her pencil and flipped the sheets in the pad back to her earlier project before she left the studio.

In the kitchen, Adam was testing his work by running water through the newly installed faucet, and checking the pipes for leaks. He was inspecting the cupboard under the sink, while crouched low and balanced on the balls of his feet, when Cadence entered the kitchen again.

"How is it going?" she asked, trying to sound lighthearted. "It looks great."

"It's all done," he replied. "I had a little trouble with the faucet, but it looks fine now."

Cadence walked closer to the sink to admire the finished product. Adam stood up, and his shoulder brushed her stomach. When she sprung back to get out of his way, he grabbed her shoulders to steady her. They ended up in an awkward, loose embrace that lasted until Cadence laughed nervously and he released her. The heat from his hands lasted long after Adam turned away to start cleaning up the tools and supplies.

She went back to admiring her new hardware. He really had done a great job, right down to the caulking and cleanup. When she turned back to him, there was a huge smile on her face.

"You don't know what a relief this is for me. I've been ordering in and using paper plates for over three weeks. I can't thank you enough."

Though Adam had a complexion like expensive

chocolate, Cadence was certain his skin got flushed. Her smile turned into a silent giggle when he turned away from her without meeting her eyes. And then she watched him rearrange and straighten the things that he had already put in order. *Maybe he's not rude at all. Maybe he's just a little shy?* Cadence thought to herself. It would certainly explain the lack of conversation.

"So," she said once the silence dragged on too long. "How long do you think it will take for you to install the dishwasher?"

Adam cleared his throat before answering.

"Not long. No more than an hour if there are no complications. You said you have a new stove being delivered?" Cadence nodded. "Let me know when it's coming and I'll install both for you at the same time."

She smiled broadly at him again, even though he still was not looking directly at her.

"That would be great! It's booked for Thursday afternoon, but I have to call again tomorrow to re-confirm," she explained.

He nodded. The doorbell interrupted them and Cadence rushed to answer it. She didn't notice that Adam had followed her until he reached out to take the hot pizza box. He also tried to slip the delivery boy a twenty-dollar bill, but Cadence blocked his way and paid the tab with an added tip.

Neither of them said anything while she set the food on the table, and got paper plates and napkins out of the cupboard. Once they were seated, Adam waited for her to put slices on both the plates and take her seat before he started eating. The now familiar silence lasted until he reached for a second slice and Cadence was picking at her crust.

"So, how do you know Calvin?" she asked.

"Through Yvonne," Adam replied briefly, until her prolonged look indicated she was waiting for more information. "She and I have been friends since high school."

"I see. That's nice that you guys have remained friends for so long. I guess you're both from Orlando?" He didn't reply, but Cadence was now used to his limited contribution to dialogue, so she continued thinking out loud. "I don't have any friends from high school that I still talk to. But that's probably because I've moved cities a few times and it's so hard to stay in touch when that happens. I run into a few people when I'm back home, but even then it's just brief conversation. And the truth is, I didn't have a lot of friends in high school. I was a bit of a loner, really."

She paused to put down her crust and pick up another slice.

"Where do you call home?" Adam asked, then elaborated when she stared at him blankly. "You said you run into people when you're back home. Where is that?"

"Oh," she said with a short giggle. "Fort Lauderdale. That's where I went to high school, anyway. Before that, we lived in Jacksonville, but I haven't been back since we moved. My mom is still there. In Fort Lauderdale, I mean. So I try to go back and visit her once or twice a year."

He nodded. She smiled back, and he looked down at his plate before helping himself to more pizza.

"I thought you weren't hungry?" Cadence teased, linking her fingers.

"Well, there was no point in letting your leftovers go to waste," he responded ironically.

Cadence couldn't help but laugh, then laughed harder when Adam joined in. She still had a smile on her face when he looked into her eyes, and she felt the heat of his golden eyes. Their smiles faded, and he looked away to refocus on his meal. Cadence continued to inspect his face, not at all timid about embarrassing him. He cleared his throat again.

They continued eating for a few more minutes before Adam stood up. He thanked her for the meal and shrugged on his shirt. Cadence thanked him again for his help, and they confirmed that he would return on Thursday evening at the same time. Within fifteen minutes, they said good night and Cadence closed the door behind him.

She stood by the door for a few minutes after Adam left, with a twist to her brow and a bemused smile on her lips. Then she made her way back to the studio and flipped the pages of her art pad back to the sketched outline of his lips. There was something about this man that fascinated her, but not just for the artistic appeal. It was a mixture of quiet strength and hidden intensity that made her want to look deeper.

Chapter 5

"What do you mean you think she's a working girl?" Calvin asked in disbelief. "Like *'a working girl'*?"

"I don't know, man," Adam said while shaking his head. "I'm just telling you what I saw. The same dude was leaving her house both times I got there. And one time, I watched him give her an envelope."

It was Friday evening, later that week. Adam had stopped by Calvin and Yvonne's house for a few minutes, but was expected at Cadence's house within the half hour. He found Calvin home alone while Yvonne was out doing an errand.

"He gave her cash?" asked Calvin.

"I don't know what was in the packet and I didn't hear what he said. But, he handed it to her while buttoning up his shirt and zipping up his pants. And they didn't act like boyfriend/girlfriend, if you know what I'm saying."

"Damn!" Calvin uttered, staring at Adam with wide eyes. "Who would have thought it? She seems so young and sweet."

"Maybe at first. But from talking to her, it's clear she's a pretty sharp girl, so she knows what she's doing, and she's obviously doing it well."

"So you're saying she has herself set up as an escort in her own house in the 'burbs, where the johns come to her?"

"Like I said, I'm just telling you what I saw," Adam reiterated. "She might not even live there permanently. There's no furniture in the place except a kitchen table and stuff in the bedroom."

"Well, she's home most of the time. In fact, Yvonne has commented a few times that Cadence didn't appear to work at all," Calvin explained. "Yvonne is going to flip when I tell her."

Adam was silent for a few minutes and took a long drink of his beer.

"Maybe you shouldn't tell her," he advised Calvin in a low voice. "I love Yvonne too, but you know how she is. Within a week, everyone will know about Cadence and have a petition to have her kicked out of the neighborhood."

Calvin chuckled because he knew Adam was right. His knew his wife thought of herself as an advocate for righteousness, and was very relentless when she found a cause. A high-end prostitute doing her business across the street, though very discreetly, was going to be at the top of her to-do list.

"Good point," Calvin granted.

"Plus, I could be wrong. And if I'm right, it's her business and she's not hurting anyone."

"Am I sensing a soft spot for our naughty neighbor?"

"Nay, nothing like that. It's just that despite what she may be doing to make money, she seems pretty cool. She has been nothing but grateful for my help. When I told her I had to come back tonight to finish the dishwasher, she insisted on making me dinner in return."

Calvin slammed his hand on the coffee table.

"Come on, man! It sounds like she's making a move to me."

Adam shook his head with mock disgust. "It's nothing like that. She's just being appreciative, that's all."

"Whatever, man. You've been out of the game so long that you don't even know the rules anymore."

"Please! You haven't seen game in over a decade, so I don't know what you're talking about."

The two men continued to rib each other until Adam noticed the time and made his way across the street. He had told Cadence to expect him around seven o'clock. It was already ten minutes after, and any later would have been a little rude. Though he had denied it to Calvin, Adam had to admit that he was looking forward to spending more time with Cadence, despite his wicked suspicions.

At first, he had been so put off by her half-naked visitor that he found it difficult to speak to her. But by the end of Tuesday evening, he was amused by her genuine delight and guileless chatter. Then, on Thursday, while he installed the dishwasher and the newly delivered stove, they talked a little more about their backgrounds. It turned out that they had a lot in common. They were both born in Florida, but from parents who were struggling Jamaican immigrants. Their breezy conversation touched on several other topics, but ended with music. They both loved old reggae, like ska, culture, rock steady, and lover's rock.

Adam was really surprised by how comfortable he felt with Cadence. He had struggled with whether or not to tell Calvin about his suspicions, but in the end, he was really hoping that Calvin would laugh, tell him he was crazy, then provide a logical explanation for why this half-dressed man was giving Cadence envelopes probably filled with money.

He now regretted saying anything at all, for fear that Yvonne would somehow get wind of it and blow a gasket.

Adam stopped at his truck to pick up the part for the dishwasher before he approached Cadence's house. When he rang the doorbell, he detected the faint throb of music, and when she opened the door, he could not help but smile. She was playing one of his favorite reggae songs by Beres Hammond, "Tempted to Touch."

"Hey," she said, smiling back.

"Hey," he replied. "Sorry I'm late."

"No problem," she replied as she closed the door behind him.

Adam followed her through the house to the kitchen. There was the distinct and delicious smell of cooking fish and hot pepper. He also noticed that Cadence was not wearing her usual casual clothes. Instead, she had on a dress that wrapped and tied like a sarong, and was made of a copper-colored African fabric. Her eyes were darkened with makeup, and her lips were shiny and wet with tawny gloss.

"I hope you like red snapper," she asked as she returned to the stove. "I finally found a market that has really fresh fish. I've gone to a few other shops in Orlando, and I wouldn't buy salted cod from them."

"I love fish. It smells really good."

"Are you sure? I've had the door to the patio open and the fan blasting all evening trying to get rid of the smell. The whole street knows what I'm cooking by now."

"It's fine. It's not strong at all."

They smiled at each other until Cadence looked away shyly. Adam cleared his throat.

"Do you want me to finish the dishwasher now, or wait until you're done?" he asked.

"Oh, now's fine. I'm pretty much done here. I'll just turn down the stove and get out of your way."

She moved to the far end of the kitchen counter and began putting together a salad. Adam got to work replacing a leaky hose, and they both worked quietly as the music played in the background. Cadence finished chopping the vegetables and added the salad to the kitchen table.

"What would you like to drink?" she asked him. "I have white wine on the table, but there's juice and water also. Or beer if you'd prefer."

"Wine is fine."

She was pouring two glasses when Adam stood up and declared the job was done. At his request, she pointed the way to the main bathroom so he could wash his hands. When he returned, Cadence was serving up steamed snapper stuffed with Jamaican spinach-like leaves called callaloo, rice, and coleslaw. He sat at the table and she placed a hot plate in front of him before sitting with her own serving.

"So I guess the stove is working okay?" Adam asked her after a few bites.

"It's great! I don't cook a lot, but it was really hard not to have a working kitchen," she replied. "Now that it's finished, thanks to you, I have to work on the rest of the house."

He looked at her quizzically.

"In case you haven't noticed, I have no furniture," she added. "There was no way I was moving my old stuff in here, so I gave it all away. I just didn't realize how hard it would be to go shopping from scratch. I have no idea what style or color I want. It turns out that I don't even know what style I like. It's pretty sad, isn't it?"

Adam smiled with her.

"I thought women were born knowing that stuff," he told her.

"I thought so too, but apparently I'm not normal."

"I'm sure that's not the case," he opposed kindly. "Anyway, it's better to take your time until you find something you're going to be happy with long-term. 'Haste makes waste'."

Cadence laughed. "My mother used to say that, too. But she also used to say: 'Pick, pick 'til you pick shit!'."

"True, true," replied Adam with a deep chuckle.

"So, which one is your life philosophy? Wait for exactly what you want, or choose the first thing that comes close?" she asked with a teasing glance.

"Well, that's a good question. I guess it depends on what we're talking about. For example, if it's furniture, I'm like most men: Whatever is functional and reasonably priced. But, there are other things that I would wait for until the perfect one comes along."

"Such as?"

Adam chewed quietly for a few seconds before responding.

"Shoes."

"What?" Cadence sputtered while trying not to spray the wine she had just sipped.

"Shoes," Adam repeated. "And I'll tell you why."

"Please do."

"They have to be the perfect combination of fit, comfort, practicality, style, and price. If you compromise on any of these, you will regret it. As a woman, you know I'm right."

Cadence continued to stare at him, trying to figure out how serious he was, but then could not stop herself from laughing heartily.

"You asked for an example and I gave you one," Adam said with a shrug and a smile. "So what about you?"

"I think my empty house speaks for itself. I am definitely the 'haste makes waste' type."

"But is that because you can't find what you want, or because you don't know what you want?" he asked.

"That depends on whether we're still talking about my furniture," she countered with a glint in her eyes. "Most of the time, I only know what I don't want. I try to learn from my mistakes."

Adam put down his fork and slowly chewed the last mouthful of rice. His eyes were on the half-empty bottle of wine, but he could see Cadence watching him without staring, as though she was trying to figure out what he was thinking about.

When their eyes did meet again, they both smiled and looked back at their plates.

"The meal was delicious," he stated when he spoke again.

"Thank-you."

"You said you don't cook a lot? That's hard to believe."

"It's not because I can't cook. I just don't seem able to make time for it. I get wrapped up in a project or some work, and I completely forget to eat until I'm so hungry that I don't have time to cook. It's either an immediate snack, or I go out to eat. I also got tired of buying all these perishables and then having to throw them out. I hate throwing away food. It's so much easier to pick up premade stuff every few days."

Adam immediately wanted to ask what kind of projects or work she did for a living, but was afraid of the answer. She could lie, or worse, tell the truth. Instead, he let the moment pass, as Cadence picked up their plates and walked to the sink. He followed with the other items on the table. When she turned around he was directly in front of her, and she jumped, clearly not expecting his closeness.

Adam did not move and Cadence eventually looked up questioningly. He stood looking down at her sultry eyes, moist lips, and petite frame with the salad bowl and dressing still in his hands. Then, he lowered his mouth to hers, brushing their lips to together and gently stroking her lower lip with his tongue. He could feel her breath catch, then escape in a rush as she released a soft moan. The sound sent his heart racing.

When her hands touched his chest, Adam pulled

back. His intention was to put the brakes on, but when he saw her closed eyes and expectant lips, his clear thinking went out the window. The salad and dressing landed on the counter with a clatter, but neither of them heard it as their mouths fused again in a deep, exploring kiss. He felt her body curve into his, and his arm wrapped around the back of her waist to pull her closer. She ended up on the tips of her toes.

Adam could not get enough. Her lips tasted so sweet and her tongue was so hot. Even her locks seemed to wrap him in soft tendrils that smelled like ripe apricots and fresh peppermint. Everything about her made his blood rush and heat rise. The way Cadence kissed him back left no doubt that she was as caught up as he was. It became impossible to separate his stifled moans from her breathy sighs.

When their lips finally parted, Adam buried his face into the curve of her slender neck in an attempt to calm his breathing, and, he hoped, lessen the pressure that was pulsing through his loins. He could not resist the feel of her soft flesh, and ended up raining kisses on her neck.

"Wow," Cadence said with a breathless giggle. "That was unexpected."

Adam straightened up to look down at her.

"I'm a little surprised myself," he replied in a low voice.

"Really? You mean you didn't come here with the intention of seducing me?" she replied playfully as she took his hand and led him back to the kitchen table. "I'm starting to think you've been trying to get on my good side."

He sat in one of the chairs and she sat in his lap.

Her arms went around his neck and they fell into another deep, searching kiss. Adam could barely feel her weight as he lifted her by her hips and her legs straddled his. His hands slid around to grasp the soft cushions of her behind, bringing her delicate core against the rigid force of his arousal. Their mouths broke apart as they both gasped at the intense sensations. Their breaths mingled as their lips remained a hair apart, until Cadence reached up and undid the knot behind her neck that held her dress in place. The fabric slowly slid down until it pooled at her waist and revealed her naked breasts.

"You're incredible," he whispered. His eyes savored the creamy caramel globes and chocolate-dipped nipples. He leaned forward and ran his tongue over one tip, and then the other. Her body shivered and a high-pitched moan escaped her lips as her head fell back. Adam took his time licking and sucking her puckered flesh, and marveled at the touch, taste, and smell of her. She was in all his senses and he could not get enough.

He swept the fabric of her dress away from her legs to reveal her panties, and brushed the thin lace aside to cup her delicate mound.

"Oh! Oh, Adam. . . ." Cadence exclaimed. Her body bucked and shivered as he massaged her with the palm of his work-hardened hands. She bit her bottom lip to stifle a scream, but then let out a long moan when he slowly thrust his middle finger deep into her wet sheath.

"You're so incredible," Adam repeated in a low, tight voice.

He felt his control slipping. It had been so long

since he felt this uncontrollable passion, this overwhelming sexual desire, that he was not sure he could hold back. The need to root his straining erection into her tightness was almost more than he could resist. But it would be over too soon, and he could not bear the shame. His need to give Cadence the pleasure she deserved outweighed his own frustrations.

The beat of her heart throbbed in the heat of her core and it matched the pace of his own. Adam slowly pulled back, then thrust his thick finger into her again, then again, until she was slick with wetness. He pressed in a second digit and used his thumb to tease the nub at her core. His eyes were fixed on her beautiful face as her skin became flushed and damp. Then she opened her glazed eyes and they locked with his. He immediately knew that she was about to fall apart.

"Come for me," he whispered urgently as he increased the speed and depth of his strokes. Her hips began rotating and thrust uncontrollably, and deep moans erupted from her throat. Their eyes were still locked, and Adam felt every explosion of her orgasm right to the center of his soul. It was more intense and more satisfying than anything he had ever experienced before.

Chapter 6

Cadence's body slowly relaxed, except for the occasional shudder. Adam buried his free hand in the tendrils of her hair, and pulled her forward into a hug. The heat of his body warmed her rapidly cooling nakedness. Then, they were kissing with soft, gentle brushes. She felt weightless and languid.

"Well," Cadence whispered in his ear while she gently bit his lobe. "Now I owe you even more. But I can think of a few ways to pay you back."

She started to slide her hand down to his pants, but Adam stopped her by covering it with his own. He pulled back and looked at her with intensity.

"You don't owe me anything," he stated simply.

"I think I do," she teased, still feeling the after-effects of shattering satisfaction. "I always pay my debts."

"This wasn't about you owing me, and I'm not interested in how you pay for other things."

There was a seriousness in his tone that made Cadence look at him more clearly. She hardly recognized him as the same man who was inflamed with desire moments before. His shoulders were stiff and the hard clench was back in his jaw. There was also a coldness in his eyes that made her pull back from their embrace. The cool air brushed against her naked breasts.

"What is that supposed to mean?" she asked, confused.

He didn't respond, but his eyes dropped down to her hardened nipples. Cadence immediately covered herself with her dress by tying it around her neck with flustered hands. His continued silence made her slide off his lap and walk a few steps away with her back to him.

"Look, I'm not sure what . . ."

"Let's not play games," interrupted Adam. "You're free to do whatever you want with your life, but I don't use sex as currency."

"What?" she shouted as she swung around. "Look, this is ridiculous! I don't know what your problem is, but I was only joking around."

He was still sitting in the chair, his legs spread casually like they were discussing the weather. But his eyes revealed a disdain that made Cadence feel ashamed of their intimacy. Her temper flared in defense.

"Like I said, let's not play games," he replied in a dead voice. "I am not going to be one of your clients. What we share is either freely given or I'm not interested."

"What clients? What the hell are you talking about?"

Adam shook his head and stood up quickly.

"This was a mistake," he stated, and Cadence felt like she had been slapped in the face.

"A mistake," she replied blankly with her arms crossed around her stomach.

"Look, this is my fault." There must have been something in her face that made him soften his tone. "This is not my scene and I shouldn't have let anything happen. I think I should leave."

Cadence looked down at the kitchen floor trying to grasp what had gone wrong. She just couldn't figure it out, but something he has said repeated in her mind.

"What clients are you talking about?" she asked, just as he passed her on his way of out the kitchen.

Adam stopped and took a deep breath before turning back to her.

"Let's be honest. There's not point denying that there is something between us, but I'm not buying what you're selling. And I don't share what's mine. So, your lifestyle is going to prevent anything more between us. Like I said, I shouldn't have let anything happen."

"My lifestyle? You don't know anything about me!"

"Right, and I don't really want to. Like I said, it's not my scene. Your body is your own, and you can sell it at whatever price you want."

She slapped him before she could control herself. Adam gave her a hard look before he turned and walked away. A few seconds later, she heard her front door close.

Cadence remained standing in the kitchen for several minutes. Her head was spinning in too many directions for her to think straight. Eventually, she walked into her bedroom, removed her clothes, then went in to the shower. The water temperature was hotter than she usually liked, but she hoped the heat and steam would help wash away some of the shame and embarrassment she felt.

I'm not buying what you're selling. He thought she was a slut! How could she have been attracted to such an ass? The idea that she would sleep with him just because he did a few errands around her house was ridiculous. Yes, she had joked about it, but it was obviously in the aftermath of their intimacy. The fact that he took her seriously, and rejected her for it, was unbelievable!

Cadence closed her eyes and tried to squelch the tears that were forming. She was such an idiot. It had been months since she had gone on a date, much less had any real interest in a man. She had tried to be so selective and Adam seemed different from the other men in her past. He was hardworking, generous, and mature. Serious and intense, but also thoughtful and interesting. By his second visit to her house, she knew she liked him, and was scheming subtle ways to let him know.

His kiss had completely surprised her and had felt so good. As did everything else that followed. While in his arms, Cadence had experience an intense and rare pleasure. She had completely opened herself up to him, and now felt the shame of that exposure. As Adam had stated, it had been a mistake.

Once out of the shower, Cadence dressed in a soft camisole with matching briefs and climbed into bed. It was almost ten-thirty PM, and she would normally be in the studio, but tonight she was too worn out to work. Instead, she turned on the television and searched for something to take her mind off Adam and the disastrous evening. She finally settled on a teen movie from the eighties that she had seen at least ten times before.

It was a typical high-school romance where the smart, good girl falls for the small-town bad boy. Of course, the heroine rejects the sensitive, geeky kid who loves her for who she is, and lets the hoodlum treat her like garbage. So typical! *Females have been idiots since the beginning of time,* Cadence thought to herself bitterly. *Why do we always want what's bad for us?* She heard it time and time again, from both men and women. The nice guys were always too boring and uninteresting. They made great friends, but there was never any chemistry. It was the brain-dead, sweet-talking thugs that turned their heads and melted their resistance. In the end, the women were left with broken hearts, feeling foolish. But they would never learn. The next man they fell for would be worst than the last.

Cadence knew her mom was the perfect example. From what she was told, Cadence's father was no good. Everyone knew he was a great artist, but too lazy to do anything for money. He was also charming and good-humored, and got by with a number of girlfriends to take care of him. When his women all found out about each other, there were already four children between them and another on the way. God knows how many brothers and sisters Cadence had by now. She was barely three years old when her father decided to stay with the mother of his oldest child and stopped coming around to see Cadence and her mom.

Within a few months, her mother brought home Ellis Rutherford and she married him within the year. Cadence's sister, Monique, was born two years later. As she grew older, Cadence found Ellis to be as useless as her father ever was, but with none of her dad's charisma. Instead, her stepfather was mean, stingy, and moody. But her mother worked hard and waited on him hand and foot. It was as though she had lost one man and was going to do everything in her power to hold on to the next. To this day, Ellis did nothing to make money except for the occasional win at the racetrack.

As soon as she had finished high school and found a full-time job, Cadence moved out of the house. It had been a very hard decision because she hated to leave her mom and sister, but there was no way her hard-earned money was going to support Ellis's lazy ass. Her mom had argued and tried to dissuade her at first, but Cadence believed she was relieved in the end.

After squirming around on the bed for almost an hour, she finally fell asleep. When she woke up the next morning, it was a few minutes before eight o'clock. Cadence lounged under the covers for a while as her thoughts returned to the night before. A very vivid image formed in her mind of Adam's face at the moment she climaxed. She could still see his intense arousal in his eyes and feel the thrust of his fingers deep inside.

She cursed and buried her face in her pillow. *It was a mistake!* She could not deny how good those moments had been, but it was never going to happen again. Adam Jackson was an absolute bastard, and she was not going to spend another minute thinking about him. With that vow, she rolled out of bed to get busy with her day.

Since it was earlier than she usually got up,

Cadence used most of the morning to do some housecleaning and laundry. She also spent a few minutes drinking tea and reading the paper, then got dressed to do a yoga session. Earlier in the week, she had noticed a yoga studio down the street from her house, and they had a few Saturday classes, one being an intermediate-level at eleven o'clock in the morning.

By ten-thirty, Cadence was entering her garage with a knapsack that held shower essentials and a change of clothes. Though she knew the morning breeze was cool, the weather forecast promised a warm day ahead, so she decided to drive her car instead of taking the motorcycle. That would also give her the freedom to do some grocery shopping on the way home, now that she finally had a usable kitchen.

She arrived at the studio about fifteen minutes before the class was to begin, giving her just enough time to pay for the session and stow her things in a locker. The instructor was getting set up when she entered the studio. There were about thirty other participants spread out in the studio, most of them women. Cadence grabbed a mat, then found an open spot near the back.

"Cadence?" a voice inquired from somewhere on her right.

She looked around until she recognized her neighbor, Erica, waving from a spot near the center of the class. Cadence waved back and Erica walked toward her.

"How are you?" Erica asked with a welcoming smile. "I've never seen you here before."

"This is my first class," Cadence explained. "I

used to go to a studio downtown before I moved, then I saw this place a few days ago."

"Oh! Well, you're going to love it. Ted is awesome," Erica told her excitedly. She used her head to gesture toward the instructor who was chatting with several class members. Cadence nodded, but eyed Ted with skepticism. He didn't look like any yoga specialist she had ever seen, and more resembled a football player with his muscular shoulders, crew-cut hair, and loose sports clothes.

Cadence smiled back at Erica, but her response was cut off when the music started.

"We'll talk after," said Erica as she rushed back to her spot.

The class lasted an intense hour and fifteen minutes, and Cadence enjoyed every minute of it. Despite her first impression, she had to admit that Ted really knew what he was doing. She felt centered and peaceful, but also toned and exhilarated.

Erica was waiting for her outside the class.

"What did you think?" she asked, and Cadence confirmed Erica's assessment of the instructor's skills.

The women talked more about their yoga experiences as they headed to the changing room, then the showers. While getting dressed, Erica asked Cadence her plans for the afternoon.

"Nothing much. Just some grocery shopping," she replied.

"I'm going to the mall. They're having a few sales, and, of course, I can't resist a good discount."

"Really? At West Oaks Mall?" Cadence asked and Erica nodded. "Maybe I'll join you, if you don't mind. I desperately need some furniture."

"I would love the company. It's rare that I don't have the two rug rats for the whole day, so it will be fun," Erica explained. "I'm sure you'll find some stuff at Sears or maybe Dillard's."

They chatted some more as they finished getting dressed, then drove separately to the mall, meeting up in one of the main entrances. The next several hours were spent buying more things than Cadence had ever purchased before in her entire life. Erica turned out to be the perfect shopping partner, with great suggestions and an eye for design. And it didn't stop with the truckload of furniture that was to be delivered within the next couple of weeks. Cadence ended up with several bags filled with clothes, two new pairs of shoes, bath products, and new makeup.

When they left the mall, Erica was headed to the other side of Orlando to pick up her sons at their grandparents' house, and Cadence made her way to the grocery store. She arrived home just as the sun was setting. By the time she unpacked all her purchases, and ate a premade salad from the supermarket, it was almost nine o'clock. She considered doing some work in the studio, but decided against it. Instead, she turned on the stereo at a volume loud enough to hear in her bathroom while she took yet another shower, washing her hair.

Soon, her dreadlocks where clean and smelling like the peppermint shampoo and conditioner she used. Cadence then blow-dried the shoulder-length mass until it was almost dry and tied it back in a thick ponytail. She smoothed rich, sweet-smelling cream over her skin and got dressed in her night clothes.

Back in the bedroom, she settled on the bed with a

couple of jars of hair products, and spent the next two hours treating her scalp with an olive-oil-based stimulator and twisting the roots on each lock with a special cream made with pure shea butter. It was a weekly grooming process that had helped her hair to grow neat and strong over the last few years. People of every culture often stopped to compliment her on how beautiful it looked, and even asked to touch it.

It had taken Cadence quite a while to get used to the attention, particularly the questions about whether she was a Rastafarian or just a "funky dread," a term used to refer to people who grew dreadlocks just for fashion. She definitely was not a practicing Rastafarian, though she highly respected many of their modern philosophies, like their respect for nature and peace. And, even though she had stopped eating pork, and tried to focus on her inner serenity, she was always going to be a good old fashioned Baptist girl at heart.

When her hair was finished, Cadence wrapped it in a protective scarf. She put away her toiletries and turned down the volume on the stereo. A wave of sleepiness overcame her as she settled under her bed sheets, and she fell into a deep sleep before her mind had a chance to touch on the disastrous events of the night before.

Chapter 7

The next few weeks went by quickly for Cadence. She had been asked to participate in the second annual Too Nubian Festival in Miami the last weekend in November. The event was a two-day celebration of art, music, and literature by African, Caribbean, and African-American artists. Too Nubian was also the name of a large black art and bookstore in Miami Beach. They already carried a large selection of her prints, and wanted her to meet customers and autograph purchases. Cadence knew it would be a great opportunity to expand her recognition, and immediately agreed to be there.

For Adam, things went back to the way they were before meeting Cadence Carter. He worked six to seven days a week meeting construction deadlines, getting home after dark almost every night. The one difference was that he started going out with friends a little more. Vince invited him out to parties almost every weekend, and other friends tried to set him up with any single or almost single women they knew.

By mid-November, he had even gone on a few dates with two different women.

On the Friday evening before Thanksgiving, Adam was at home getting dressed to go to the movies on a double date with Yvonne and Calvin. They were introducing him to Alexa Beauchamp, a former coworker of Yvonne's who was described as gorgeous and lots of fun to hang out with. It seemed harmless enough, so Adam agreed.

Alexa also lived in downtown Orlando, so they were all meeting at the large movie theater near Adam's apartment. They had decided in advance to see a newly released crime drama, so Adam arrived early and purchased four tickets for the seven o'clock show. He was standing near the front entrance when the others arrived at six-forty. As they got closer to him, Adam had to admit that Alexa really was beautiful. She was tall and curvy, and with a complexion a shade darker than his. Their eyes connected and she smiled wide, showing beautiful white teeth between full lips painted the color of dark red wine.

After they all said "hello," Yvonne made the formal introductions and Alexa and Adam shared a friendly hug. Adam handed out the tickets, then they walked over to the concession stand to decide which snacks they would buy. The two men joined the line to make the purchases, and the two women went off to get seats in the theater.

"So what do you think?" Calvin asked when the girls were out of earshot.

"Not bad," replied Adam in a neutral tone.

"Oh, give me a break!" exclaimed Calvin. "Alexa is hot! And I say that as a happily married man."

"Alright, she's pretty tight."

"And she's pretty cool, too. A little high-maintenance, but probably well worth the work," Calvin added with a sly chuckle.

Adam laughed too, but he wasn't thrilled by that added description. The *last* thing he was interested in was a high-maintenance woman. He had been married to the queen of vanity for almost eleven years, and had absolutely no interest in going down that path again. It would really surprise him if Calvin turned out to be right. Yvonne knew exactly the type of woman his ex-wife, Rose, had been.

It was about five minutes before the movie was scheduled to start when they joined the women, carrying sodas and popcorn. The girls were sitting side by side in the center of a row near the front, so the guys sat at either end of them. Adult contemporary music played softly in the background, and the screen flashed the typical premovie ads. Alexa and Adam used the few minutes to have a conversation about movies in general and reviews they had heard about the one they were to see. They finished talking in a whisper as the lights went down and the movie trailers began.

Adam tried to pay attention to the story line and get into the characters, but his mind could not stay focused. Alexa kept asking him questions as she clearly struggled to understand every new twist in the plot. After a while, he stopped trying to explain and stopped watching the movie altogether.

His mind ran in circles, thinking about Alexa and the other two women he had gone out with in the last few weeks. Dating was not as bad as he thought it was going to be, and he knew his friends were all relieved that he was getting out more. There was no doubt that he found the three women physically attractive, but that was about it. None of them did anything more for him, though it was still too early to say for sure with Alexa. He knew right away that he could continue dating them casually or he could never see them again. It really didn't matter to him.

Emotionally, he felt nothing, but Adam was used to the void. It was a numbness that had settled in long before his marriage fell apart almost two years before. He had wanted to believe it was all Rose's fault. His self-centered, spoiled wife had turned his heart to stone with her manipulation and greed. But it was now six months after the divorce, and it was starting to dawn on Adam that maybe *she* had been right—his cold, passionless personality had driven her into another man's arms.

Either way, Adam was now comfortable with, and even grateful for, his inability to feel. From the stories told to him by his other single friends, women in the dating scene went for the jugular. He had no intention of becoming one of their victims.

As they had several other times over the last few weeks, his thoughts eventually settled on that disastrous evening with Cadence Carter. It was the perfect example of the complications that came with uncontrollable passion, and what Adam wanted to avoid at all cost. He didn't dwell on why that particular woman made him lose his control. He chose instead to blame it on the combination of unexpected events and prolonged celibacy.

The lights came up as the movie ended. Adam cleared his thoughts and joined the crowd as they shuffled out the exits. The two couples met in the parking lot and decided to walk over to a nearby restaurant and get something to eat. They were seated at a booth with Yvonne and Calvin on one side, and Alexa and Adam on the other. When their waiter arrived, the group requested a round of drinks and a selection of appetizers.

"So, Adam," said Alexa, once their order had been placed. "Yvonne said you own a home-building company. That sounds pretty exciting. How long have you been doing that?"

"We're a pretty small shop, so it's not really that exciting," he replied with a modest smile.

"Oh, please!" Yvonne interjected as she brushed away his comments with a wave of her hand. "He's just being modest. His houses are beautiful. Calvin and I wished we could buy one, but they are way above our budget."

Alexa turned back to him with sparkling eyes.

"So, are you an architect? Do you design the houses yourself?" she asked.

"No, but I was lucky enough to hire someone very talented while he was still unknown. I'm a general contractor," he stated simply. "What about you? Are you still working in insurance like Yvonne?"

"No, I'm actually in human resources. I got a job with a manufacturing company after I left the insurance company that Yvonne works at. We make plastic household products," added Alexa with a giggle.

"Very interesting," Adam replied, but his tone and smile were ironic and she laughed harder.

"I know, garbage cans and stepladders aren't very glamorous, are they?"

"Well, we do what we have to do to make a living, right?"

"For now," she told him with a more serious tone. "But I don't plan on working like this for the rest of my life. There's too much to see in the world to be stuck in the office every day listening to people's problems. Living is more than just paying bills and getting by."

Adam looked at her silently for a few seconds, surprised by her depth and passion.

"So, what's your plan?" he asked. "Because I see what you're saying, but most of us have no choice."

She shrugged, looked down at her glass and slowly mixed her frothy cocktail with the stir stick.

"It's not about a plan, necessarily. It's about recognizing opportunities and taking advantage of them. And, I'm a smart, resourceful girl, so sometimes it's about creating opportunities."

The conversation was cut off when the waiter delivered their assortment of finger foods. It prompted a group discussion about their favorite appetizers, meals, and restaurants. Then they talked about their worst food experience, until the details got too gross and Yvonne threatened to leave and take the car with her. Adam and Calvin were used to her weak stomach and empty threats, so it didn't stop them from adding a couple more stories and exaggerating the facts.

It was after eleven by the time they paid their tab and walked back to the theater parking lot. Yvonne and Calvin got into their car while Adam walked Alexa to hers.

"I had a very good time tonight, Adam," Alexa told him when they stopped beside her driver-side door.

"I did, too."

"Why don't you give me a call, and maybe we can go out again some time?"

Adam nodded, then waited as she reached into her handbag and pulled out a business card. She then wrote her home number on the back side before handing it to him. He slipped it into the back pocket of his pants.

"Drive carefully," Adam told her, thinking she was about to get into the car.

Instead, Alexa remained standing in front of him, waiting. It took him a few seconds to read the clue, then he leaned forward and kissed her. It lasted for a couple of seconds, and she smiled up at him when they pulled apart.

"Good night, Adam."

He nodded again, then stepped back a few steps and watched her drive away.

Yvonne and Calvin were patiently waiting for him when he got back to their car, and Yvonne had a grin that went from ear to ear. It was obvious they had seen the kiss. The three of them decided to hang out at Adam's place for a little bit, so Adam made his way to his vehicle, then Yvonne and Calvin followed him home in theirs.

At the apartment, Calvin went to use the bathroom. Adam knew Yvonne would use that time to grill him about the evening.

"So, what do you think of Alexa?" Yvonne asked as soon as Calvin was out of earshot.

"She seems all right," Adam replied neutrally.

"All right," she repeated in the same flat tone he used. "Just all right? Adam, give me a break! She is the most beautiful single woman I know. I'm not going to let you get away with your typical 'I'm not affected by anything' attitude. You're going to have to do better than 'all right.'"

Instead of responding, Adam walked to the kitchen and grabbed three beers. Yvonne followed him, determined to get some kind of response. When he turned to face her, he looked at her intently.

"What's that supposed to mean?" he asked quietly.

Yvonne sighed loudly.

"Adam, I've known you for a long time. I was there in high school when all the girls drooled over your serious, bad-boy image. It worked. You had them all convinced that you were too cool to catch on fire. But I know different. Quit acting like you don't have a pulse!" She took a deep breath, then rushed forward when he didn't respond. "Adam, any woman you meet will want to feel connected to you, like they know you inside. If you never open up, you will never have a relationship of any value. You'll end up with someone like Rose all over again."

Adam clenched his jaw tight, then looked away from her to uncap two bottles. He handed her one and took a drink from his own. Though his eyes glowed with intensity, his lips curved into a lop-sided smile.

"Yvonne, you're taking this a little too seriously. Fine. Alexa is gorgeous, and she seems quite nice. I will gladly go out with her again. Is that a better response?"

"Don't try to charm me," she replied, and reprimanded him with a punch to his shoulder. "I'm worried about you."

"Well don't be. I will never end up with someone like Rose again."

Calvin walked into the room at that point. His steps slowed as he felt the tension in the air.

"I hope you don't, Adam," stated Yvonne. "But, you know that Rose and I used to talk, and one of her biggest beefs with you was that you were so cold and unapproachable. Don't interrupt! Let me explain! I know she was spoiled and selfish. I'm just saying that it's only natural for a woman to feel insecure if she doesn't feel important."

Adam looked at her, expressionless, while she looked at the floor, and Calvin looked back and forth between them.

"It's getting late," Calvin stated after a minute of silence.

"I'm sorry. I shouldn't have said anything. . . ." said Yvonne, clearly uncomfortable with the mood she created.

"Don't even worry about it," Adam dismissed with wave of his hand. He handed Calvin the last beer, and each of them took a sip.

Eventually, Calvin started a discussion about their plans for Thursday, which was Thanksgiving. He and Yvonne were hosting a family dinner, then on Saturday they were leaving for vacation in Jamaica for two weeks. It was a trip that the couple had been planning for over a year. They were going to the Sandals resort in Montego Bay.

Adam's plans were not nearly as exciting. He was going to catch up on some work and sleep. A few of his houses were closing in less than a month, and more were scheduled in early January. It was going to be a crazy few weeks with very little time for holiday celebrations, he explained. Unfortunately, his friends had heard the same story many times before, and just rolled their eyes.

Yvonne and Calvin said their good-byes once their drinks were finished. Though it was almost one o'clock in the morning, Adam was still wide awake. He changed into cotton pajama pants, and switched on the television in the living room to see what was on. Once he found a rerun of a crime drama, he slouched on the couch and got comfortable.

He managed to stay focused for about ten minutes, before the discussion with Yvonne filled his mind.

Adam wasn't angry. He knew that she was truly concerned about him, and she had not said anything that wasn't true, or that he didn't already know. But he was the way he was. There was no way to change his nature, nor did he really want to.

Chapter 8

"Mom, I'm really sorry I can't make it."

"I know, Cadence. I don't really have anything special planned for Thanksgiving, anyway. Will you be able to stop by over the weekend while you're in Miami?

"I don't know, Mom. It's going to be pretty busy. I won't be finished at the festival until Sunday evening, then I have to drive back to Orlando."

"Oh." Cadence could hear the disappointment in her mother's voice.

"But maybe I can drive down again in a couple of weeks and stay for the weekend," she suggested.

"That sounds nice, baby."

"Listen, Mom, I have to run. I'll call you from the hotel on Friday, okay?"

"Okay, baby. Have a good time. I love you."

"I love you, too, Mom."

Cadence hung up the phone and threw it on her bed. She had been running late when her mom called, and now she was way behind schedule. It was Wednesday evening, the day before Thanksgiving, and she was getting ready to meet Steve and some friends at seven o'clock to celebrate Steve's birthday. All she needed to do was finish her makeup, slip on her shoes, and she would be out the door. She hoped she would not be embarrassingly late.

The group was meeting for dinner at a trendy restaurant in a luxury downtown hotel. The food was supposedly top-notch, and there was live jazz most nights of the week. Cadence had never been there, but knew the type of people who went there: very trendy, high-end people. She was pretty sure Beverley had picked the spot, because Steve would definitely have picked a noisy rib joint instead.

The traffic through the city was light, so Cadence was able to push her dated Honda and skim several minutes off the trip. By the time she left her car at valet parking and walked through the lobby toward the lounge, it was only twenty minutes after seven. She approached the maître d' and was ushered to the reserved table right away. There were eight people already seated, and three empty spaces.

Steve was at the head of the table with Beverley beside him. He stood up as soon as she approached. Cadence gave him a big hug and wished him happy birthday, then shared a light embrace with Beverley. Most of the other people in the group worked with Steve at the publishing company. She waved at each of them before claiming one of the available chairs in the center of the table. Her back was to the entrance of the restaurant.

"So how are you doing, Cadence?" asked one of her former colleagues, Greg, who was sitting to her right.

"I'm okay, Greg. How are you? Steve told me you're now assistant art director. Congratulations!"

"Thanks," he replied with a nod and a shy smile. "But it's crazy, though. My hairline was receding before, but now, I'm officially bald *and* going grey. And it's only been four months!"

"Whatever, Greg," chimed in Natalie, another former coworker who was seated on Cadence's left side. "You were bald and grey long before the promotion!"

The rest of the group laughed loudly while Greg's pale skin turned red and he broke out in laughter as well. Their waiter arrived at that moment with a variety of appetizers that had been ordered earlier, and he also took a drink order for Cadence. Natalie then launched into a series of updates and gossip about each member of the dinner party and several other coworkers who were absent. They were all laughing uproariously at a story about Steve when Beverley jumped up with a squeal as she waved toward someone near the front of the restaurant. The chuckles faded away as everyone looked toward the focus of her attention, and watched as a couple approached them.

"Alexa, you made it!" stated Beverley before the two women embraced.

"Sorry we're late," said her friend when they broke apart. "Hi Steve! Happy birthday."

While Alexa hugged Steve, Beverley made brief introductions to everyone else.

"This is my best friend, Alexa. And this is . . . Adam, right?" she asked.

Cadence was sure Adam had confirmed with a nod or something else, but her back was to them and she wasn't about to turn around again.

What the hell was he doing here? When she had

looked over her shoulder and saw him walking across the dining room, everything had frozen. Even though he had been several feet away, their eyes had met almost immediately, and the copper heat in his seemed to burn right into her. It took several seconds for the reality of the situation to sink in, and Cadence turned her head away as soon as the shock wore off. She had hoped he was here as a coincidence, eating dinner at another table. But Beverley's introductions snatched that optimism away.

To make things worse, Cadence watched out of the corner of her eye as he and his date took the empty seats across from her and slightly to her right. Her heart rate increased as his gaze fell on her. She felt the constant focus while the others around them continued chatting, oblivious to the tension. Cadence forced herself to keep her eyes fixed on her plate, at least until she could decide how to handle the situation without embarrassing herself, or snatching her purse and running out of the room.

After several minutes of fidgeting with the food on her plate, and two large sips of red wine, Cadence finally looked toward him. Adam was still watching her, though not in a way that anyone else would notice. He nodded in acknowledgment, and she quickly looked back at her plate.

Cadence knew the only way to get through this dinner was to ignore him completely. She took another sip of wine, which fortified her resolve. There was absolutely no reason to speak to him, or even acknowledge his presence. And since he was obviously here on a date, he should not have any interest in her, either.

Eventually, Michelle and Greg pulled Cadence into a discussion about a particularly difficult writer they had all worked with. Their waiter came around to take their entrée orders, and their meals were delivered surprisingly quickly. It was starting to look like avoiding contact with Adam was definitely doable.

Adam, on the other hand, felt distracted at every turn.

When he first saw Cadence at the table, looking at him over her shoulder, he had been surprised by her presence, but also taken back by her appearance. He had a very clear image in his head of the last time he saw her—her face almost bare of makeup, but flushed with excitement and anger. She had seemed untamed and earthy, completely comfortable with her arousal and sexuality. But tonight, she looked beautiful, sophisticated, and untouchable.

Her dreadlocks were styled and curled so they swept to one side and hung in individual spirals. Her face was flawlessly made up with smoky grey eye shadow and lips the color of pink cotton candy. Even her dress, from what he could see, was made from crisp white linen and skimmed her body with tailored lines.

By the time he was seated at the table beside Alexa, Adam was finding it difficult to keep his eyes off Cadence. Clearly, she did not wish to acknowledge his presence or that they knew each other, and he was okay with that, for now. But he kept wondering what she was doing there and her connection to the others at the table.

Adam also wanted to know how Cadence was doing and make sure her kitchen was still working okay. He had planned to give her a call over the last few weeks. He had even dialed her phone number a couple of times, but then thought better of it. Her name had come up a couple of times with Calvin and Yvonne, but Adam had avoided any real conversations about her, even though he was tempted to ask all sorts of questions.

"How is your steak, Adam?" Alexa asked once they were halfway through their meals. They had not spoken much since their arrival. Alexa and Beverley had been in their own private conversation, conveniently leaving Adam to his thoughts.

"Very good," he replied with a smile. "Do you want to try some?"

"No, thanks, I'm not a big steak fan. Here, have some of my pasta."

Before he could object, her forkful of noodles was pressing against his lips. Adam had no choice but to let her feed him while she gazed into his eyes.

"Good, isn't it?" she asked.

Adam nodded quietly while continuing to chew, then went back to his steak and mashed potatoes. He did not miss Cadence's glance toward them, then the look of disgust on her face before she looked away. He smiled to himself.

"So, you've told me about Beverley and her boyfriend Steve. Do you know anyone else here?" he asked Alexa once their dinner was finished and the waiter started to remove the plates.

"Not really," Alexa said. "Most of them work with Steve at the publishing company."

He was about to ask more questions when Beverley tapped her wine glass to get everyone's attention. The other conversations died away until they were all looking at her expectantly.

"Hi, everyone. Thank you again for coming out tonight." She paused while the group clapped and a few people cheered, causing several of the patrons around them to turn and look at them. "Most of you have known Steve for a long time, much longer than I have, so you know what a special man he is. So I'm sure you will join me in wishing him all the best for his birthday and the year to come."

Beverley leaned forward and gave an embarrassed Steve a big sloppy kiss, while the rest of his friends applauded. Several jokes were thrown around about his advanced age and limited physical capabilities. Steve laughed good-naturedly along with everyone else.

Their waiter then arrived with a big chocolate cake decorated with sparklers, and a stack of dessert plates. While servings of the dessert were handed out, Cadence took the opportunity to excuse herself and go to the bathroom.

Adam waited about five minutes before he excused himself also. He waited in the lobby for another five minutes before he saw her standing at the end of a hallway. She was on her cell phone and turned away from him. He couldn't hear what she was saying, but her emphatic hand gestures suggested it was an important call and she wasn't thrilled with what she was hearing. At one point, she stood listening for a length of time, and that was when she noticed him leaning against the wall near the entrance to the men's bathroom.

Cadence quickly turned away with her back to him. She ended the conversation several seconds later.

Adam was just going to wait in that spot since she would have to pass him to get back to the restaurant, but when she stood where she was, still turned away, he walked quickly toward her.

"Hi, Cadence," he said when he was directly behind her.

Finally, she turned around and looked directly up into his face.

"Adam," she said simply.

He smiled, amused by her attempt to be icy and detached. Her flared nostrils said differently.

"How are you?" he asked with deliberate politeness.

Her eyes narrowed suspiciously, and Adam added a smile. He was having fun ruffling her feathers.

"Just fine. Wonderful, actually. And how are you?" she replied.

"Good, good."

Cadence nodded, then walked around him to head back to the group.

"I've been meaning to call you," Adam said softly before she could pass him.

She paused, then looked up at him again.

"Why. Did your financial situation change?" The scorn in her tone was unmistakable, and Adam raised his brows in a silent question. "You said you weren't buying what I'm selling, remember? So why would you call me? With the dirt under your nails, you cannot afford anything I have to offer, so I have to assume that something has changed. Did you win the lottery? Bingo maybe?"

Adam's polite smile spread into a sly grin. *Ouch*, he thought.

"Actually, I was just going to make sure your plumbing, and other things, were still working okay. When I do a job, I make sure it's done right, so I hope you were completely satisfied."

He watched her cheeks flush and her smoky eyes burn venom at him before she turned on her heels and marched away as fast as her tiny frame could take her.

Adam decided to put some space between them, so he went into the men's bathroom, used the urinal, and washed his hands. He could not resist checking his hands for any dirt under the nails, then shook his head at his misplaced vanity.

When he got back to the table, Alexa smiled sweetly at him and pulled him into a conversation she and a few others were having.

"Beverley and Steve are planning a vacation to the Caribbean in December, and I was telling them that, since you're Jamaican, maybe you can give them suggestions," Alexa explained. "I've heard Negril is a lot of fun."

"Well, it depends on what you're looking for. Have you guys been to the Caribbean before?" Adam asked the couple.

They both shook their heads to say 'no.'

"We were originally thinking of Cancun because we've both been there and really enjoyed it. But my friend Cadence suggested Jamaica," Steve explained while gesturing over to where Cadence was sitting, quietly finishing her slice of cake. "She's also from there," Steve explained.

"Really?" asked Adam, taking the opportunity to

openly give Cadence a once-over. "Like I said, it really depends on what you want to do. The resorts in Negril are great for partying and lying on the beach, so are the ones in Montego Bay and Ocho Rios. But, you should also consider some of the less commercial areas like Port Antonio."

"Funny. Cadence recommended Port Antonio as well. She said it's quiet and peaceful, but still with lots to do."

"But are there any nightclubs? It sounds a little boring," Beverley added with a slight pout.

"Well, it's definitely not like Negril or Cancun, but no matter where you go in Jamaica, there is always somewhere to dance and listen to music," Adam told her.

Alexa and Beverley then launched into a story about their trip to Cancun several years ago, but were interrupted when Cadence approached them.

"Hey," Steve said as he stood to greet her. "You're not leaving, are you?"

"Sorry, Steve. I have to. I still have a ton of things to get done by Friday. But I had a lot of fun."

"Well, I'm glad you were able to come out," he told her while they shared a big hug.

Beverley stood up as well.

"Yeah, thanks for coming, Cadence," she added, before leaning in to kiss both cheeks.

"I left my portion of the bill with Michelle," Cadence told her discreetly.

Beverley nodded, then sat back down as Cadence said good-bye to everyone else, deliberately avoiding any eye contact with Adam.

Chapter 9

Adam's eyes followed Cadence as she walked purposefully from the restaurant. He continued to look into space for several minutes as conversations continued around him.

After the initial date with Alexa on Friday evening, Adam had been indecisive about whether to call her again. She was nice enough, and quite attractive, but he sensed that she was not the sharpest tool in the box. In the end, he convinced himself that he was being too picky and critical, and left her a message on Sunday afternoon. She called back right away, and they had a pleasant conversation for about an hour.

They spoke again on Monday night, at which time Alexa invited him out on Wednesday night. Adam was not able to commit right away, since he had been planning to catch up with some work before the holiday. But, after checking with the team on Tuesday, he realized that their most urgent projects were on schedule. He called her back that evening and confirmed their plan.

During that conversation, Alexa told Adam a little about her best friend, Beverley, and her live-in boyfriend Steve. According to her, the two women used to be inseparable, partying and vacationing together. That was until Beverley and Steve became serious and moved in together. Though the women were still very close, their lives had taken different directions, and they only saw each other a couple of times a year.

Adam detected some resentment in Alexa's tone, particularly as she over-emphasized how glad she was that Beverley had met someone special. He was tempted to ask her more about it, but let it go. Alexa did not strike him as the type who would be honest about her true feelings, anyway. She gave him the impression that she wanted him to think she was easygoing and uncomplicated. It was hard for him to tell if the image was real or not.

Their conversation did cause Adam to remember how things had been for him and his ex-wife, Rose, once they got married. They had stopped partying and hanging out with their mutual friends, much to the exasperation of Vince, Yvonne, and others. Everyone accused them of changing, and it was true, to some extent. Adam turned into a man obsessed with making money to give his wife the kind of life she was used to, while Rose decided she wanted to be a true society woman and that image did not include her middle-class college friends. In the end, they both changed into unhappy, unfulfilled people who couldn't remember why they fell in love to begin with.

"Are you okay?" Alexa asked Adam, pulling him out of his thoughts.

He looked at her with an easy smile.

"Sure," he replied.

"You looked like you were a million miles away."

"Sorry. Just thinking about work."

The others around them must have heard his response.

"What do you do, Adam?" Steve asked.

"Oh, Adam owns his own building company," Alexa answered for him with obvious pride in her voice. "He builds residential homes all over Orlando. I haven't seen any yet, but apparently they are absolutely gorgeous. Where are some of your houses located, Adam? Maybe Steve and Beverley have seen them."

"Right now, we have a project in Altamonte Springs, but we've done some lots around Lake Apoka and in several other suburbs," answered Adam. "What about you, Steve? You're in publishing, right?"

"Yup. I'm the art director at Edison Publishing, and we publish books for children right up to young adults. Actually, almost everyone here is part of my art team. Except for Beverley, of course," Steve explained. "And Cadence, the woman who just left."

"Oh really, she doesn't work with you?" Adam asked, trying not to sound too interested. "So how do you know her?"

"She works with us, but only on contract."

Adam waited patiently for more information, but Steve only took a drink from his beer bottle.

"What sort of contract work is there in publishing?" Adam was forced to ask.

"She's an illustrator; our best illustrator, actually.

I would love to have her on the team permanently. But once her paintings started to sell, I had to settle for the occasional special project."

At that point, Steve excused himself to answer a question from one of his friends; otherwise, Adam would have asked a dozen more questions. Thank God that Alexa was too busy gossiping with Beverley to notice his lapse into deep thought, again.

What an unbelievable ass he was! His brain was running a mile a minute, revisiting all his interactions with Cadence since he met her at Yvonne's house. He had taken everything he saw about her and assumed the absolute worst. No wonder Cadence looked at him with such loathing tonight. It was surprising that she didn't slap him again. Adam knew he was going to have to apologize to her, but he couldn't imagine what he could say to make up for his nasty accusations.

And once he told Calvin the truth, his friend was never going to let him forget his jaded imagination.

She's an artist, and apparently quite successful, too. Adam smiled at the thought. She was spontaneous, untamed, and unconventional. All the pieces fit together so well. He really was an idiot.

It was almost ten o'clock before Adam gave in to his urge to leave the dinner party. Alexa's friends seemed very nice, but he was distracted, and it was starting to appear rude. After a round of quick good-byes, Adam drove them to Adam's apartment in Alexa's car. He had offered to drive his own, but conceded that her sporty Mitsubishi would be more comfortable than his pickup truck for the evening.

He pulled into the visitor's spot closest to his building, stopped the car, but left the engine running. She unbuckled her seatbelt and turned to face him.

"Thanks again for coming out tonight, Adam," she told him with a warm smile.

"My pleasure," Adam replied courteously.

"It was my pleasure. I had a good time."

Alexa placed a hand on his thigh and leaned a little closer.

"I had a good time, too. Are you going to be okay to drive home? I can drive you to your house, then take a cab home."

Alexa shook her head to say 'no,' but pulled back a bit when he didn't seem to notice her overture.

"I'll be fine. It's just a few blocks away, and I've only had one glass of wine."

Adam nodded, then opened the driver's door. She did the same, and they both walked around to the front of the car. He pulled her into a hug that ended with a friendly squeeze.

"Talk to you later?" she said when they pulled apart.

"Sure. Drive safely, okay?"

"I will," promised Alexa.

Adam stepped aside to let her get into the car and watched her drive away. He then jogged up to his apartment, and once inside, began stripping off his clothes before he jumped into the shower. Twenty minutes later, he was pulling on a cotton polo shirt over faded jeans. After a spritz of cologne, he grabbed his wallet and keys and was out the door again.

It was eleven thirty-five PM when he stopped his truck in Cadence's driveway.

Adam sat behind the wheel with the engine running for a couple of minutes, wondering if this was a good idea. Reality set in, and he realized that it was really too late to show up at her house uninvited. *Maybe I should call first,* he thought. But it would be too easy for her just to hang up the phone.

He sat there for another couple of minutes before he put the truck in park and turned it off. There was no point in turning back now. He was already there and so he might as well go talk to her. The worst she could do was slam the door in his face. Or punch him in the eye. Or call the police.

Adam smiled again. When did his imagination become so overactive? He walked quickly to her door and rang the doorbell before he changed his mind.

He knew the minute Cadence realized who it was, and he could feel her standing in her foyer trying to figure out what he was doing there, and whether to open the door. Adam let out a deep breath when he heard the bolt unlock.

"What do you want?" she asked aggressively with the door only open wide enough to show her frame. Cadence had also changed her clothes, and was now wearing white cotton shorts and a matching camisole. Her face was free of the makeup she had on earlier.

Adam smiled, amused by her attack, and knowing he fully deserved it.

"Hi, Cadence," he replied.

She stared back at him, clearly refusing to speak again until he answered her.

"Can I come in?" he asked.

Her eyes flashed.

"Why?"

"Because we need to talk."

Something in his voice must have swayed her. She

turned around and walked back inside, leaving the door open. Adam followed her in, after taking off his shoes at the door. By the time he reached the kitchen, Adam could see that the house had gone through a drastic change. Previously empty rooms now had living room and dining room furniture.

Cadence was standing next to a new plush couch in the family room. A midsize flat-screen television was now set up in an entertainment unit.

"Well?" she insisted, pulling Adam's attention back to her.

"Well . . . it looks like I owe you an apology," he stated seriously, but could not help but smile when her eyes widened to the size of saucers. "It turns out that I was very wrong about you, and what you do for a living."

Cadence sat down on the arm of the chair and looked at the floor, silent for several seconds.

"Really?" she finally replied. "And how did you come to this realization? What is it you think I do for a living now?"

"Okay, I deserve the sarcasm. I admit that I was an ass and I acted very badly. But, in my defense, you could have just told me the truth." Smoky eyes flashed fire again as Cadence finally looked up at him. "Seriously! Why didn't you just tell me you're an artist?"

"You're serious? You want to blame me for your ridiculous assumptions and wild imagination? You are unbelievable!"

"I'm not blaming you, but you must admit, it did look pretty suspicious. There was a half-dressed man regularly leaving your place in the middle of the day. Never mind the envelop I saw him give you. It looked like a payment to me."

"It wasn't a payment, it was an invoice from the modeling agency!" Cadence interjected hotly.

"I'm just saying, you could have corrected me, that's all," Adam defended himself. "Why didn't you?"

Cadence crossed her arms over her chest. It was clear that she was trying to decide whether to give him an answer or just tell him to go to hell. Finally, she shrugged her shoulders and let out a long sigh.

"To be honest, I didn't even understand what you were talking about at first. I just thought you were pissed off about something I said and took it out of context. But a few days later, it occurred to me that you might actually think I'm some sort of . . . of . . . prostitute!" The last word was spit out with disgust.

"All right, I already admitted that I was an idiot. But that still doesn't explain why you didn't just correct me," Adam insisted.

"Are you for real? After what happened, and the things you said to me, you still think I owed you an explanation? At that point, I was pretty glad that I would, I hoped, never speak to you or see you again. Unfortunately, my luck wasn't that good."

Adam had the good sense to realize that his approach was not getting him the results he wanted, and decided to change it.

"Well, for what it's worth, I really am sorry, and I am really glad I was wrong."

Cadence stood up and walked a few steps away.

"Really? Why is that? What difference does it make either way? We barely know each other," she replied with her back to him.

"You're right, we barely know each other, but I would like to change that."

Adam walked toward her but stopped a step away, waiting for her to turn around or respond in some way.

"Cadence, let's just put our cards on the table. Despite what I thought was true, I know there was something between us. I don't think it's too late for us to see what that is. Why don't we spend some time getting to know each other more? You can tell me all about yourself so I don't have to use my imagination."

She whipped around, ready to attack, just as he knew she would. Adam used the opportunity to give her a slow smile, showing that he had baited her on purpose.

"What do you think? Do you forgive me?"

Cadence didn't answer right away, but she did uncross her arms and relax her stance.

"So, what other assumptions did you make about me?" she asked instead.

Adam laughed.

"Trust me, I've learned my lesson. No more assumptions, I promise," he replied.

Sensing that her mood had lightened, Adam reached out and took her hand. She didn't resist his touch, so he pulled her closer to him.

"I'm pretty sure that the real Cadence Carter is much better than anything I could make up."

"Oh, pleeeeeese!" she exclaimed while her face twisted in disgust at his shameless fawning.

Adam laughed again and Cadence finally smiled back.

"So, what now?" she asked.

"Well," he replied. "Why don't we start with this?"

Adam swept his free hand along the length of her neck and into the thickness of her hair. He then leaned down and placed his mouth on hers.

The first kiss was soft and sweet; a simple brush of their lips that lasted a few seconds. Hot currents sparked between them immediately, and the second kiss was hot, wet, and deep. His tongue thrust in and out of her mouth, stroking and teasing against the sweet roughness of hers. Cadence's hands slid up his chest until they locked behind his neck. They remained in the steamy embrace until their moans got louder and deeper.

When they finally pulled apart, they were both breathing heavily. Adam rested his forehead against hers.

"What are your plans for tomorrow?" he asked.

Chapter 10

Cadence woke up on Thursday morning feeling a little light-headed. It could have been the two glasses of red wine at Steve's dinner party, or the fact that she was up much earlier than usual. But, after lying under the covers and letting her mind wander for several minutes, she knew it was the surreal visit from Adam Jackson the night before.

She had been surprised to see him at the restaurant, but completely stunned when he showed up at her door. It didn't help that, until he had shown up, Cadence had been sitting on her couch re-examining every interaction between them, that night and back in October. Though she had made a conscious attempt to curse him as a total ass and put him out of her mind, it had not worked. It was impossible to forget his kindness, quiet strength, and good conversation. That was not even mentioning the magic his hands did to her body.

Cadence grabbed the television remote control off her side table and turned on the unit in her bedroom. She then rolled over onto her stomach and plumped her pillow under her head so she could watch the morning news comfortably. The weatherman promised a clear, warm day with a light breeze in Orlando, and the same in Miami for the weekend.

The rest of the holiday news broadcast was filled with heartwarming stories and turkey cooking tips, but Cadence was barely listening. Her mind was wondering how the day would unfold now that she was going to spend most of it with Adam. They hadn't discussed exactly what they would do, but he was coming by her house in the afternoon and they would decide then. That only gave her a few hours to complete her list of "to do" items before she got on the road to Miami.

Cadence had exaggerated a little when she told Steve she had a ton of things to get done before the weekend festival. It had made a good excuse to leave the get-together early. She really only needed to pack her clothes, then organize and price the small inventory of originals she was bringing with her. Now, she would have to get all that done within the next few hours.

When Adam called, she was in the studio debating which of her newly framed paintings she liked the most. She had already packed her suitcase with everything she needed, except for toiletries and a few last-minute items.

"Hey there," he said in a low voice after she picked up the phone. "Happy Thanksgiving."

"Hi Adam. Happy Thanksgiving to you, too," she replied.

"I was thinking that I can be by your place by around two-thirty," Adam stated. "Is there anything in particular you want to do? It's going to be a nice day."

Cadence looked at her watch, and it was a few minutes after one o'clock in the afternoon. She thought quickly and decided she would need another twenty minutes or so in the studio. That would give her about an hour to get ready.

"Two-thirty sounds good," she told him. "I'm pretty open to anything."

"Okay, well, I have an idea. Just wear comfortable clothes and shoes and plan to be outside," he said.

"Okay. . . . So what's the idea? What are we doing?"

"I'll tell you when I get there. See you in a little bit."

With that cryptic statement, Adam hung up the phone.

He was ten minutes late when he rang her doorbell. Cadence let him in, and she was relieved to see him in dark jeans and a polo-neck top. She had not been sure what he meant by comfortable clothes, but was happy she had chosen loose tan-colored capris and a white cotton T-shirt.

The two said hello politely, then stood awkwardly in the foyer for a couple of seconds before Adam pulled her into quick hug and placed a kiss on her cheek.

"Are you ready?" he asked.

"Um, I think so. But where are we going? Do I need to bring anything?"

Adam smiled, clearly enjoying the suspense. He looked up in thought for a moment before responding.

"Bring a bathing suit, and a change of clothes."

Cadence stared at him, wanting to question him more, but knowing he wasn't going to tell her anything. Finally, she turned away and walked back to her bedroom to throw a few things in a bag.

"Are you hungry?" Adam asked when she returned. He was now standing near the kitchen.

"No, I had lunch. Are you?" she asked.

"No, I'm good. Are you all set?"

"I guess," she replied.

After she locked her door, they walked to his truck parked in the driveway. It was a big Ford pickup with a spacious cabin that seated up to six adults in two rows of seating.

"I hope you don't mind if we take my truck?" Adam stated as he opened the passenger door for her and helped her up into the seat. "It's not the smoothest ride."

"Not at all. I've been in worse, I'm sure," she replied.

Adam put her small tote bag into the back seat next to his duffel bag and another knapsack. He then hopped in, and they were on their way.

A compact disc loaded with classic reggae played loudly as they drove with the windows down. Neither of them said much until they were headed north on the Florida Turnpike for about twenty minutes. Adam then took the exit to Highway 27 north toward Leesburg.

"So, are you going to tell me where we're going?" Cadence asked loudly.

Adam turned the music down so he could hear her. She repeated her question.

"You'll see soon enough. We'll be there in about twenty minutes," he replied briefly.

"You're not even going to give me a hint or anything?"

"I already did. I told you to bring a bathing suit and a change of clothes," Adam replied. "Don't you like surprises?"

"I don't know, to be honest with you. I don't get surprised often. I usually make my own plans."

He looked at her briefly, then back at the road.

"You make your own plans for dates? That doesn't sound like much fun. Are you a control freak?"

"What? Why? Because I don't get a lot of surprises?"

"I'm just saying that if you're always the one making the plans, it may be because you need to be the one in charge."

"Okay! Clearly, you can't stop yourself from judging people and jumping to extreme conclsusions," Cadence stated in a heated tone.

"It wasn't a conclusion, it was a question," he replied quietly and slowly.

She took a deep breath while looking out her window.

"I wasn't referring to dates," Cadence explained after a few moments. "I just meant that I don't know a lot a people who plan surprises or elaborate schemes. If I want to do something, either with a friend or on my own, I usually make the plans. And only because I'm good at organizing things, that's all."

She added the final statement only after Adam slid her a know-it-all glance. It made him laugh quietly, and made her want to hit him.

"Okay, so that means you're due a good surprise, right?" he told her. "So sit back and relax. You said you were up to anything, so as long as you don't mind the great outdoors, I think you'll have fun. Unless of course, you're one of those women who prefers air conditioning to fresh air."

Cadence had to laugh because she knew exactly the type of women he was referring to. Those who could not stand being outside because perspiration might ruin their makeup, or humidity could ruin their perms. That was her mother and sister in a nutshell. Their only exposure to the sun came from the walk from the car to the closest mall entrance. It was such a waste of Florida weather.

"Don't worry, I won't melt in the sun," she assured him. "So Adam Jackson, do you often ambush women and abscond with them to a secret location in the country? Maybe you're the control freak."

"Abscond?" Adam repeated with a burst of laughter. "Trust me, this is not something that I have done often. I'm probably the total opposite of you. I'm not very good at making plans, romantic or otherwise. I'm the guy who usually goes with the flow, or defers to what others want to do."

"Really? Why is that?"

Adam shrugged but didn't say anything more. To Cadence, he appeared a little uncomfortable, either with his statement or with her question. She looked at his profile for a few moments, but looked back out her window when he still didn't elaborate.

Eventually, he turned up the volume on the stereo again for the rest of the ride. They turned off the highway a couple of miles past Leesburg. Less than ten minutes later, they pulled into the driveway of a house on a residential street. Cadence could smell the lake in the air and feel its breeze through the window.

"We're here," Adam stated as he parked the truck and walked over to her door to help her out.

"And where exactly is 'here'?" she asked suspiciously.

"Welcome to Fruitland Park," he announced.

"Never heard of it. Whose house is this?"

By then, Adam had unloaded their things from the back seat. She picked up her tote, while he grabbed the two other bags.

"Adam, whose house is this?" Cadence asked again while she watched Adam unlock the front door to a two-story brick house.

"It belongs to my company," he told her briefly before heading back outside.

Cadence followed Adam down the hall into the house while looking around. The space in front of the door was very open and topped by a high, vaulted ceiling. Adam turned into the kitchen on the right of the hall, and a staircase on the left led upstairs to the bedrooms, she assumed. There was a living room with a couple of couches and a television at the rear of the house, and a den or library next to it.

When she joined Adam in the kitchen, he was unpacking various items from the knapsack into the fridge.

"This is really nice. Does it belong to your boss? He must be doing well in the construction business," she commented, but elaborated when Adam looked at her questioningly. "You said it belongs to the company you work for. A construction company, right?"

He looked away before nodding. He put a few more things in the fridge, then left a few pieces of fruit in a bowl on the counter.

"Well, it's great that employees can use it." Cadence commented. "Do you come here often?"

"Not really. Just a couple of times in the last year or so," Adam replied. "Do you want one?"

He held up a large golden delicious apple. Cadence nodded, then watched him wash two and polish them with a paper towel. He gave her one, and they both bit into the juicy fruit.

"Come, let me show you around the place."

They walked through the center of the house and Adam pointed out some of the rooms that she had glimpsed earlier. He also showed her a small powder room near the front door, then explained that there was also a larger bathroom off the family room and two more upstairs. In the family room, Cadence got her first look at the incredible waterfront view of the property.

Adam opened French doors that led to a large solarium enclosing a spacious swimming pool and cozy hot tub. Then, a wide backyard stretched about thirty yards before sloping to the edge of the lake. There was a splatter of boats on the water, but otherwise it was completely peaceful and secluded.

"Wow!" Cadence said as they stepped out of the solarium and onto the grass. "This is breathtaking."

Adam smiled at her while still chewing his apple, then continued leading her across the lawn until they reached the water's edge. Two oversized Adirondack chairs were planted near a wooden pier, overlooking the view. He gave one to Cadence and sat in the other.

The two sat quietly for several minutes, absorbing the warm sun and fresh air.

"Thank you for bringing me up here, Adam. It

was definitely worth the surprise," Cadence told him sincerely. "I can't understand why someone wouldn't live up here permanently."

Adam shrugged, waiting a few seconds before responding.

"Some people find it too isolated and rustic. There's not much to do up here other than boating or hiking. And there isn't much nightlife either."

"Well, I think nightlife is overrated," she told him. "Plus, Orlando is only an hour away. It's perfect."

He looked at her with a fixed gaze, but didn't say anything.

"What?" demanded Cadence when she became uncomfortable with his assessment.

"You're very different from most of the women I know," Adam stated simply.

"Really," she replied, but looked away, uncomfortably. "And I'm sure you've known a lot of women."

Adam laughed with a short burst before he responded to her.

"Actually, not very many at all."

"Whatever!" Cadence retorted, clearly dismissing his claim as modesty. "Anyway, how am I different?"

He laughed again, this time with genuine amusement.

"Are you looking for compliments?"

"Not really. Different isn't necessarily a good thing," she told him. "I've been different all my life, particularly within in my family. My mother had no idea what to do with a rebellious, ambitious daughter with little interest in marriage and babies. And whenever I talk to my little sister, she just looks at me like I'm an alien."

Cadence smiled at Adam, but there was a trace of sadness in her eyes. He listened silently.

"They don't understand why my career and independence are more important than having a man in my life," she explained further. "They love me, but they feel sorry for me at the same time."

"Well, I meant it as a compliment," Adam told her in a quiet voice.

"Okay," said Cadence, more to fill the gap than anything else.

"I don't think I've met anyone as easygoing and uncomplicated as you. No, I'm serious!" he defended when her eyes opened wide in reaction. "I noticed it immediately. You're easy to be with."

She was speechless for a few minutes. No one had ever described her as easygoing before. It was not that she didn't know how to have fun with the friends she was close to. But men usually found her unapproachable and women found her baffling.

"Somehow, I knew that you would like it up here," Adam continued.

"So, this isn't your typical first date?"

"I was serious about not knowing a lot of women, Cadence. Up until about eight months ago, I had been married for eleven years."

Chapter 11

Cadence could only look at him with a shocked expression and completely speechless. Finally, one thought came to mind.

"How old *are* you?"

Adam broke into a deep laugh.

"I'm serious!" Cadence insisted. "Please tell me you're not, like, forty or something."

"No, I'm not forty. I just got married really young," he replied between chuckles.

"So what happened?" she asked.

When Adam glanced at her, the smile was still on his lips, but his eyes had lost their glint. He looked back out over the water.

"We just grew apart. We fell in love before we really knew who we were and what we wanted out of life. In the end, I don't think we had anything in common."

"Do you have any kids?"

"No. We were pregnant once, but she had a miscarriage."

Cadence could not think of anything to say, nor did she want to pry too much, so she remained silent.

"Now it's your turn," he finally announced.

"Sorry, no marriage, divorce, or kids to talk about. And I'm not forty years old, either. Thank God, or my mother would really be disappointed with my life."

They both smiled at her ironic humor.

"Are you hungry?" Adam asked her. "I'm going to start up the barbecue for dinner."

"That sounds great. What can I do to help? Make a salad or something?"

"You can go for a swim if you'd like. Enjoy the rest of sun before it sets."

He stood up and gave her a hand to help her out of her seat. Then they walked back to the house. Adam stayed outside to fire up the grill, while Cadence grabbed her bag from near the front door and went to the bathroom off the solarium. She stripped off her clothes to pull on a two-piece bathing suit in a vibrant sky blue. While standing in front of the vanity mirror, she twisted and tied her locks into a thick bun on the top of her head.

She also thought back to what Adam told her while they had been sitting in front of the water. *He had been married for eleven years!* That was so unbelievable to her. Despite her joking comment about his age, she knew he could only be in his early thirties, at the most. That meant that he must have been married by the age of twenty, maybe? That was so young! Cadence could not imagine marrying any of the men she had dated, or even thought she loved, at that age. She could clearly look back now and see that they would not have worked out long-term.

Cadence checked the fit of her bathing suit again, then went out the exterior door of the bathroom. She walked around the edge of the swimming pool until she reached the shallow end, then sat at the edge and sank her feet into the cool water. The sun was getting low on the horizon, and the fall air was cooling down. But the glass enclosure of the solarium kept the covered patio comfortably warm.

She had just jumped into the water when Adam came into the room carrying what looked like several white towels.

"Is everything okay?" he asked as he put them on a lounge chair near the Jacuzzi.

"Perfect," Cadence told him. "Are you sure you don't need any help with dinner?"

"Nah, it's pretty much done."

He then disappeared back into the house.

Cadence spent the next thirty minutes or so floating around in the pool. She couldn't remember when she had last had time for such leisure or relaxation. Her days were usually split between working on her art portfolio, meeting deadlines for the publishing contracts, and getting life errands done in her spare time. This unexpected afternoon with Adam felt like a minivacation, and she was enjoying it completely.

When Adam let her know dinner was ready, Cadence dried herself off with one of the towels, but she also found a fluffy terry robe. It was way too big for her tiny frame, but she wrapped herself in it anyway, then went back into the house.

Adam led her to the dining room, where he had set the table with their meal, which included steaks, grilled vegetables, a salad, and a bottle of red wine.

A cluster of glowing container candles sat in the center of the table. He invited her to sit in the seat adjacent to his while he took the chair at the end of the table.

"Adam, this looks incredible," she told him with genuine surprise. "How did you do all of this in such a short time?"

He smiled while uncorking the wine bottle and filling their glasses.

"Come on. You can't expect me to reveal all of my secrets in one day."

Cadence smiled back, shaking her head at his teasing.

They spent the meal talking in the same manner they had when they had first met weeks ago, and discovered their common interests in things like movies, television shows, and other activities. Eventually, Adam asked to hear more about her career as an artist, and asked question after question about where she got her talent, her inspiration, and her motivation. That led Cadence to reveal more about her family history and her biological father. She deliberately avoided mentioning her stepfather and her contempt for him and his treatment of her mother.

They were talking about her gallery showings when Cadence told Adam about the festival in Miami that weekend.

"It's called the Too Nubian Festival, and it's a display of everything African, Caribbean, and African-American. The organizer owns a large art store in Miami, and he's asked me to be there to meet people and sign some of my prints. I'm also going to bring a few originals that I've just completed and see if there are any interested buyers. There will be lots of art and music, tons of food, too, so I think it will be fun."

"It sounds like a good time. I haven't been to Miami in years," Adam replied. "How are you getting there?"

"I'm driving," she told him. "I rented an SUV for the weekend."

"You're not driving by yourself, are you?" he asked with a furrowed brow.

She nodded, then explained further, before he could voice the objection clearly written on his face.

"Remember, my mom still lives in Fort Lauderdale, so I've made the trip tons of times on my own. It's only about four hours, max."

Adam was silent for a few minutes, but Cadence could see that he was debating something in his mind.

"What?" she finally asked, teasingly. "You're not worried about me, are you?"

Adam shook his head.

"No. I was just thinking that you should have some company for a weekend like that."

The look he gave her told her clearly that he was offering to go with her. Cadence was speechless. It had never occurred to her that someone would want to go with her to this event, or any of the other showings or gallery openings she had participated in over the last few of years. She created her work in isolation, and got used to doing the marketing side of the business alone also.

"I'm leaving tomorrow afternoon. Don't you have to work?" she asked.

"It's Friday, but it's technically a holiday. I was

going to put in a few hours, but I could do that in the morning."

"You're serious," Cadence stated, still really surprised by his suggestion.

"Why wouldn't I be? Like I said, it sounds like a good time. Unless of course, you would rather not have company."

"No, that's not it. But, I'll be pretty busy on Saturday and Sunday at the event, and it's probably going to be really boring for you."

"It's Miami, Cadence. I'm sure I can find a way to keep myself occupied. So, it's settled? What time do you want to get on the road?"

They spent the rest of their meal discussing the travel details. Cadence told him the hotel she was booked in and what she knew about the schedule of the festival, but it took a while for her to accept the fact that he was serious about coming with her. Despite the surprise date he had put together for the afternoon, and his offer for the weekend, Adam just didn't strike her as the spontaneous type.

She was usually pretty good at reading people, and her first impression of him had been that he was stable, thoughtful, and reliable. He was a humble guy with a humble and respectable profession. Those were the attributes that had most attracted her to him, on top of his general physical attractiveness, of course. This impulsive side made her wonder what else she didn't know about him. It made her nervous and excited her at the same time.

They cleaned up the table and washed the dishes together, then Adam suggested they take a soak in the hot tub. It was just before six o'clock, and the sun was setting over the water, providing a beautiful horizon of red, gold, and dark blue. The plan was for them to relax for about thirty minutes, then get ready to be on the road again by around seven o'clock.

Cadence was already soaking in the frothy warm water when Adam joined her, dressed in loose swimming shorts. She could not help but admire the perfect cut of his body. He was lean and toned, with sculpted slabs of muscles right down to the hair-sprinkled flesh of his lower abdomen. She knew right away that it wasn't the heat from the tub or the red wine that caused her temperature to rise several degrees.

Adam settled into the seat beside hers, then pulled her over into his lap while his arms wrapped loosely around her waist. Her hands settled on the tops of his thighs. They sat like that for several minutes, both enjoying the pressure of the jets, the view, and the feel of the touching skin. Eventually, outside was pitch black and the only light in the solarium came from a low-voltage lamp near the French doors.

"It feels like we're the only people on the earth," Cadence said in a lazy voice.

Adam responded by placing a feathery kiss on her temple and she let her head fall back onto the top of his shoulder. He pressed his lips to the exposed length of her neck, his tongue brushing the skin and his teeth nipping at the tight tendons. She stifled a groan and dug her fingers into his legs. Then he sucked hard on her flesh and she let out a deep gasp.

"I've wanted to do this all day," he whispered into her ear.

Cadence shifted her weight so they could look at each other in the dimness. His open mouth immediately fell on hers, and his probing tongue entwined with hers. The depth of his penetration caused her heart to race and her head to feel light. Soon, her lips were sucking his and her tongue stroking his with abandon.

Once they parted from the kiss, they remind so close that their breath mingled in the air. Cadence was immediately flooded with the sensations around her. Her nipples were like hard pebbles as the water teased their edges, and her lower stomach was trembling with excitement. She also felt Adam's arousal as it brushed her naked back through his shorts. Her eyes looked into his as she arched her spine to caress its rigid length.

"I want to touch you again," he told her. "I can't stop thinking about how good you feel."

Cadence shifted in his lap again so that she could relax back against his firm shoulders, giving him permission to explore her eager body. His strong hands cupped her breast and she groaned softly. She bit her bottom lip as his fingers kneaded the firm mounds and his palm scraped their erect tips. Her hips filled with warmth and wetness. She closed her eyes and immersed herself in the delicious stimulation.

By the time Adam undid the bra of her swimsuit and tossed it aside to stroke her naked flesh, her breaths were coming in sharp catches, and her hands were clutching and stroking his legs with abandon. She rotated her hips in slow circles, loving the feel of his thick penis at the base of her spine.

When one of his hands slid down her stomach and under the fabric of the bikini bottom, Cadence sucked in a sharp breath. His fingers parted her feminine lips and slid against the delicate nub at the apex. She let out a low moan. He brushed light kisses along her neck and licked the swirl of her ear. She moaned again, then slid out of Adam's arms.

Cadence turned to face him, and with slow, deliberate movement, slid the rest of the bathing suit off her hip and stepped out of it. She then climbed back onto his lap fully naked, straddling his hips with a knee resting on either side of the seat. Their eyes met in the dim light, and she could read her desire clearly reflected in his eyes. She leaned forward and kissed him hard and urgently.

Between pecks and licks, Cadence let her hands wander all over the contours of his body, exploring its hardness and smoothness. Eventually, she allowed them to brush the rigid plane of his stomach until one rested over his firm erection. She stroked her tongue deep into his mouth while her fingers traced over the sensitive tip and down the thick length. Adam expelled a sharp breath, then was completely still as she reached beneath his shorts to stroke his hot, naked shaft.

He responded by pulling her to him so their wet bodies there meshed. His hands ran up and down her back, then rested on the swells of her bottom.

Soon, the sounds of their mingled groans echoed in the solarium.

"I want to touch you," Adam said again as he set her body back from him and ran his mouth along her collarbone, then down to one of her breasts.

His teeth scraped her nipple mercilessly, while his

hand cupped between her legs. With gentle pressure, he stroked her delicate flesh, learning each fold and contour, discovering every sensitive hot spot. He played with her until she was slick with her arousal, then he thrust his long middle finger deep into her core, pulled back and thrust it forward again.

"Oh God!" she screamed as her hips bucked forward to meet his deep penetration. "Oh, Adam."

Cadence was completely unprepared for how quickly her body spiraled out of control. She was clutching his shoulders and looking deep into his eyes when the tremors of climax coursed through her body, one crash on top of another in never-ending waves.

Chapter 12

"You're incredible," Adam whispered over and over again while dropping light kisses over her shoulder and neck.

His finger was still buried within the tight heat of her body and he was hesitant to withdraw it. Her orgasm had been so powerful that he had felt it like it was his own. Though his loins were still twisted with arousal, there was a part of him that was completely sated, for the moment.

Finally, her body was completely relaxed and Adam pulled her into a hug while her head rested on his shoulder. They sat quietly for a few minutes.

"Are you okay?" he finally asked.

"I'm very fine," she replied.

He could hear the humor in her voice, and he smiled into the dark in response.

"Come, I think we've been in here long enough," he told her.

They both stood, then shared a gentle kiss before Adam stepped out of the hot tub and then helped her out. He picked up one of the towels and used it to dry Cadence off, first her shoulders and arms, then each leg and foot, before wrapping it snugly around her torso. He shed his own wet swim trunks and wrapped another towel around his hips.

She took his hand and they walked together into the house. There was very little light, but Adam guided her into the front hall, where he left her for a moment, stopping briefly to retrieve a travel bag from his duffel, then going off to the dining room. When he returned, he was carrying one of the candles from their dinner, and he then led her up the stairs to the second floor.

When they entered a large bedroom, Adam sat her on the edge of a king-size bed, then rested the candle and travel bag on a dresser in front of it. He removed a tube of skin lotion from the bag before turning back to Cadence. Neither of them spoke as he knelt before her and slowly began to rub the rich lotion over her skin, starting with her feet and moving up her legs. When he reached her thighs, he urged her to stand so he could remove the damp towel, then he continued the slow, sensual rubbing up her body.

While his hands roamed her caramel body in small circles, Adam admired the beauty of her nakedness. Cadence was petite and delicate, barely reaching his collarbone, but beautifully sculpted, with feminine curves. Her legs were slender but toned, and extended from gently flared hips and a round bottom with high, full cheeks. Her stomach was flat, but with a soft curve, and her breasts were full and high, tipped with thick nipples dipped in chocolate.

He stood up once he reached her arms, then turned her around to give the same attention to her back. His hands lingered over the lushness of her bum, and he swept lubricated fingers between their shadowy cleft, seeking to explore all of her secrets. The heaviness between his thighs tightened and rose hard.

Still, Adam tried to take his time. He reached up and gently undid the twists holding up her hair until the mass of tendrils spilled down her back. Then he turned her to face him. They kissed again, slowly and sensually, tasting the heat between them and savoring the flames. Their hands roamed everywhere they could reach.

Eventually, Adam pulled back, breathing hard, but resting his forehead on hers to try to cool down.

He let out a short, humorous laugh.

"Cadence, I'm trying to go slow here, but I don't think I can," he whispered urgently.

She leaned forward and licked one of his nipples, then bit it gently. A shiver coursed through his body, and he groaned quietly.

"Why go slow?" she asked.

Adam was speechless for a moment, since her tongue was making it hard for him to think.

"Because," he finally replied. "I want it to last; I want it to be good for you. I don't want to hurt you. You're so tiny."

His last words came out in a harsh, low voice. He could see her soft smile in the candlelight as she loosened his towel and let it drop to the floor. She then took his hand as she backed up and lowered herself to the bed.

"I'm not as delicate as I look."

Adam could not think of a response. He turned toward the dresser and quickly slipped on the pro-

tection that he had ambitiously thrown in the travel
bag that morning. He then lowered himself onto
the bed beside her. Cadence immediately curved
her body into his, one leg thrown over his hip and
fusing their loins together. He lost his ability to
hold back at that point.

She wanted him as much as he wanted her. Her
urgency matched his and she let him know with her
hands, lips, and every arch of her body. She took
and gave pleasure so openly and naturally that
Adam felt humbled by her honesty. It was easy to
give up control and let their bodies take over.

They rolled around on the bed in abandon until
Adam finally placed Cadence under him, dying to
feel himself encased in her sweetness. With her legs
wrapped high around his waist, he put his weight
on his knees, and gently rubbed the engorged tip
of his penis along the slick folds of her core. She
felt like liquid fire and she writhed her hips in response. He stroked it again and again until they
were both panting and quivering.

"Adam!" Cadence begged, arching her back to
welcome his thrust, her eyes clenched tight.

"Look at me," he asked tightly, then held her
drugged gaze as he slowly pressed the tip of his
swollen shaft into her wetness. It took all his power
not plunge to the hilt, but she was so tight that he
held back, instead pushing slowly and pulling out
as her body opened to him.

Finally, Cadence thrust her hips forward, taking
every thick inch of him into her core. They both
moaned loud and long, then remained still for several seconds.

Adam felt like he was sheathed in heaven and

wanted to stay there for the rest of eternity. He leaned forward and rained kisses over her forehead, then the side of her face.

"Oh, Cadence, you feel so good! Please tell me I'm not hurting you."

He felt her shake her head, then flex her hips to let him know it felt good to her, too.

Adam groaned again, slowly withdrew, and plunged into her again. Then, he lost all control. Every thrust into her body was so deep that he felt like part of her, and every stroke took him closer to a cliff he knew he had never been to before. When he reached the edge, he leaped over it with complete abandon. Then Cadence's release caressed him into a flight of ecstasy that he didn't know was physically possible.

It felt like forever before reality came back to them. They remained entwined in the dim light, not moving until the sweat on their bodies created a chill. Adam pulled the blanket on the bed over them until they were wrapped in a cocoon, and they fell into an exhausted sleep.

When they awoke, the candle had burnt out and the room was completely pitch black. Cadence opened her eyes first, then shifted slightly to get more comfortable. Her movement woke Adam up immediately, but he just pulled her back into his arms. They lay like that for a few minutes.

"What time is it?" Cadence finally asked.

She wasn't wearing a watch, and Adam could not read his in the dark.

"I have no idea, but it looks late. I guess we should get up, huh?"

Cadence heard the regret in his voice, and felt

exactly the same way. She would have loved to stay where they were in the dark cocoon that still held the scent of their lovemaking. But tomorrow was going to be a long day, and they needed to get back to the city.

Adam finally unwrapped himself from the bed and reached over to a lamp on the bedside table. Blinding light flooded the room.

"It's almost eleven o'clock," he told her. "Do you want to take a shower before we head home?"

"That would be great," she agreed.

"Okay, there's a bathroom through there," he told her, pointing toward a second door in the bedroom. "I'll go grab us some more towels."

Once he was gone, Cadence scampered off the bed and went into the bathroom and turned on the shower. When the water was warm, she stepped in and did a leisurely wash, using bath gel that was sitting on the edge of the bathtub. She heard Adam enter the room and found a new towel waiting for her on the counter.

He had also left her tote bag for her in the bedroom along with the lotion he had used on her body earlier. The clothes she had worn were folded neatly inside the bag, and her wet bathing suit was in a plastic bag. Cadence pulled on the extra clothes she had brought, then rummaged in the bathroom until she found a new toothbrush and a tube of toothpaste. She wished she had some deodorant, but didn't worry since they would be home within the hour.

When she got downstairs, the lights were on and Cadence could see Adam locking up the solarium and the other external doors at the back of the house. When he joined her near the staircase, he looked freshly showered and was also wearing new clothes.

"Are you all set? Did you find everything you need?" he asked.

Cadence nodded, then looked away, suddenly feeling shy. It was a little ridiculous, considering the intimacy they had recently shared. To hide it, she walked over to get her purse, which she had left in the kitchen when they had first arrived. Adam followed her, and she saw that he had already packed away some of the things he had brought for dinner in his knapsack.

He is so organized and efficient, she thought.

"Do you want some water for the drive?" asked Adam while holding up a couple of chilled bottles.

"Sure," she replied and accepted one.

"Okay, I think we're all set," he said, then led the way to the front door, turning off the lights behind them.

Ten minutes later, they were driving on the road that would take them past Leesburg and on to Orlando. Adam turned on the radio, and tuned it to an all-day news station so they could get an update on traffic and the weather. When the announcer mentioned the forecast for Friday, including Miami and the rest of southern Florida, Adam glanced at Cadence. They hadn't really said much to each other up to that point.

"So, are we still on for tomorrow?" he asked her.

"For Miami? Of course. If you're still interested in coming," she replied, but twisted the final statement to sound like a question.

He looked at her with an assessing gaze, a look

she now recognized as his attempt to understand the meaning behind her words.

"I would very much like to go with you," he stated simply, but solemnly.

Their eyes met again, but Adam looked away to focus on the road.

"This feels a little weird, doesn't it?" she stated. "I was comfortable and relaxed this afternoon, and now I feel . . . awkward."

"Well, a lot has happened since this afternoon," Adam replied, and there was a teasing smile on his lips. "It started out as a simple, official first date and ended as something more."

Cadence turned in her seat to look at him. Her brows were furrowed in bewilderment.

"I have no idea what to make of you," she told him.

"What does that mean? In what way?"

"I don't know. I usually have a good read on people. I can get a sense of their basic personality, but you keep surprising me. When we met at Calvin and Yvonne's, you seemed so serious and almost angry. Then, at my house, you were quiet, but helpful and kind. And let's not even mention that . . . insulting incident!"

"I'm never going to live that down, am I?" Adam groaned.

"No, you're not!" she threw back, but only half serious. "But through all that, I never would have guessed you could be so spontaneous and almost insightful. Thoughtful, yes. Deep, no."

"I'm not sure if you've insulted me or not."

"I'm just saying that every time I think I have a read on you, you throw me for a loop," she explained.

"Does that bother you? Do you need to label me? Maybe once you really know someone, it's not always possible to easily categorize their personality."

She stared at his profile until he glanced at her.

"See what I mean? You would barely put together two sentences for me when we met, and now you're questioning my thoughts on human behavior!"

Adam laughed, his white teeth flashing in the night.

"To be honest with you, I hardly recognize myself over the last couple of days. I freely admit that I am not at all spontaneous, quite the opposite, actually. Nor do I often debate other people's thoughts or opinions, except at work. So I guess the only difference in the last forty-eight hours of my life is you."

"Me!"

"You," he repeated. "I told you earlier that I feel more comfortable with you than I have with any other woman. I was married at the tender age of eighteen, and for almost all of my adult life, so you know that I was being honest with you. The only answer I have to why you can't get a read on my personality is that I'm not my usual self when I'm with you."

Adam had his eyes fixed on the road, but Cadence could not take hers off his face. Everything except her hard-earned cynicism told her he was telling her the truth. The possibility of it made her heart race and her mouth dry. Sitting beside her was a strong, reliable, and sexy man and the only one she had ever met who might actually steal her heart.

Chapter 13

Adam was in the office by seven o'clock on Friday morning. He was the first one there, but his assistant, Tamara, was there by eight o'clock. Tamara had been with him since the beginning and was clearly surprised to see him in the office at all, never mind that early. He was usually on a construction site except when it was mandatory to be behind a desk.

"Good morning, Adam," she said when she stuck her head through his door. "I'm surprised to see you here. What's going on?"

"Hey, Tamara. Come in; sit down," he replied. "How was your Thanksgiving?"

"Good! We had my whole family at the house, and miraculously, no one got attacked or injured."

They both laughed. Tamara came from a very hot-blooded Cuban family, and her stories were always entertaining, if not a little shocking.

"That's good, but there's always Christmas!" Adam reminded her with a grin. "Listen, what time are you expecting Tony? I want to have a meeting with him and Peter at around nine-thirty this morning."

"That should be okay. They're both usually in before nine o'clock."

"Good. I'm going to be out of town this afternoon and for the weekend, so I want to make sure everything will be covered."

Adam didn't miss the look on Tamara's face. She was clearly curious.

"Okay, but what's going on?" she finally asked.

"Nothing, just spending a couple of days in Miami," he replied.

"Miami? What's in Miami? Is everything okay?"

"Everything's fine. I'm just taking a couple of days off."

Tamara stared at him for a few seconds.

"Really? Adam, I've worked for you for almost five and a half years, and I don't remember you ever taking a day off, much less a whole weekend. Don't get me wrong, I think it's great! You know I've been bugging you to slow down, take a real vacation. It's just surprising that you're taking off on such short notice, that's all."

Adam shrugged, not sure how to respond. It did seem odd to him now that he had not taken any time off in such a long time. How did he become so consumed with work that he didn't even know how to relax?

"Well, it's no big deal," he finally replied. "Everything looks on schedule and Tony is more than capable of handling any problems. That's why I hired him."

"Everything will be fine," Tamara agreed. "I'll go send out an e-mail for the meeting."

She left the office and closed the door behind her. Adam swung around in his chair until he was facing the window at the back of the room.

He had hired Tony Esposito almost six months ago to act as his right-hand man and construction manager. It was just after his divorce had become final and Adam wanted to change the pattern of his life and cut back on the hours he spent working. It was also around the time he bought the Fruitland Park house with the intention of spending his weekends there. It was exactly the type of place he thought was ideal for relaxation, and exactly what his ex-wife would have hated.

But things hadn't worked out as planned. Adam had found it harder than he had expected to leave his company in the hands of his employees, even for a weekend. He also realized that he didn't enjoy doing nothing all day—relaxation wasn't very relaxing, particularly by yourself. So, he put his intention to have a more leisurely life on the back burner, and did what he knew best: he worked harder.

Tamara was right. He should not have spent so many years without a vacation or any real time off. It had always been an issue in his marriage to Rose. Certainly not the reason things fell apart, but he could not deny that it was a contributing factor.

Adam's thoughts were pulled back to work when his phone rang. It was Sandra Evans, the bank manager for his corporate accounts.

"Hey Sandra, how are you?" he asked, a little surprised by the call.

"Good, Adam. Listen, I've been meaning to give you a call. Do you have a few minutes?"

"Well, I'm about to go into a meeting, but I can postpone it if needed. What's this about?"

"No, it's not urgent. I just wanted to go over a few things with you and propose a few new products the bank is offering. When would be a good time for you?"

"Next week sometime should work. Why don't I have Teresa give you a call on Monday to set something up?" Adam proposed.

Tony stepped into his office at that moment.

"Sounds good, Adam. Have a good weekend," Sandra told him before their call ended.

"What's up, boss?" asked Tony.

It was a couple of minutes after nine o'clock, so Adam waved him into one of the chairs in front of his desk. A few seconds later, Adam's financial controller, Peter Tulic, also entered the office and sat in the seat beside Tony.

The two men were complete opposites in almost every way. While Tony was young, big, and boisterous, Peter was the quintessential image of an accountant: middle-aged, mild-mannered, and with a slim, small frame. But they were both hardworking, easy to get along with, and very good at what they did.

Adam spent the next hour reviewing the status of the current projects, and going over what needed to be accomplished by Monday. He was in the office for another forty-five minutes, then he drove toward the building site in Altamonte Springs. By one o'clock in the afternoon, he was headed home to get dressed and packed for the trip. The plan was for Cadence to pick him up at around two-thirty so they could be on the road by three o'clock.

He was toweling off from a shower when his

phone rang. Adam answered it in his bedroom. It was Alexa, and they spoke casually for a few minutes before she got to the point of her call.

"A friend of mine is throwing a party tonight at a club downtown. I thought maybe you and I could go. Are you free tonight?"

"Actually, I'm going out of town for the weekend," Adam replied.

"Oh . . . okay. Well, maybe we can do something next week, then," she suggested. Adam heard the disappointment and curiosity in her voice, and he didn't quite know how to respond.

"I'll give you a call on Monday," he replied finally.

Their call ended shortly afterward, but Adam continued to think about it while he finished getting dressed. It was hard to believe so much had changed since his date with Alexa on Wednesday evening. Part of him felt bad that he might have somehow led her on, but there was no way he could have known that Cadence would re-enter his life. Plus, he and Alexa were just getting acquainted. There were no expectations or promises, were there?

Finally, Adam just shook his head and tried to put it out of his mind. He had no clue how these things were supposed to work and he never had. It was probably the reason he had married young, despite the warnings from everyone around him.

Cadence arrived at around quarter to three. Adam had finished getting dressed and packed, and was putting together a few snacks and drinks for the drive when he heard her knock. He opened the door to find her leaning against the door jam, looking like a young teenager. She had on loose cargo pants, a snug black cotton knit top and orange flip-flops. Her face fresh and clean of makeup.

Adam invited her in, and there was an awkward moment when neither knew how to act with their new intimacy.

"Did you find the building okay." he asked as he led her into his living room.

"Yeah, it was pretty easy," Cadence replied. "This is a great apartment. Have you been here long?"

"Just a few months. It's temporary for now. I'm subletting from a friend of mine."

She looked at him speculatively, and Adam knew she was remembering his recent divorce. But she didn't comment further and he chose not to elaborate.

"Are you all set?" she asked instead.

"Yup. I'll just grab my bag from the bedroom."

When Adam came back, Cadence was looking out the window at the swimming pool in the center of the building complex. She turned toward him, and her eyes fell immediately on the leather week-end bag slung over his shoulder.

"Nice bag," she told him.

Adam looked down at it for a few seconds. It was part of a set Rose had purchased for them a couple of years back. He knew it was one of those expensive labels, but hadn't paid much attention. The look on Cadence's face told him it was a big deal.

"It was a gift," he told her simply.

"A very generous gift."

He shrugged, then made his way to the front door, picking up the bag of refreshments on his way. Cadence followed him as he locked the apartment and led the way down to the visitors parking area, where she had parked the large SUV she had rented for the weekend. She had lowered all the rear seats to make room for twelve canvas paintings, all stacked lying flat, faceup, then individually wrapped for protection. There were also a few boxes of promotional materials.

They spent a few minutes loading Adam's bag next to her suitcase, then shifting their things to put Adam in the driver's seat.

"How did everything go this morning? Did you get all your errands done?" he asked as they stood near the rear of the truck.

"Pretty much. I had confirmed two gallery showings earlier this week, so I was really worried about getting the promotional flyers done on time, but they had them ready this morning. So, it all went smoothly. I guess things worked out for you to get the time off work?"

"It was no big deal. I got a lot done by noon, anyway. To be honest, I hardly ever take time off, and definitely not last-minute, so everyone was just glad to see me get a life," he told her, while chuckling at himself. "Pretty sad, huh?"

Cadence smiled back, revealing her button dimples. "Yeah, very sad! You need to learn how to have more fun."

Adam took her hand and pulled her into a loose embrace.

"Are you going to teach me?" he teased.

"I'll see what I can do."

He leaned down to kiss her for the first time since dropping her home the night before. Her lips tasted just as sweet as he remembered. Adam urged her mouth open and teased her tongue with his. By the time their lips parted, Cadence was clinging to his shoulders, and his hands were roaming her back.

"I'm having more fun already," he told her while tickling her ear with his lips.

She laughed.

A few minutes later, they were pulling out of his parking lot and on their way to Miami. Cadence had a CD playing in the stereo and they started a relaxed conversation about various topics. Adam was very curious about her art career, particularly since he had yet to see any of her work, and spent some time asking about when and how she had decided to become a full-time artist. He also brought up her use of models, particularly nude ones, which then led to a lighthearted debate about his first impressions of her.

Just over four hours later, they reached the outskirts of Miami. It was after seven o'clock and neither one was hungry yet, so they decided to wait until they were checked into the hotel before having dinner. This led to a discussion that Adam admitted he had been hesitant to broach earlier.

"I called the South Beach Marriot hotel this morning, and they were fully booked. I figured I could check again when we arrived, and if there were still no rooms, I would check out other hotels nearby. I'm sure there will be something nearby," he assured her.

"Adam, I really don't mind if you stay in my room," Cadence told him simply.

He gave her a quick glance to read her true feeling. That was what he had hoped she would say, but he wasn't going to suggest it himself. Though everything had felt natural and right over the last day or so, he didn't want to seem too pushy or demanding. Although he wanted to spend as much time with Cadence as possible, he was realistic enough to know it wasn't necessarily a good thing at the beginning of a relationship. She might end up seeing some annoying habit of his that would completely turn her off forever.

"It's up to you, Cadence," he finally replied. "But I really don't mind getting another room. This is your weekend, and I'm just along for the ride. The most important thing is that you're comfortable and rested."

"Let's see what's available at the Marriot. Then we can decide."

The high-rise hotel was located on the bay, and they arrived shortly afterward. The front desk confirmed that there were still no rooms available for Friday and Saturday nights. Cadence gave Adam a brief look before deciding they would share her room. While she finished the check-in, Adam went to the concierge desk to get a recommendation for dinner. He wanted to take Cadence somewhere nice, with great food and some music if possible. He told her the options as they rode up to the room in the elevator, and they both decided on a Cuban restaurant a few blocks away.

Their room was a spacious suite with a king-size bed, a large sofa, a desk, and a beautiful view of the beach. Adam put their luggage on the sofa and immediately removed his clothes to hang them in the closet, then offered to hang hers up also. Cadence handed him her items gratefully, but kept the dress she intended to wear and laid it on the back of a chair. She then headed for the shower with the hotel robe and her toiletry bag.

When she returned to the room, Adam was watching television, and had ironed both his clothes and her dress, leaving them draped neatly over the bed.

"Adam, you didn't have to do that," she told him with obvious surprise and gratitude.

"It's no big deal. I was doing mine, anyway," he said, dismissing her comment with a shrug.

"Still, it was very thoughtful."

"Don't worry about it."

Then he was gone, into the shower, leaving Cadence staring at the perfectly pressed clothes in wonder.

Chapter 14

It really should not have been a big deal, but Cadence felt completely blown away by Adam's actions. She could not stop thinking about it while she got dressed.

While growing up, she had never seen her stepfather do anything for himself. Her mother dressed him, cooked for him, and cleaned up after him. Ellis did a few things around the house like mow the grass, and he tinkered with things in the garage, but otherwise, he was like a grown child. As Cadence and her sister, Monique, grew older, he started to expect them to cater to him, too. Monique didn't seem to mind her father's behavior, but Cadence would not stand for it, particularly since Ellis rarely had a job. It was the cause of many fights.

Since leaving home, Cadence had dated a few men who seemed to be looking for a nursemaid or a replacement mother. Somehow, they always wanted an invite to her house, expecting her to cook, or would spend days in her apartment without lifting a finger to clean up after themselves.

Those relationships always ended fairly quickly, and usually with them telling her she was selfish, or bitter, or not a real woman. It got to the point were she stopped inviting any men to her apartment until she was sure they had some ability to fend for themselves.

Then there were the few men who had seemed promising, like Carlos. But of course, they always had other issues. In general, the few she got close to appeared self-sufficient, even somewhat independent. They wouldn't ask much of her, and appeared to respect her time and dedication to her career. But in the end, that independence was covering up things, like other women, or just a general lack of interest in a real relationship.

Yet, through all these experiences, she had never met a man who would spend his time doing something just for her without her asking, even something as small as ironing her clothes.

When Adam came out of the shower, Cadence was almost finished getting ready. Her dress was a simple silk sheath in a deep burnt copper with spaghetti straps and a plunging neckline at the front and back. An oversized black belt cinched her waist, emphasizing the high curves of her bare breasts, and the soft swells of her hips and behind. The sensuous fabric clung to her body with every move. Cadence could see the appreciation in Adam's eyes as she swept past him into the bathroom with her makeup case.

"Wow, you look beautiful," he told her when she reappeared in the room ten minutes later.

"Thank-you. You look pretty good yourself," she replied, as she stopped in front of where he sat on the bed putting on his dark brown leather shoes. He was wearing dark tan slacks and a crisp cream shirt tucked into his belted waist. Modest gold cuff links twinkled at his wrists, and he left the collar open a couple of buttons to reveal the top of his chest.

Cadence sat beside him to put on her high-heeled black sandals. Instead, Adam took each of her naked feet and slipped the shoes on for her, buckling the delicate ankle straps with ease. He then pulled her into his lap so her legs were draped over his.

"Can I kiss you or would it ruin your makeup?" he asked with his eyes fixed on her full lips covered in a rich red lipstick.

She responded by reaching behind his head and pulling his mouth down on hers. Within seconds, his hands were brushing over her silk-covered breasts, teasing and tweaking them into hardened points. Cadence groaned against his lips and ran her hands over his chest until her palms were over his nipples. She played with him until Adam was groaning also.

"Okay, either we stop now, or we're going to have to get room service," he said in a deep, husky voice.

"Hmmm, room service sounds great," she replied, licking his lips with a wet tongue.

"Cadence, you're killing me! But I promised you a Cuban dinner and that's what you're getting. We can always have room service for dessert."

"Great idea. I love dessert."

Adam laughed while lifting her off his legs and onto her feet, then laughed even harder when he noticed the damage their kissing had done. Cadence looked in the mirror to see that the lipstick was almost gone except for a ruby stain on her fair skin. His lips looked almost as bad.

After they spent a few minutes cleaning up their faces and adjusting their clothes, Cadence grabbed a light black sweater in case it got cooler later in the evening, and they headed to the lobby to grab a cab. The restaurant was only a few minutes' drive from the hotel, and they were seated beside each other in a booth near the back where the light was dim and the lively music was not too loud for conversation.

They had ordered their meals and were sharing a bottle of rich red wine and shrimp enchilada appetizers when Cadence brought up something that had been on her mind since the night before.

"Adam, who was the woman you were with at Steve's party on Wednesday night?"

He smiled mysteriously, then took another sip from his glass.

"Do I detect a bit of jealousy?" he eventually replied.

"Give me a break," she muttered.

"She was pretty hot, wasn't she?"

This time, Cadence punched him in his shoulder.

"Jealous and violent! That's a pretty hot combination."

"Forget I asked!" she retorted hotly.

Adam must have sensed that she really wasn't kidding, because he placed his hand over hers, and put down his glass. The annoying smile was still on his face.

"Seriously, her name is Alexa, and we were on our first date. Well, maybe our second. She's a friend of Yvonne's and I had met her last when the four of us went to the movies."

"Really," she replied, still tight-lipped and stiff.

"Cadence, I was only teasing you. Alexa is a nice girl, but in case you didn't notice, I couldn't take my eyes off you all night."

She allowed him to lace his fingers through hers, and by the time she looked at him again, her posture had loosened somewhat.

"So, what happens now?" she asked him.

"What do mean?"

"I mean with Alexa. Things have developed really quickly with us and I just want to make sure I understand where we stand."

"Okay. I'm going to explain something to you," Adam stated in a more serious tone. "I've been divorced for almost eight months now, and separated for a year before that. In spite of constant urging and pushing from my friends, I can count the number of dates I've been on with my fingers, and with digits to spare. And that's including our date yesterday. I'm not interested in dating every night of the week and collecting phone numbers at nightclubs. So to answer your question, nothing happens now with Alexa. She is just an acquaintance I met through Yvonne, and that's it."

Cadence nodded to accept his words.

"Is that because there was no chemistry, or because of what happened between us?" she asked.

"Does it matter?" he returned.

"I think it does."

"Because you want to know if I'm going to keep her on the back burner, right? Just in case things don't work out between us?"

Cadence just looked at him. He raised his eyebrows, taunting her to respond.

"Be honest," he finally urged.

"Okay. Yes. So now you have to be honest with your response."

"People always say honesty is the best policy, until they get the truth and it hurts."

"True, but it hurts a lot less than being lied to."

Adam gripped her fingers.

"Like I said, Alexa is a nice girl and very attractive, but beyond that there was no great attraction. But the reality is that if you and I had not run into each other again, I probably would have continued dating her, mostly because there would be no reason not to."

She took a sip of her wine, trying to understand what that meant.

"It just got to the point that I knew I had to get out there again," he continued. "Particularly after that evening we had."

Their meals arrived at that moment, and Adam and Cadence focused on their own thoughts for a few minutes while they started eating.

"So, I guess I should ask you the same question," stated Adam, the teasing tone was back in his voice. "Are you seeing anyone else right now? And keep in mind that I prefer the truth also, even if it is painful."

Cadence shook her head while finishing a mouthful of roasted chicken.

"No," she finally said. "I've been too busy over the last few months to date."

"Do you usually date a lot, when you're not so busy?"

"Sometimes. If I meet someone I like, or can have fun with, I'll go out with them a few times."

It was Adam's turn to nod while digesting her words. "What about relationships? Anything serious?"

"It depends on what you mean by serious. There have been a couple of guys I dated for a while, like a year or longer, but nothing like moving in together, or getting engaged."

"Why is that?" asked Adam.

"I don't know. There are lots of reasons. I've always been more focused on my art and my career than getting married. And I didn't meet anyone that I want to tie my life to. Not to mention that a lot of men find me too liberal for their liking, particularly Jamaican men."

"Really?" He sounded genuinely surprised. "Why is that?"

"I don't know, maybe because I don't cook very often?" Cadence guessed. She wasn't willing to dig into the real issues, so she deliberately made her response sound humorous. Adam laughed.

"That explains it! We really love our food."

"I didn't say I can't cook, just that I don't."

"Okay," he acknowledged while chuckling some more.

The conversation took a lighter tone as they continued on the topic of Jamaican men and women, then some of the traditions they grew up with. Adam spoke for a few minutes about his mother who still lived in a small town in St. Catherines's, Jamaica. She came up to visit him every year for about a month, but he admitted that he hadn't been back home for almost eight years.

When their meals were finished and the table was

cleared, Adam and Cadence sat closer in the booth and sipped the remainder of the wine. His arm fell across her shoulder and her head rested in the crook of his arm. Her legs were crossed toward his.

"Do you want any dessert?" he asked after the waiter dropped off the dessert menu.

Cadence looked up at him with a slow smile and ran a hand over one of his tight biceps.

"I thought we were going to have some back at the hotel."

She could feel the heat from his eyes as their copper color glowed bright. He ran his fingers down the side of her leg, over the silk of her dress to the hem, then up the bare skin to her midthigh. They kissed lightly and repeatedly while his hand inched higher under the cover of the table. Cadence uncrossed her legs, silently inviting Adam to play more. He let his hands roam her sensitive flesh while they listened to the rhythm of Cuban music.

Eventually Adam dared to roam higher until his knuckles brushed the mound between her thighs. He sucked in a deep breath in disbelief.

"Jesus, Cadence, you're not wearing any panties!" he gasped into her ears. He brushed over the small spatter of hair that rimmed her hidden lips, then slid down into her dewy valley. "Jesus!"

"I didn't want any panty lines under my dress," she explained breathlessly, then bit her bottom lip to stifle the moans in her throat.

"God, you're killing me!" he muttered. "Let's get the bill!"

Ten minutes later, they were outside waiting for a taxi. When it arrived, Adam told the driver where they were going, and they were barely seated before he pulled her so close that one of her legs lay over his. The five-minute ride was spent stroking and touching places that they hoped their cabbie couldn't see, and trying to keep the signs of arousal off their faces. The look the driver gave them when they were leaving the car said they had failed miserably. Cadence and Adam burst out laughing with embarrassment and made their way to the elevator as quickly as possible.

Adam pulled her into his arms the minute the elevator doors closed. He immediately reached under her dress to hold and caress her bare bottom. Cadence closed her eyes to savor his touch.

"This is the sexiest thing I've ever felt," he told her. "I don't think I can see you in a dress again and not image you naked underneath."

"Maybe I will be and maybe I won't. It will be up to you to find out," she teased.

Thankfully, there was no one in the hall when the doors opened on their floor. Once in their room, they fell into each other's arms kissing wildly. Adam picked her up high until her legs wrapped around his waist, then turned until her back was against the wall next to the door. He ran his lips over her collarbone and licked the valley between her breasts. Then his mouth was sucking her breasts through silk, first one, then the other, then back again.

Cadence felt consumed by their passion and abandon. She couldn't breathe, couldn't think. All she wanted was more. Her eyes met his between embraces and she knew he felt the same.

Chapter 15

Cadence unhooked her legs from around Adam's hips, then turned them around so he was against the wall with her between his legs. She slowly started to unbutton his shirt while kissing the naked flesh she revealed. At his waist, she pulled the rest of the fabric out of his pants, removed the garment completely and threw it on the floor. She then took her time stroking and caressing his shoulders, chest, and stomach. Special attention was paid to the sensitive places that made him groan and quiver.

When she had worked her way down to his waist, Cadence undid his belt buckle and the button of his pants. She looked up at him while sliding his zipper down. His eyes were blazing and his lips clenched tight. He let out a deep hiss when she stroked her tongue over the skin at the base of his abdomen, then groaned loudly as her hands covered the thrust of his penis under the cotton of his boxers.

Cadence cupped the firm erection through the underwear and ran her hand up to the thick head.

It seemed to swell impossibly larger between her fingers. Then she pulled his erection free from his clothing and brushed her palm in small circles over the sensitive tip.

"God, Cadence," Adam groaned, and sunk his fingers deep into her hair before lowering his mouth to hers for a deep, probing kiss.

Her hand stroked and caressed him until he could only bury his face in her neck, his breath coming in deep bursts. He then seemed to freeze as Cadence slid down his body until she was on her knees. She took his rigid flesh into both her hands, then ran a wet tongue over the top and down the side. Adam moaned loudly, his hand braced against the wall as though holding on. Finally, she slid her mouth over the quivering thrust, and encased him to her full capacity.

"Uh, Cadence, Cadence! Oh God!" he muttered over and over again.

His reaction urged her on, and she enjoyed as much of his hard, hot flesh as she could. Cadence took her time bathing it with her tongue, teasing it with her lips, and stroking it with her hand. When she started sucking on him with deep strokes, Adam abruptly pulled her up into his arms and carried her to the bed. He sat her down, then proceeded to remove the rest of his clothes. His rigid penis stood impossibly thick, still shiny from her mouth. Cadence couldn't take her eyes off his incredible body, and her own breath now came in deep pants.

Adam turned away to slip on protection, then he was standing between her legs. He picked her up like she weighed nothing and turned her around so she was on her knees and facing the head of the bed. His hands started a path up from the ankle strap of her shoe, over her calves, and up her thighs under the skirt of her dress. They finally came to rest between her thighs, where he ran circles with his thumb while brushing his lips over her shoulder.

Cadence could not help but thrust her hips back, silently begging him to touch her at her core. But Adam continued to tease and stroke her everywhere but where she wanted it the most. Finally, he urged her down onto her hands and pushed her dress up to her waist so she was completely revealed and open to him. Even then, he only cupped her bottom and lightly stroked her thighs.

"Adam," Cadence finally pleaded, then moaned loudly when he only ran a gentle finger along her wet, trembling flesh.

"God, Cadence, you're so beautiful. You feel so good. I want you to want me as much as I want you," he whispered into her ear.

"I do," she promised. "Adam!"

He slid a long finger deep into her and she nearly screamed, tossing her head and arching her back.

"Jesus, Cadence."

Adam pulled her up and cupped both of her breasts, then thrust himself into her quivering body with one long stroke. Cadence didn't try to hold back her moans as they came out loud and long with each of his deep, slow penetrations. He was taking and filling her so completely that she could not get enough. Soon, both their voices were ringing in the room. The pace of their thrusts increased until she knew she was going to fall apart. She tried to hold it off, not wanting the incredible ride to end, but craved the shattering summit she knew she would reach. And when it came, it took the breath and control from her body.

Somewhere between the mind-shattering waves of absolute pleasure, Cadence felt Adam explode with similar intensity. The pulse of his release led her into a second wave of explosions, less intense but equally satisfying. When her body final came to rest, she found herself wrapped tightly against Adam's chest. She could feel the racing beat of his heart against her temple.

They lay like that for several minutes, each of them relishing the peace and stillness that came after the storm.

"I think I'll have to get your dress dry-cleaned," Adam finally said.

His tone was so rational and practical that Cadence burst out laughing.

"What?" he asked, but she was laughing too hard to explain.

He eventually gave up trying to understand and let her giggles die away on their own.

"Are you thirsty?" he asked, once she had calmed down.

"Now that you mention it, I could do with some water," Cadence told him.

"Okay, I'll go get some ice."

He kissed her cheek before rolling off the bed and strolling naked into the bathroom. She heard him splashing around before he was back. He then pulled on his boxers, pants, and shirt before heading out the door. Cadence used the few minutes alone to freshen up and slip into a black satin teddy. She was coming out of the bathroom when Adam returned.

She climbed into the bed and turned on the television while he poured bottled water over the ice in two glasses. Once settled under the covers, they spent the next half an hour or so watching the news until they fell asleep.

Saturday was a hectic day and went by swiftly. The festival was being held at Bayfront Park in downtown Miami, and was scheduled to run from eleven o'clock in the morning to eight o'clock at night both Saturday and Sunday. Cadence had made arrangements to be at the booth most of Saturday, then at specific intervals on Sunday.

She and Adam arrived just after ten o'clock on Saturday morning, and got busy setting up Cadence's original paintings and promotional items next to the Too Nubian Art and Book Store booth. She had brought several easels with her, and set them up around the space like a gallery, then added small cards with the title of each piece and the price. It was the first time that Adam had seen her work, and she watched his face as each piece was unwrapped and put on display.

Finally, just minutes before the event was to start, she could not stand his silence any longer. She walked up to him while he stood staring at one canvas for a long time.

"So?" she demanded.

Adam turned to look at her for a couple of seconds, then back at the painting. It was called *Heat in Autumn* and was one of her favorites. It was the second in a series of six she did earlier in the year that focused on the passion and sensuality between

a man and a woman. This was her first time showing them.

"Cadence, I don't know what to say. Your paintings are unbelievable! I didn't know what to expect,
but I'm blown away," he finally said without taking
his eyes off the image in front of him. "I want to buy
this one."

Cadence just looked at him.

"I haven't done any prints for it yet, but I'll set
one aside for you when I do," she replied.

"No. I mean that I want this one. The original.
Can you put a 'Sold' sign on it or something?"

"Adam, it's priced at $2500. I . . ."

"I know, and I want it. I'll write you a check when
we get back to Orlando."

Cadence was too surprised to respond. Oliver
Lindo, the organizer of the festival and the owner
of the art store, arrived at that moment. Cadence
thanked him for including her in the event and introduced him to Adam. She and Oliver then spent
a few minutes going over their business arrange-
ment before the crowd arrived.

The rest of the day was very busy. From her table,
Cadence could see the stage and hear all the different performers. There was a constant stream of
people through their area and most came with
their wallets. All of the vendors agreed it was a cul-
tural and financial success.

Adam spent part of his time walking around,
shopping and enjoying the music. During the rest
of the time, he brought her food and refreshments
as needed. He even manned the table for her when
she needed to use the bathroom.

By eight-fifteen that evening, Cadence was exhausted and dying to get off her feet, but thrilled at how things had turned out. She had sold tons of autographed prints through Too Nubian and two of her smaller originals. There was also a lot of interest in gallery showings scheduled for the New Year.

It was almost nine-thirty by the time Adam and Cadence got back to the hotel. They ate dinner at the hotel restaurant, then went for a leisurely walk on the beach. It was a beautiful night with a cool, gentle breeze blowing in off the Atlantic Ocean. Back in their room, they took a long, hot shower together, making love under the spray of the water. It was just as urgent and explosive as their other times together, and left them physically sated before they fell asleep naked and wrapped in each other's arms.

Sunday at the festival was as busy as the day before, but Cadence had more free time away from her table. The Too Nubian staff took care of her display while she spent the time with Adam listening to a few performances and meeting some of the other artists. She even managed to pick up a few items for Christmas presents.

By six-thirty that evening, Cadence had sold another original painting, and was ready to pack up for the trip home to Orlando. Oliver agreed to keep the remaining originals on consignment at the store, along with some of her promotional cards. She and Adam were packed up and on the road home by a few minutes after seven o'clock. There was an awkward moment while Cadence rewrapped *Heat in Autumn* and Adam helped her to secure it in the back of the truck. It was the only painting going back with them. She was dying to question Adam about how he could afford such an expensive impulse purchase, but didn't know how to bring up the subject, so she left it alone. Maybe construction work was very lucrative, she told herself, but somehow knew that wasn't the case. She also knew that he wasn't the type to spend that kind of money just to impress her.

The drive went smoothly. They stopped outside of Miami to have a quick meal, then drove nonstop the rest of the way. Adam did most of the talking and Cadence really enjoyed this talkative and animated side of him. *How did she ever think of him as quiet and brooding?* she thought to herself. He talked quite a bit about the artists he met and the bands he got to see. He was pretty excited about the various music CDs he had bought of Cuban and African music. And, he seemed genuinely impressed with her art and ability to interact with customers, complimenting Cadence repeatedly.

They hadn't discussed what would happen when they got back home. Cadence could not believe how well the weekend had gone and how much fun she had. They had spent most of their time together for the last four days, but what would happen now? Would they continue to see each other every day? Or would it be the occasional date once a week? Things had happened so fast that she really didn't know what to expect from him. She also had not had time to think about what she wanted to happen.

A week ago, if asked, Cadence would have said she didn't have any time for, or interest in, a committed relationship. But that was before experiencing this harmony and companionship with Adam. She honestly could not remember being so comfortable with another person. And then there was the sex! Mind-blowing, intense, and addictive sex.

Before leaving for Miami, she had decided to enjoy the time with Adam without any expectations. She told herself that she wasn't ready to put too much attention or energy into a man, no matter how good-looking and seemingly nice. Now, as they pulled into the parking lot of his building, she could not stop thinking about what it all meant. Was he going to ask her to spend the night with him? Should she tell him that was what she wanted? Or should she play it safe and go home to her bed and her regular life?

"Can you carry my bag up while I carry the painting?" Adam asked, pulling Cadence out of her thoughts. He had turned off the truck and was stepping out the door.

"Sure," she replied.

In his apartment, Cadence took the opportunity to use the bathroom. When she came out, Adam was in the kitchen and offered her a cup of tea. She accepted, and was about to sit in a chair at the breakfast bar, when he handed her a check. It was for the full amount of the painting. Cadence stared at the piece of paper for several seconds.

"Adam, are you sure about this? It's a lot of money."

"It's an incredible painting and worth every penny," he replied, dismissively. "I'm not very good at decorating and stuff, so you'll have to tell me the best place to hang it."

She really wanted to ask him more questions, but let it go. His finances were really none of her business, anyway. Instead, she sat in front of the kitchen counter and sipped at the tea he handed her. He eventually came over and sat on the stool beside her.

"I really appreciate your help this weekend," Cadence told him. "I've done so many of these events by myself over the last couple of years."

"Thank you for letting me go along. I've never gone to anything like that before," he told her.

"Really?" she asked, genuinely surprised. "Why not? There are so many smaller ones that happen in Orlando."

He shrugged.

"I don't know. Yvonne and a few other people have invited me over the years, but I just never had any interest, to be honest. I can just imagine their reactions when they find out I went with you. They have this impression of me as being a bit of a hermit and downright boring. I have no idea why."

His last sentence was ironic and clearly self-deprecating.

"You keep saying that, but I find it very hard to believe," she replied.

"Really? So, you're not bored with me yet?"

He leaned forward and placed a warm palm on her thigh. The other hand swept under her chin so she would look up at him. Cadence shook her head. Her lips parted in anticipation of his kiss.

"Good, 'cause I'm not ready to let you go. Stay with me tonight."

Chapter 16

"Hey, sis," Monique yelled as she walked into Cadence's house.

"I'm in the kitchen," Cadence yelled back. "Are you hungry?"

"I could eat something. What're you making?"

"Just heating up some leftovers," said Cadence.

Monique breezed into the kitchen and gave her big sister a hug before checking out the food on the stove. The resemblance between the two women was subtle, but obvious to anyone who looked closely. Monique was taller and several shades darker than Cadence, but she had the same smoky eyes and dimples in each check.

It was just after noon on Friday and almost a week before Christmas. They had plans to go shopping for gifts over the weekend and Monique was going to stay over that night.

"Salted mackerel, boiled banana. Looks good."

"So, what's going on, Monique?"

Monique opened the refrigerator and poured a glass of juice.

"Nothing, really," she responded.

"Well, I haven't seen you in almost three months, and suddenly you want to spend the weekend together," Cadence summarized with skepticism.

"You know you missed me."

"Yes, I missed you, but I'm more worried about you. How are things with Andre?"

Monique shrugged and continued to drink her juice. Cadence shook her head with exasperation.

"Monique, why do you continue to stay with him? How long do you think it's going to be before he hits you again?"

"Honestly, Cadence, I really don't want to talk to you about this. And I'm sorry I told you about that incident. It was months ago, and it was really just an accident. It's not going to happen again. And, where am I going to go? I still don't have a job, and Andre likes to take care of me."

"You can stay with me," Cadence offered. "And I still think you should sue that company for wrongful dismissal. Iris Homes, Iris Builders? Whatever. They can't just fire you because you refused to sleep with the owner. That pig should pay!"

"Okay, okay! We've been over this before, sis. It was over six months ago, and no one is going to believe me, anyway. This guy is rich, and it's not worth the energy. Just drop it, please."

Cadence released a deep breath. Monique was right. They had gone over it before, several times, and it did no good. While she was outraged by what had happened to her sister, Monique didn't seem all that bothered, and just wanted to move on. It was another example of how different the sisters were.

"Fine, I won't bring it up again. And I won't bring up Andre either, as long as you're okay."

"I'm fine, I promise. Actually, I'm better than fine," revealed Monique with a secret, devilish smile. "I think I'm in love."

Cadence looked at her, clearly confused. Her sister had been living with her boyfriend, Andre, for about eight months. Their love was not that much of a surprise.

"His name is Michael Donovan, and he is soooo sweet!"

Cadence's eyebrows shot up.

"I know what you're going to say," Monique interjected. "But it just happened. We met at the building company and were just friends at first. But, then it developed into something more."

"Oh, Monique! Does Andre know?"

"No! Of course not."

"So, what are you doing?"

Monique shrugged.

"I'm just taking care of myself, that's all. Like I said, Andre has been good to me, and he likes to take care of me, but he works too much. Michael is available and wants to spend time with me. What am I supposed to do? Stay home every night by myself? I told Andre I was lonely, but he won't listen. So, it's his fault that I found someone else."

Cadence could only look at her and shake her head. What could she possibly say to her sister that made any difference? Monique had never listened to her before, and definitely not about men.

"Just promise me you will be careful," she finally replied.

Monique just smiled like there was nothing in the

world to worry about, and changed the subject. Their mom and Ellis were going on a cruise over the holidays, so the sisters were staying in Orlando for Christmas day. They agreed to spend brunch together at Cadence's house. Cadence and Adam had not discussed any plans, but she was pretty sure they would spend the rest of the day together.

After eating, the women discussed their shopping.

"So where are we going first? I want to get Michael one of those tiny iPods."

They decided to go to Cadence's favorite shopping spot: Park Avenue in Winter Park, a cozy town in the northeast end of Orlando. It was a street lined with expensive and high-quality stores and boutiques. She had never been able to afford buying anything there before, and was really looking forward to splurging a little. They could also stop at a few stores along Colonial Drive on the way back home. If they didn't find everything they wanted, the plan was to hit the outlet malls downtown on Saturday, and the Mall at Millennia as a last resort. Neither of their shopping lists was very long. Other than gifts for her mother, Ellis, and Monique, Cadence only needed something for Steve and Beverley, then, of course, Adam. She also planned to pick up a few smaller items for her neighbors, like Yvonne and Calvin, and of course Erica and her husband and their two little boys.

The sisters eventually ended up in a trendy shoe store after shopping for several hours. Their love of shoes was probably the main thing the two girls had in common. After trying on several pairs, Cadence wandered over to the men's section.

She had been wondering what to get Adam for

Christmas and nothing appropriate came to mind. In the past, her gifts to her boyfriends had been small and fairly inexpensive. After being burnt a few times, she had developed a rule a long time ago not to put herself out financially and think it would make a man love her more. But things were different now. She was not as cash-strapped as in past years, and she really wanted to get him something nice. Something that would show him how much she enjoyed their time together, and appreciated how well he treated her.

"Dad would never wear those," Monique commented when she noticed the designer loafers Cadence was admiring. "And I don't think he's ever heard of Prada."

Cadence laughed. There was no way in hell she would ever spend that kind of money on her stepfather. She put down the shoe. It was not something that Adam would appreciate, either. Way too flashy and pretentious. *Even though he carries a Louis Vuitton weekend bag?* Cadence asked herself.

"It's not for Ellis," she replied to Monique as she walked along the display.

"Really? Who are you shopping for, then?"

Cadence smiled, but looked away.

"You have a new man, don't you?" Monique accused her. "Cadence, how could you not tell me! It has to be serious if you're thinking of getting him a gift. What's his name, how long have you been seeing him? You sly dog!"

"It's no big deal, Monique. You're acting like I've never had a boyfriend before."

"Then why are you being so secretive?"

"I'm not being secretive. I just haven't had the chance to tell you yet, that's all."

"Oh, please! You've had all afternoon, and I've told you almost everything there is to know about Michael. So, what's going on?"

"All right! All right. His name is Adam, and we met a couple of months ago. But we've only been dating for the last few weeks."

"Wow, he must be something. Three weeks and you're buying him something? That goes against every rule you've ever lectured me about."

"I don't lecture," Cadence replied defensively. "And I haven't bought him anything. Yet."

"Whatever. Let's go get some ice cream and you can tell me what makes this guy so special that you're willing to break your sacred dating rules."

"They're not rules," Cadence protested again, but Monique ignored her and led the way to a small café around the corner.

"Okay, out with it," Monique demanded between licks of a mocha almond fudge cone.

"Like I said, we met back in October at my neighbor's house. He's gentle and sweet and we have a lot in common. What else is there to say?"

"What does he do?" Monique asked.

"Something in construction," replied Cadence. Her cone had two scoops of mango sherbet.

"Construction? What kind of construction? You said his name was Adam, right?"

There was such unexpected alarm in her sister's voice that Cadence was taken aback for a moment.

"I don't know. Regular construction I guess. Brick-laying? I don't know, I never asked. Why?"

"So, he's not well-off or anything like that?"

"Sorry to disappoint you, Monique. He's just a regular blue-collar guy. No fancy car or big house."

Monique shrugged as though suddenly losing interest.

"Can I ask you something?" Cadence asked after a few minutes of ice cream licking. "What do you get a guy you've only know for a few weeks?"

It was probably the first time she had ever asked her younger sister for man advice, and Monique smiled smugly at the opportunity to share her knowledge.

"Well, it depends on how serious you guys are. How often do you see him?"

"A lot, I think. A couple of times a week, and we've spent the weekends together."

It was Monique's turn to raise her eyebrows in surprise.

"Really? It sounds serious." Cadence shrugged, almost shyly. "Okay. Is it like hanging out and going to the movies? Or like wild, kinky sex every night?"

"Monique!"

"What? It makes a difference, trust me. And I can tell by the look on your face that you guys have been doing more that hanging out at bookstores."

"Well, I wouldn't say it's been kinky, but definitely not boring. And we do lots of other things besides just that."

"Good, 'cause kinky sex could mean there's nothing else. And in that case, he already got his gift," analyzed Monique with a wink.

"You're too much," Cadence responded.

"It sounds like you should get something meaningful, but maybe not too expensive. It's only been a few weeks, after all."

Cadence nodded. Her sister's advice actually sounded pretty reasonable.

"Listen, you're welcome to stay over tonight, but I'm going out with Adam and I probably won't be home until tomorrow morning," Cadence told Monique.

She had been looking for an opportunity to explain this ever since her sister had asked to stay over.

"That's cool. No need to change your plans for me," Monique replied smoothly.

The girls finished their desserts and spent another hour shopping. Cadence found the perfect gift for her mom, then picked up a few bottles of expensive wine. She and Adam were going to a get-together at his friend's house that evening, and she thought the wine would be a nice gesture.

They were back at the house just as the sun was setting. Cadence was supposed to pick up Adam at seven o'clock, so she had over an hour to get ready. She got Monique set up in the guest bedroom, then headed into the shower with a few new bath products she had picked up at a specialty soap store that afternoon. Adam had told her the evening was going to be casual, just a few friends hanging out, but she still wanted to give special attention to her appearance, especially since she was going to spend the night at his place afterward.

Cadence left her bedroom dressed in black cotton pants and a tailored white shirt with ruffles down the front and along the cuffs. She was surprised to find Monique standing at the front door, obviously dressed to go out, and talking on her cell phone.

"You're heading out, too?" Cadence asked when Monique got off the phone.

"Yeah, Michael is picking me up and taking me to dinner and a club."

Suddenly, Cadence understood everything. Monique had asked to spend the night because she wanted to go out with her new man, and didn't want Andre to know. No wonder she was okay with Cadence being out for the night.

"Sis, are you sure you know what you're doing?"

"I know exactly what I'm doing. But I hope you don't mind, I told Michael that I lived here."

"Monique!"

"It's no big deal, I promise. But I had to tell him something. He was starting to think I'm homeless."

"Well, if you're thinking of bringing him back here tonight, forget it."

"Don't worry, he has a nice little apartment. I'm sure you'll be back before me in the morning."

A car pulled into the driveway at that moment, and the headlights shone though the glass of the front doors.

"Don't do anything I wouldn't do!" Monique teased as she danced out the door.

Chapter 17

Adam was waiting downstairs for Cadence when she pulled up on her motorcycle. He didn't recognize her at first, though she stopped right in front of him. He did, however, notice the beautiful Yamaha with its low lines and sparkling chrome. The minute she pulled off her helmet and her dreadlocks spilled out over her shoulders, his jaw dropped. The look on his face must have revealed his shock because she giggled.

"Do you need a ride?" she asked as she released the kick stand and swung off the bike.

"Oh, my God!" he exclaimed, still a little dazed.

He walked around the sleek bike and ran a hand over the smooth seat.

"Is this yours?" he asked, still admiring the ride.

"Yup! Do you like it? Have you ridden one before?"

"Not since high school. She's beautiful!"

"Good," Cadence stated. "Because . . . look what I brought for you."

She opened the underseat storage and pulled

out a helmet like hers but larger. Adam pulled her into a bear hug and literally swung her around. He was like a kid in a candy store!

"How long have you been riding?" he asked from his seat behind her as they were rolling slowly out of the parking lot.

"Almost five years," she told him.

They couldn't really speak again until they reached his friend Vince's apartment about ten minutes away. Adam gave her directions and she parked the bike in a spot close to the doors. The minute they dismounted, he embraced her again and kissed her with a loud smack.

"Thank you," he told her while resting his forehead on hers.

"For what?"

"For reminding me of one of the things I loved but stopped doing anyway."

He squeezed her tight again. Cadence took a moment to take off the small knapsack on her back and removed a bottle of wine from it. Adam then led the way into the building.

"Why did you stop riding?"

Adam shook his head and took a deep breath. He was hesitant to go into too much detail at that moment.

"It's a long story, but I was newly married and trying to be responsible."

"Ahhh," Cadence declared. "Your wife didn't like it."

"Not at all! And neither did her father. The funny thing is that it had been fine while we were dating. I even think my beat-up old bike was one of the things that attracted her to me. But, apparently, good husbands don't do those things."

They had reached Vince's apartment, and the door was opened a few seconds later. Vince gave them a wide smile and the men exchanged dabs of their fists. He then turned to Cadence with a teasing smile.

"Well, well, well, this must be the Cadence I've heard so much about," he stated before pulling her into a hug.

Vince was a big guy, a couple of inches taller than Adam, but with an additional fifty pounds on his frame, at least. Cadence looked even smaller while enveloped in his thick arms. She laughed when he finally let her go, then handed him the red wine as a gift. They all walked into the house. Vince was taking Cadence's leather jacket when he noticed the motorcycle helmets in both their hands. He immediately started laughing and tapped Adam on the back.

"You did it, dog! You finally got back in the saddle. I knew it was only a matter of time."

He was so enthusiastic that it took several tries before Adam was able to correct him.

"No, man, it's not mine. We rode Cadence's bike here," Adam was finally able to explain.

Vince looked confused for a moment.

"For real? You ride a bike?" he questioned, looking hard at the tiny woman beside his friend. "Damn! No wonder you hooked up with her."

His last comment was directed at Adam.

"Honestly, Vince, I didn't even know she had a bike until she showed up with it tonight."

Vince just shook his head, and he eyes said he could not believe that this fine black woman in front of him was a rider. Finally, he wrapped an arm over

Cadence's shoulder, and led her into the apartment. He also started to tell her all about Adam's high school years and his infamous motorcycle.

"I don't know if Adam told you this, but he was the only kid in high school who rode a motorbike. I still remember when he showed up on the first day of our sophomore year. You have to understand; we lived in Winter Park and back then there were just a handful of black kids in our high school. So this guy shows up, new to the neighborhood, and riding this loud, dusty bike, looking like a black James Dean. Of course, he was all serious and sincere, and all the girls fell in love with him right away."

Vince laughed at the memory and Cadence laughed along with him, giving Adam a quick glance as he strode behind them rolling his eyes.

They had just reached the main part of Vince's apartment, a general room with a living room and dining room in one. The dining chairs had been moved to the living area to provide additional seating. There were four people there already, one of whom was Calvin. Adam went over to shake his hand and say "hi" to the others—a couple, Dwayne and Celine, and a mutual male friend, Eric. He was introducing Cadence to the group when Yvonne and another friend, Cynthia, came out of the kitchen to say "hello."

While the others got seated in various places, Adam went into the kitchen to get Cadence a glass of white and a beer for himself. When he got back, he gave her the glass and sat in the chair next to hers. Yvonne was in the middle of telling them about the trip to Jamaica that she and Calvin had returned from the week before. She raved about the Sandals resort, the beach, and the food. The other couple, Dwayne and Celine, also talked about their Sandals vacation to the Bahamas the year before. Vince brought up his last vacation to New York, and wanting to go to the Caribbean.

"What about you, Cadence, have you gone anywhere interesting?" Yvonne asked.

"I wish," she replied. "I haven't really had time or money for a real vacation, to be honest. But I did go to New York earlier this year. It was only for a couple of days, but it was great. And Adam and I went to Miami a few weeks ago for the weekend."

Adam felt everyone's eyes fall on him. Vince already knew, but the others looked at him like he was an alien, Yvonne in particular.

"I was working, but we had a really good time anyway," Cadence continued.

There was silence for about a minute. Yvonne gave him a look that said they definitely had to talk! Adam gave her a smile and shrugged like it was no big deal. He had not had the chance to update anyone other than Vince about much over the last three weeks, so he wasn't surprised by Yvonne's reaction. As of the last real conversation with Yvonne or Calvin, he was going on his second date with Alexa. Then he surprised them this morning with a message to say he was bringing Cadence with him tonight.

"So what were you doing, Cadence?" asked Cynthia, the only single woman there. "What sort of work?"

"I was participating in an art and music festival," she replied simply.

"She's an artist," Adam interjected. "She paints

the most amazing pictures. I was totally blown away when I saw her stuff. We brought down some of her paintings, and she was able to sign some of her prints. It was great."

He knew he was gushing a bit, and even had to stop himself from going on. Cadence gave him a sweet smile and he squeezed her free hand with his before realizing what he was doing. There was more silence.

"So, is that your hobby, Cadence? What do you do full-time?" continued Cynthia before another bout of silence became too prolonged.

"That is what I do," she replied. "Occasionally, I do some illustration work on contract, but my painting and various promotional events keep me pretty busy."

"Wait a minute!" burst out Celine. "It's Cadence, right? Oh my God, I have one of your prints! Dwayne, it's the one that I put in the dining room. The one I got from that art store in Florida Mall. I love that piece!"

Celine went on to describe the picture to everyone and then the conversation splintered as they broke out into smaller discussions. The doorbell rang, and Vince brought in the pizza and wings he had ordered. Yvonne finally got the chance to descend on Adam as everyone went to get a plate of food, and Cadence went to the bathroom.

"Okay, out with it," she demanded.

"What?" he replied defensively. "I ran into Cadence again before Thanksgiving, and we started going out."

"And? There is obviously a lot more to the story.

You guys went away for the weekend? You? When was the last time you went out of town for fun?"

"I don't know, but isn't this what you've been telling me to do? So we went to Miami for a couple of days. We have a good time together, so what's the big deal?

Yvonne let out an exasperated breath.

"You're right, it shouldn't be a big deal, but Adam, I barely recognize you. You're relaxed and smiling. And you're being . . . affectionate with her!"

He had to laugh, then responded sarcastically.

"You make it sound like a bad thing." Yvonne punched his arm in protest. "It's true, though. I am relaxed. Cadence is so different from any woman I have ever met, and I've never felt so comfortable. I don't even remember what I was like before I met her."

Yvonne looked at him with her mouth a little slack.

"I guess I'm just worried about you, that's all," she told him in a calmer tone. "I don't want you to get hurt."

"Don't worry, I'm a big boy and I don't get bruised very easily. Don't forget that you guys introduced me to her."

"No, Calvin did. Until tonight, I didn't even know what she did for a living. She was definitely not on my list of women for you."

Adam was puzzled by Yvonne's statement. It almost sounded as though she didn't like Cadence, or somehow disapproved of her. The subject of their discussion walked by at that moment, preventing him from responding to Yvonne. Instead, he dropped the subject and joined the others around the food in the kitchen.

After eating, the men started a game of poker in the dining room while the four women sat in the living room talking and listening to music. From the way they told stories, Cadence got the sense that they had known each other for some time. There was about thirty minutes of talk and shared jokes that she just could not understand or participate in, so she sat quietly and listened. Eventually, she started to feel like she was invisible.

"So, how long have you guys known each other?" she asked when there was a slight gap in the conversation.

"Adam, Vince, and I went to high school together," Yvonne replied. "Then Vince met Eric and Celine in college, I guess about eight years ago. Cynthia, you worked with Celine at one point, right? But we've all been hanging out for years now."

"How long have you known Adam?" Cynthia asked Cadence.

"Not long. Just a few weeks. We met at Yvonne's house, actually, back in October."

"At the housewarming, right? I thought I recognized you," Cynthia continued.

"She lives across the street from us," explained Yvonne.

The others nodded in acknowledgment.

"So, are you guys dating now?" continued Cynthia.

Cadence was a little surprised by the question, but the three women continued to look at her, waiting for the response.

"We've been seeing each other."

"Good for you!" This time it was Celine who responded. "Adam is a great guy, and it's nice to see him with someone who cares about him, not what he has to offer. I could tell immediately that you were good for him."

"I know," added Cynthia. "I was pleasantly surprised when I met you, to be honest. I was afraid he would pick up with another high-maintenance princess. I can't stand those women who only care about what a man does and how much money he has to offer."

"Well, I have to admit that I do kind of like the fact that Adam does construction," Cadence told them with a playful smile. "He's great with his hands and pretty good with tools, too. Money isn't everything."

The girls burst out laughing at her joke, except Yvonne, who smiled, but gave her a puzzled look. After a moment, the subject changed to more general topics like tabloid news and television shows. The men joined the women again about an hour later, and they all sat together to watch a movie they found on satellite.

Chapter 18

By eleven o'clock, the group started packing up and getting ready to go. Celine and Dwayne were the first to leave, but not before Celine made Cadence promise to come by their house and autograph the back of their print. Eric left next and Cynthia soon after. Adam and Cadence stayed to help the others clean up, and it was after midnight when they got back to Adam's apartment.

On the ride back, Cadence let him take the driver's seat. Adam was a little rusty at first, so they took back streets. He was handling the bike like a professional by the time they parked it in front of his building. When they hopped off the bike, they were both breathing hard from the adrenaline and excitement.

"How did I do?" he asked after taking off the head gear.

"That was great! You handled it really well. How long has it been since you stopped riding?"

"God, it has to be at least ten years. But honestly, it feels like yesterday."

Adam handed her his helmet, and Cadence tucked it into the storage container after removing her small knapsack. She had brought along a change of clothes to wear home on Saturday morning.

"So, why didn't you tell me about the bike earlier?" asked Adam while they were going up the stairs of his complex. "For someone who says she's not into surprises, you really know how to pull one off."

Cadence giggled.

"Honestly, I wasn't sure how you would react. I was afraid you would think I was too wild or something. Some guys are actually put off by it. Or they don't want me riding because they think it's dangerous."

As they stood in front of his door, Adam took her into his arms and placed firm hands on either side of her face. He looked into her eyes for several seconds, his expression unreadable. Cadence could feel his heart racing.

"Cadence, I don't think there is anything about you that could put me off."

His lips claimed hers with hot intensity. She was limp as his tongue explored her mouth, entangling with hers over and over. He slid his hands down her back until they cupped her bottom, pulling her up onto her toes. Their bodies were fused, and Cadence could feel that long length of his arousal against her stomach. The kiss got deeper and their breathing became harsher, but neither wanted to stop long enough to go inside.

When Adam finally unlocked his door, they practically rolled inside, breaking apart only long enough to kick off their shoes and turn on the light in the foyer. They were then back in each other's arms with him kissing and biting at every sensitive spot of her neck and ear. Cadence responded by running her hands up under his sweater to feel the ripples and folds of his taut body.

They stumbled blindly into the main room until Cadence was backed up against the breakfast bar. Adam used the opportunity to slowly unbutton her shirt, pressing his lips over the soft, scented skin that was revealed.

"Ummm, you smell so sweet! What is that?" he asked, while burying his face just above her cleavage.

"New bath products," she uttered as he ran his tongue over the top of her breast.

"I like it," he muttered. "It makes me want to taste you everywhere."

Adam then picked her up and sat her on one of the bar stools. He pulled off her shirt and threw it on the floor. Cadence let her back rest against the high counter, and she watched with dazed eyes as he undid her pants and pulled them off her body as quickly as possible. They landed in the general direction of her shirt. Adam then pulled off his sweater and tossed it away also.

He stood between her legs and looked her up and down. Cadence felt the heat of his eyes like a touch as it hovered over her swollen lips, then traveled down to the curves of her breasts displayed perfectly in a white push-up bra. She looked back up at his face and felt empowered and glorified by the look of adoration it revealed. His fingers brushed over both dark nipples visible through her bra, and her eyes fell closed. The touch was urgent and sweetly rough, sending her senses spinning.

"Oh, oh, yes!" she begged. "Oh, Adam."

"Does it feel good?" he demanded with his mouth hot against her flesh at her neck.

"Yes, yes, yes . . ."

His lips replaced his hands on her breasts; and Cadence groaned, arching her back with delight. She wrapped her legs around him and urged him closer to her heat.

"Sweetheart!"

Adam suddenly picked her up, and quickly walked her over to the sofa, placing her, sitting, in the center. He paused for a moment to remove his pants and underwear and slip on protection from his wallet. She moaned in protest, immediately missing his touch, but purred with contentment when he returned, sitting beside her. With his help, she removed her underwear and bra, then he pulled her across his lap, settling her knees on either side of his hips. They kissed again, his tongue stroking hers, demonstrating his deepest desire.

Then he brought her hips down and encased himself deep inside her. Their lips parted and they held their breaths, motionless until Cadence rocked her hips.

"Cadence. Oh, Cadence, you feel like heaven," Adam muttered, his faced buried in her breasts.

He groaned deeply when she thrust onto him again.

"Do you like that? Does it feel good?" she asked.

His response was incoherent. He could only utter throaty moans as Cadence took the lead to ride him with long, slow thrusts. They both reached their peaks with stunning force before collapsing in exhaustion. Eventually, Adam found enough energy to pick her up and carry her to his bed.

Saturday morning, Adam had to leave Cadence before she woke up. He was having breakfast with his bank manager, Sandra, at nine o'clock at a restaurant near his office. He was on the road by eight, but left a note and a key for Cadence on the night table in his bedroom.

Sandra Evans had been managing Adam's accounts ever since he rebuilt his first house. They had become friends over the years as she watched him develop Iris Custom Homes into a sizable competitor in the Orlando housing market. She had also been there to advise him when his marriage fell apart. Still, Adam was surprised when she asked to meet with him, and it took a few weeks to coordinate their schedules.

He was seated at their table sipping his coffee when Sandra arrived. They greeted each another with a hug.

"You haven't been waiting long, have you?" she asked.

"No, it's fine. I was a little early," he told her.

She also ordered a coffee, and they caught up on their lives for the next few minutes. Sandra was married with three kids under the age of eight, so her home life was pretty crazy. But eventually they got down to business.

"I was going over your business account for the last year or so, and I think we can find some better ways to manage the balance," she explained.

"Okay," he replied politely.

She then went into a description of several short-term and long-term investment strategies that would ensure the business profits could grow with aggressive interest, but be easily liquidated for new projects and cash flow when needed. Adam listened intently and occasionally interjected a few questions. In the end, he was quite interested in her proposal.

"This sounds promising, Sandra. I'll talk to Peter on Monday, and maybe we can come up with amounts and a timetable to start transferring funds. We're just entering negotiations for another project, so we can probably put something in place for January," he told her.

"Sounds good. I'll have my assistant contact you to set up the accounts. Now, the other question is how you would like to handle the interest earned. We can deposit it back into the business account, or keep investing it separately. What are you guys doing with it now?"

"Doing with what?" asked Adam, suddenly confused.

"With the interest you're currently earning on your investments? I know they have been rather short-term, so I assume the returns have been high in order to make the risks worthwhile. And that's the main reason I was concerned. I would hate to see you lose such large sums of money in risky transitions."

"Honestly, Sandra, I don't know what you're referring to," he finally told her.

"Well, we'll look into the numbers and figure it out," she said dismissively. "You transferred out about two million dollars so far this year with no losses yet . . . well, except for the $500,000 still outstanding from last month."

Adam could only look at her. He really had no idea

what she was talking about, but was hesitant to let Sandra know it. The company was not doing any outside investments, so either she was mistaken, or there was a logical explanation. He would just sit down with Peter on Monday and go over the accounts.

Adam wrapped up the meeting with Sandra, then went back to the office to review Peter's reports for the last year. There was nothing in them that suggested the type of transactions Sandra mentioned. Eventually, he shook his head, puzzled, but not worried, then moved on to examine the latest development proposal he was involved with. He took a break just before noon and called Cadence on her cell phone to say "hi."

Cadence and Monique were just finishing a late breakfast when she answered the phone.

"Hey there," she said with a smile on her face when she recognized Adam's number. "How's your day so far?"

"Pretty good. But that's because I had such a good sleep," he replied.

She laughed, delighted, but stifled her grin when Monique looked at her suspiciously from across their table. Cadence turned away to get some privacy.

"Sorry I had to leave you so early," he added. "Did you get out okay?"

"It was fine. Thanks for letting me sleep in."

"How is the shopping going so far?"

"Well," she replied slowly, "we haven't really started yet. We're getting something to eat."

Adam chuckled.

"All right. Give me a call when you guys are almost done. I was thinking we could rent a couple of movies or see what's playing at the theaters."

"Okay, sounds good. I should be home by around four o'clock."

They hung up, and Cadence went back to her meal, avoiding her sister's knowing looks.

"Cadence is in love," Monique sang in a little-girl voice, and was hit by a pack of sugar in retaliation.

The teasing continued throughout the afternoon and until they were on their way back to Cadence's house. Andre called at that point, and put Monique into a totally different mood. Her voice became agitated and short, and Cadence could hear his angry voice through the cell phone as they argued back and forth. It was clear that Monique's boyfriend was not too thrilled with the night spent away from home.

"Is everything okay?" Cadence asked when the call ended.

"It's fine," replied Monique with a tight smile. "He just misses me, that's all."

"You don't have go back, you know. You can stay with me as long as you need to. No, listen," she demanded when Monique tried to protest. "I have a really bad feeling about this whole thing. I know you don't want to believe it, but Andre could really hurt you, especially if he ever found out about this other guy, Michael."

Monique didn't respond. She just looked out the passenger window. They pulled into the driveway shortly afterward and Cadence parked the Honda in the garage. They carried their purchases inside.

"Look, I'm not judging, okay? I'm just worried about you," said Cadence, trying again to get through to her sister.

"I know, but it will be fine, I promise. I have to get

going," she replied, then went to the spare bedroom to get her stuff.

The doorbell rang, and Cadence checked her watch, wondering who it could be. She was pleasantly surprised to see Adam's profile through the glass of the door.

"Hey," she said in welcome as he stepped inside.

Adam pulled her into a kiss before responding.

"Hey, yourself. I was nearby, so I thought I would see if you were home yet. I hope that's okay."

"Of course! We just got in, actually. My sister is just grabbing her stuff before she leaves, but you'll get to meet her."

They walked into the living room just as Monique was coming out of the bedroom carrying her overnight tote bag. She stopped in her tracks when she saw them.

"Adam, this is my sister . . ."

"Monique?" he questioned, cutting Cadence off.

Cadence looked back and forth between them for a second, taking in his confusion and Monique's obvious shock.

"You two know each other?" she finally asked.

"Monique Rutherford," Adam repeated before turning to Cadence. "You two are sisters?"

"Yeah. We have different fathers," Cadence explained. "But how do you guys know each other?"

There was a pause as her sister and boyfriend looked at each other, but neither spoke. Monique looked away first, down at the floor, and Cadence knew something was really wrong.

She heard Adam take a deep breath before he responded.

"Monique used to work for me," he told her.

"Work for you? When, where? Monique, what's going on?"

Monique looked at Adam again, then finally at her sister.

"Look, I really have to get going. Andre is waiting for me," she said stiffly, then tried to walk by them.

Cadence stopped her with a grip on her arm.

"Wait a minute. What's wrong?" But Monique didn't answer, so she turned to Adam instead. "When did she work for you?"

"Cadence, she worked for me for a few months this summer."

Monique snatched her arm out of her sister's grip.

"I have to go," she pleaded before she practically ran out the door.

Cadence turned to Adam with her arms crossed.

"What on earth was that about, Adam?"

"Look, I'll let Monique explain her side to you, but she's probably embarrassed because I had to fire her."

"What? You fired her? From that building company? She told me it was the owner who did it."

She watched Adam clench his teeth and look away before he answered.

"Cadence, I *am* the owner of the company."

Chapter 19

It all fell into place within seconds. Cadence dropped her hands and stepped back from him.

"Look, Cadence, I know I should have told you the truth earlier . . ."

"What truth is that, exactly, Adam?"

He let out a deep breath and smiled humorlessly while stepping toward her. She stepped back, farther out of his reach.

"Sweetheart, it's not a big deal, really. You thought I was a construction worker and I didn't correct you. Construction is what I do, what I've always done. What difference does it make that I work for my own company?"

She just stared at him, remembering all the things that had not made sense. The house near Leesburg, the expensive luggage, his buying her painting. He had been playing games with her and she had fallen for it.

"If it didn't make a difference, why did you deliberately mislead me? On several occasions, Adam?"

"I don't know, Cadence. It seems silly now, but I

guess I like the idea that you didn't care what I did.
It's been a long time since I felt that way."

"You know what? I don't care! Not only are you a
liar, but you are a sleazy bastard. Just because you're
rich, you think you can prey on young women?
Men like you make me sick."

"Whoa, what?" Adam protested, clearly baffled.

"You heard me! Monique told me all about it.
You fired her because she wouldn't sleep you. You
are so lucky she didn't sue you like I told her to."

"What the hell? Cadence, that's crazy."

"Really? Well, forgive me if I don't believe you."

She walked away from him toward the kitchen,
then turned back with her hand wrapped around
her waist.

"I think you should leave."

"Cadence, come on, don't you think you're over-
reacting? This is me you're talking to. I don't know
what your sister told you, but it was definitely not
the truth. I admit, I made a mistake, but . . ."

"I don't know who you are! The person I thought
I had met clearly doesn't exist. I want you to go."

"Cadence, sweetheart, let's just talk about it.
Once I explain, you'll see that . . ."

Adam took steps toward her, his hands out pleadingly. She took another step back, her face showing
a mix of anger, disbelief, and fear.

"Don't come anywhere near me! Just get out.
Please!"

"I'm not leaving you like this! You're upset, I understand that. But, I promise you, I don't know
what your sister is talking about. Cadence, I swear
to you, nothing like that ever happened."

She didn't believe a word he said, and the more

he talked the more she realized how much she had been misled.

"None of this was real, was it? It was all just a game to you. What did you want from me, Adam? A good time from a cheap date? I was better off when you thought I was a hooker!"

"This is crazy, Cadence. Of course it was real! I have never felt anything so real in my life."

Cadence covered her ears, afraid he might say something to soften her outrage. She suddenly felt embarrassingly close to tears.

"I need you to leave," she told him with punctuated words, and with her eyes focused on a spot behind his ear. "If you don't go, I'm going to call the police."

Out of the corner of her eyes, she saw him clench his jaw. His outreached arms fell to his side.

"Everything that happened between us was real," he told her in a low, raw voice before he turned and walked away.

The water did not well up into her eyes until she heard the door close behind him. Cadence fell into the nearest chair in the living room. Her eyes were unfocused as the silent tears poured down her face.

How the hell had she let this happen to her? How could she have fallen for such a fraud? The signs had been there, but she hadn't paid attention. She was too caught up in the perfect words, the caring façade, and her own need to find someone who could understand her. And now, she was left without her dignity or her heart. How could she have allowed this?

Cadence could not tell how long she sat in the chair, but when her eyes dried up, it was completely dark outside. Eventually, she stood up to make her way to her room, then saw the bags of holiday shopping on the floor where she had put them when she got home. In one of the large bags was a big red toolbox, and in that was a top-of-the-line cordless drill with every conceivable attachment. It was a gift that would make any laborer drool, or so the salesman had assured her. *What a joke,* she told herself before stomping to the bedroom and crawling under the covers after removing her clothes. She turned on the television for company, but could not pay attention to anything being played.

The same thought ran through her mind over and over again. How was it possible for her to have such intense feelings for someone who was a fraud? Shouldn't her instincts have protected her? She understood lust, animal attractions, and physical passion. If that was all it had been, Cadence would be angry, but able to see it for what it was. But this was different. She had felt such an intense connection, both physical and emotional, that she felt as betrayed by her body as she did by Adam's deception.

Eventually, Cadence fell asleep, but her dreams were saturated by images of Adam fixing her kitchen, carrying her in his arms, and walking naked across the room. She woke up still tasting him on her lips and throbbing from the memory of his touch.

The week went by agonizingly slowly. Cadence tried to stay busy around the house and on the phone with art stores and galleries. She even took a couple of extra yoga classes to pass the time. But, as hard as she tried, she could not paint. She spent hours staring at half-finished pieces, blank canvases and sketch pads. Nothing would come to her. By the following Saturday, she was starting to get worried. Her talent was the one thing she had always been able to count on, and now she couldn't find it. This was the time she needed it the most. The injustice of it made her angry and hurt all over again.

Sunday was no better, but Cadence was forced to get up and get out of the house by ten-thirty in the morning. It was Christmas Eve and Steve had invited her to brunch to exchange gifts and would not take "no" for an answer. It was a beautiful day, and normally she would have ridden her motorcycle, but when she opened the garage door and looked at the sleek, black machine, all she could think of was riding behind Adam, clinging to his waist, as he led her through the downtown streets. She took the old Honda instead.

Steve was a few minutes late, so when he arrived, Cadence was halfway through a cup of tea. To her surprise, Beverley was right behind him. They all hugged and exchanged the small gifts they gave each other every year.

"So, how are you, Cadence? It's been weeks since we've really spoken," Steve said once they were seated and their breakfast was ordered. "How was that event in Miami?"

Cadence couldn't look him in the eye. She felt guilty about avoiding Steve over the last few weeks. She had not been ready to discuss her relationship with Adam, nor did she want to pretend she wasn't seeing someone. So, she took the cowardly way out.

"It went well. We sold four originals, and lots of

prints. I'm definitely going to do it again next year if they will have me."

"Good. So, what else is new?" he asked.

"Nothing much, just lining up some things for next year," she replied. "What about with you guys?"

Beverley seized the opportunity to detail every social event she had gone to in the last month. Her stories lasted until their food arrived.

"What are your plans for the holidays?" Steve asked Cadence when there was a pause in the conversation.

"Nothing much. Monique and I are staying in Orlando, and we'll get together tomorrow. Other than that, I'll probably just relax and finish some projects around the house. I'm not a big holiday fan, anyway," she confessed with a shrug of her shoulders. "What about you guys?"

"We're staying in town, too. Beverley's mom is here, so we're having a big Christmas dinner. We also want to take her to a few places like Disney World, maybe even Busch Gardens in Tampa."

"Emily will really like that," added Cadence.

They talked some more about different events going on around the city until Beverley changed the subject halfway through their meal.

"Did Steve tell you that we've been going house-hunting?" she asked Cadence. "We've looked everywhere for something special and I think we've found it."

Cadence looked at her and smiled. She found it weird that Beverley looked like a cat that ate a fat canary, and Steve only had interest in his biscuit.

"It's a little bigger than we were looking for, definitely at the high end of our budget, but it's beautiful. I didn't really want to go brand-new, but when I saw the model home, I just fell in love. And the plot we want will be on the perfect cul-de-sac, and with a backyard that can easily hold a large swimming pool. I am so excited, aren't you, Steve?"

Steve just nodded, chewing his food. Cadence had to bite her lips not to laugh.

"It sounds really nice, Beverley. Where is it?" she asked instead.

"In Altamonte Springs. My friend, Alexa introduced us to the builder."

Cadence froze, dreading the direction Beverley was heading. She remembered exactly who Alexa was, and had a strong suspicion about the builder also.

"You met him, too, Cadence. At Steve's birthday dinner, remember? He was Alexa's date," Beverley continued, completely unaware that Cadence was doing everything not to cringe. "He's a really nice guy, considering he's doing so well. He even agreed to meet us at the site and show us the model homes himself."

"Really," Cadence felt compelled reply.

"Yeah. I was really impressed with the way he did business. I mean, he's so young, but has accomplished so much. Right, Steve? Alexa says he's loaded, but you would never guess that he is so wealthy. He acts just like a regular guy. Apparently, his ex-wife was from this really wealthy family, but she was a total bitch. You know, one of those 'society' women? Designer everything, catered brunches, expensive country-club memberships. I just can't imagine Adam with someone like that. No wonder they got divorced."

Cadence nodded occasionally, trying desperately

not to listen, but absorbing every word. It sickened her that Adam had felt comfortable confiding in Alexa about his real life and his marriage, and now Beverley DeSouza knew more about him than Cadence did.

"Anyway, I think we're going to buy one of his houses. . . ." Beverley continued, but at that point Cadence really stopped listening, regardless of how rude it appeared.

She felt physically sick. Her stomach was rolling and her hands felt clammy. By the time they left the restaurant, Cadence knew she would throw up and she almost didn't make it to the bathroom at home. There were several long and miserable minutes spent bent over the toilet before she stripped off her clothes and took a hot shower.

Cadence spent the rest of the day wrapping a few gifts and trying to keep busy around the house, but she felt so tired and listless that she could only move at half speed. It was only after eight o'clock in the evening when she gave up and crawled into bed, but no matter how much she wrapped herself in the comforter, she still felt cold. Eventually, she realized that the nausea and fatigue weren't just a reaction to hearing about Adam. She was coming down with the flu.

Christmas Day came, and Cadence slept through the morning. When she did wake up, it was to find Monique hovering over her with a look of alarm and concern on her face.

"Cadence, wake up!"

"I'm up, stop shaking me!" she replied in a thin, shaky voice.

"God, you scared me. I've been trying to get you up for at least ten minutes. What's wrong with you?"

"I think I have the flu."

"What?" Monique asked and leaned closer to hear.

"The flu! I'm pretty sure it's the flu," Cadence repeated, trying to talk louder, but her words only came out as a whisper.

"Oh no! Do you need anything? Do you want something to drink?"

Monique was gone before Cadence responded, then came back with a glass of orange juice. She sat on the edge of the bed while Cadence sat up and sipped the liquid.

"I guess this means we're not having brunch."

"I'm sorry," Cadence replied miserably.

"Don't worry about it, sis. It's not your fault. Instead of ackee and salt fish, I'll make us some pancakes."

"Thanks, but I don't think I can eat anything."

"Well, you have to. And I know you're just saying that because you think I can't cook. My pancakes are amazing, or so I have been told."

Cadence didn't respond. Instead, she put down the orange juice after only a few sips, and buried herself back under the covers. She knew Monique was still talking, but her voice sounded fuzzy and faded.

The annoying and persistent shaking returned in what seemed like seconds later. When Cadence opened her eyes, Monique was standing over her again. There was a plate of food in her hands.

"Come on, sit up. You have to eat something," she was instructed.

Cadence followed instructions, and tried to eat at

least a couple of bites of Monique's meal. She couldn't taste anything, but swallowed reflexively.

"I left you several messages last week. Why didn't you call me back?" Monique finally asked after a few minutes of silence.

Cadence let out a deep, loud breath.

"What happened after I left? Is everything okay with you and Adam?" continued Monique.

Cadence let out another loud breath.

"Cadence, what happened?"

"Did you know who he was when I told you I was dating him?" Cadence finally asked.

"Sis, I really didn't know." There was a pause. "I did consider it when you mentioned his name, but then you said he was just a construction worker. . . ."

The rest of the explanation faded away.

Cadence forced another chunk of food down her throat.

"Was he really mean to you?" she asked Monique a moment later. "I mean, when you guys worked together."

"To be honest, I didn't see very much of him, but when I did, he seemed nice enough. Look, there is something I need to tell you," replied Monique.

Chapter 20

Adam was sitting on the covered patio of the Fruitland Park house, drinking a fresh cup of coffee. It was Christmas morning, and the air was clean and cool. He had arrived late the night before and only packed away the perishable food he had brought before heading to bed. Now, sitting under the rising sun, he questioned his decision to come there by himself.

The last week had been so hectic and busy that Adam could only operate on autopilot. It was for the best, since it had left very little time or energy to think about Cadence and the last time he saw her. Yet, the image of her face, and the look of mistrust and anger on it, found its way into every spare minute. It also haunted his dreams at night.

He took another drink from his mug and tried to turn his thoughts in another direction.

This was exactly how Adam had planned the first Christmas after his divorce. In his head, the idea of getting away by himself to do some boating or fishing had seemed relaxing and ideal. But the reality was already lonely, and he had only been up for about an hour. Still, it was a drastic difference from the fiasco with his in-laws the year before.

He and Rose had already been separated for several months before the holidays, but she had not told her parents yet. She claimed not to want to ruin her holidays listening to them preach about how right they had been all along. After weeks of begging, he had given in and went along with the charade of pretending their marriage was still working.

It was the last time he did anything Rose asked of him, and it was disastrous. Adam's relationship with his wife's parents had always been awkward and chilly, at best. He had been an average kid who had somehow gotten their precious daughter to fall in love with him, then married into their exceptional and elite family. Their interactions had gone from hostile to barely tolerable over the years, and it was clear there was never going to be real acceptance.

Adam had not realized how much their intolerance and scorn had molded him during his eleven years of marriage until he had been away from them and Rose for the first few months of his separation. It all came to a head last Christmas.

He could not remember all the details of the day, but was clear about the exchange with his father-in-law that had put Adam over the edge. Every year, the Stuarts put on a huge Christmas feast for friends, family, and neighbors. It was a pretentious affair at their stately house in Winter Garden, including ice sculptures, an army of servers, and even valet parking. Adam had arrived as close to dinner as possible without being rude, and spent the first thirty minutes out on the patio drinking a rum on ice. Eventually, Jameson Stuart, Rose's father, approached him, and immediately started criticizing a recent decision Adam had made not to participate in a residential project on Florida's east coast. The location did not fit in with his vision, and the cost would have required a huge increase in his line of credit along with most of his liquid capital.

"If you had listened to me, kid, you would have gotten that contract in West Palm Beach. You're small-time, and you'll never be anything else. You don't have the vision or the balls."

Adam had given him a hostile glare, but kept his mouth shut and tried to tune out. Jameson kept prodding and prodding until his final words were something about Adam being a lazy island boy who had no business being with his daughter. Finally, Adam responded as he had always wanted to.

"You know what, *Jameson*, I'm quite happy as an island boy, as you put it. And you're right; I have never deserved your daughter. No man deserves to be controlled and manipulated by that greedy bitch that you and your wife spoiled rotten. So you can have her back, I don't want her anymore."

Adam shoved his glass into the man's chest and walked away. He left the house without saying another word, and never spoke to or saw any of them again. The divorce was finalized a few months later.

Becoming a single man was a lot more difficult for Adam than he thought it would be. He enjoyed the peace of being alone, particularly since he could finally do many things that he had been forced to eliminate from his life. He also appreciated the opportunity to be his own person again. But Adam really missed the idea of being in a relationship and having that special connection to one person. That was probably why he had waited so long to start dating again. It seemed impossible that he could find someone to share that with again.

Then he met Cadence and it changed everything, including his appreciation of solitude. It was just lonely.

Adam was still finding it difficult to accept or understand what had happened last Saturday. For whatever reason, he hadn't really thought that his not being just a construction worker would be such an issue. He knew he would have to come clean and correct some of Cadence's assumptions, but her response to the truth had taken him completely by surprise.

Then, there were her accusations regarding her sister, Monique. Adam had no idea what to make of it, but was certain that it could be cleared up if only Cadence would discuss it with him. Yes, he had been forced to fire Monique, but there had been nothing inappropriate or illicit about it.

Adam had tried all week not to call Cadence, to give her time to calm down. He even hoped that at some point before Christmas, she would call him to talk. But he did not hear from her, and she did not pick up her home or cellular phone on Sunday when he finally did call her. He left a brief message, but she didn't call him back, either.

Before he left Orlando the night before, Adam had made a few stops to drop off gifts. The first was to Vince's place. Vince had his son, Aaron, for the whole holiday week because Carol had gone to Mexico with her new man. Aaron opened the door when Adam arrived.

"Hi, Uncle Adam!" yelled his godson as he wrapped his slender arms around Adam's waist. "Are you staying with us for Christmas? Daddy says this year it's just us men. We're going to go go-carting, and maybe even play laser tag. Are you going to come? Do you remember last time? You killed Daddy right away and he was so mad!"

Adam could not help but laugh along with Aaron, then chuckled some more at the stream of chatter that followed. He nodded at Vince, who was in the kitchen on the phone, then went ahead and put Aaron's large gift under the Christmas tree. That sent Aaron into a guessing game about what his present could be.

Eventually, Aaron went off to play with his toys, allowing Adam and Vince to sit down in front of the television and talk. Vince was the only one of his friends with whom Adam would discuss the inside details of his business. Vince had been a bus driver for the Central Florida Transit Authority for the last twelve years. He got the job right out of high school and loved it because it paid the bills and allowed him to meet people. But Vince had the mind of a true entrepreneur and an excellent intuition for business. Adam had offered him a job dozens of times in the last five years, but he always turned it down. He could not stand the idea of being tied to a desk all day.

"Man, I'm scratching my head over this thing with the bank accounts. I would bet my money that Peter was telling me the truth. We pulled all the banking reports for the year and went over the accounts together. There was nothing there. Every transition was legit," Adam explained to Vince.

The friends had spoken last Saturday after the meeting with Sandra. Vince's first reaction was that something was going on and Adam needed to get more involved in the day-to-day operations. The last time they had discussed accounting, it was earlier in the year, and Adam was deciding whether or not to install a new software package that would allow his contractor to get paid by online bank transfers rather than checks. Vince agreed that it was necessary to get more modernized and paperless, but told Adam that automation was not always a good thing. Iris Custom Homes had too much cash in the bank and so many payments going out. There would be an increased opportunity for mistakes. Adam had nonetheless installed the software in the summer and it seemed to be working well.

"It's probably just a mistake by your bank manager. Or maybe she's just looking for a way to increase your business with her," Vince replied.

"Maybe."

"Is there any way for Peter or anyone else to fudge the numbers?"

"What do you mean?" Adam asked.

"I don't know. Can they be doing banking transactions that you're not aware of?"

"No, I asked our systems guy, Michael, the same thing when we were installing the new software. He assured me that the reports would be pulled directly from the bank records, and there would be no way to modify then, only to work with the numbers, depending on the types of reports we want. It was one of the main reasons I agreed to it."

Vince just nodded, but Adam could tell he was deep in thought, looking at every angle.

"Well, I wouldn't worry about it for now. If there is no money missing, then just keep an eye on things."

The men moved on to discuss other things going on in their lives, including Cadence. Vince was clearly impressed by her and the change in Adam since they had started dating. He only had one caution: don't fall in love.

"I've been telling you for months now, get out there and have some fun. I know it's not in your nature, but these days, it's the only way to go," he told Adam. "I've never been married, so for me, at thirty, it's time I start thinking about taking that step. But my life is more complicated. Aaron has to love the woman as much as I do, if you know what I'm saying. And she would have to be willing to put up with Carol's craziness. You, on the other hand, just need an airtight prenuptial agreement."

Adam laughed ironically. He knew Vince was making reference to his divorce settlement and the amount of business equity that was paid out to Rose in the end. It seemed ridiculous, since she had come into the relationship with a hefty trust fund that Adam could not touch. Then, she left with half his money and the same trust fund plus interest.

"Don't get me wrong," Vince continued. "Cadence seems like a great girl. You just don't want to fall for the rebound, that's all."

"Vince, Rose and I have been over for almost a year and a half. It's hardly a rebound."

"Eighteen months is a long time for any other guy, but not you. I'm just saying be careful and be smart, that's all."

Adam let it drop. If he defended himself any

more, his true feelings for Cadence would become obvious. He was already in love with her, but it was too fresh and raw to discuss with anyone, not even his best friend, especially considering she wasn't talking to him at that moment.

It was after eight o'clock that evening by the time Adam left Vince's place and drove to Ocoee to see Yvonne and Calvin. He was already packed up to spend most of the coming week in Fruitland Park, and was planning on being on the highway by ten o'clock that night at the latest. In the back of his mind, there was still the possibility that Cadence would call him to work things out, and they could spend the week together, but, as the evening went by, the chance got slimmer.

Adam only intended to drop off his gifts and stay for a few minutes, but Yvonne pulled him into another conversation about Cadence. They were sitting in the living room and Calvin was in the kitchen.

"How is Cadence?" she asked only a few minutes into his visit. "She dropped off a really nice bottle of wine for us a couple of days ago."

He nodded, but didn't say anything, unsure of what direction the conversation was going in.

"I asked her what you guys were doing for Christmas, but she only said something about being busy and then rushed to leave. What's going on with you guys? Is everything okay?"

Adam hesitated. He really didn't want to say anything to Yvonne, particularly since she thought his biggest problem was that he was noncommunicative and cold. She was not going to be impressed with his less than honest behavior toward Cadence.

"We had a disagreement last week and we haven't really spoken since," he finally replied.

"Is it serious? What happened?"

He let out a deep breath and bit the bullet.

"She found out a few things about me that I hadn't really told her before, and she got upset."

Yvonne slammed her hand on the arm of the sofa.

"I knew it! You didn't tell her about who you are, did you?" Yvonne accused him.

"Cadence knows exactly who I am. She knows the important things," replied Adam with a spark of resentment in his voice.

"That's not what I'm talking about. She didn't know anything about your company, did she? We were talking about money-hungry women last week, and I just got this feeling that she didn't have a clue about your wealth. Why would you want her to think you were just a construction worker?"

"What difference does it make, other than to complicate things? As long as I'm hardworking and self-sufficient, it shouldn't matter what I do or how much money I make."

"Adam, don't be naive! It shouldn't matter, but it does. I know you don't want to hear it, but your success and money are part of who you are today. Look at how much time you spend working, how focused and single-minded you have been in building your business. All of that has an impact on your relationship with a woman. She would have to understand that in order to be with you and be happy. You know that hiding that part of your life is lying about who you are."

What could he say? Yvonne was right, and Cadence had every right to be angry about his lack of honesty.

"I don't know if Cadence is the right woman for you long-term, Adam. I like her and I think she has been good for you so far. And I know for sure that she is completely different from Rose. She is not looking for another Daddy or a man to take care of her every whim. She's not the type to judge you based on your bank account and I know you know that, too. So, why would you hide the truth?"

Adam was saved by Calvin's return. He stayed for another thirty minutes, and before he left, he called Cadence's house again. She still did not answer. The idea of her joining him for the week seemed impossible at that point, so Adam went to his car and returned to give Yvonne a small baby-blue gift bag.

"Do me a favor?" he asked from the front door. "Can you drop this off at her house tomorrow for me? Tell her I've gone up to Leesburg for the week."

Yvonne must have heard the dejection in his voice, because she agreed without any additional questions or comments.

Adam got up from his seat on the patio and went into the house. He planned to call his mother and a few other relatives, but otherwise had no specific plans. The rest of the day and week stretched empty before him.

Chapter 21

Cadence did not hear the agitation in her sister's voice as Monique announced there was something she needed to talk about. She only felt a new wave of exhaustion and chills.

"Monique, can we talk later? I can't think right now."

Cadence closed her eyes and tried to find a comfortable position in which to fall asleep.

"Okay," Monique acquiesced. "Get some rest. Do you need anything?"

"Some Tylenol, please. Thanks," she mumbled.

When Monique returned, Cadence was on the edge of sleep, but swallowed two pills with a gulp of water. Vaguely, she heard Monique say she would hang around for a couple of hours and wake Cadence up before she left.

It was the doorbell that pulled Cadence out of her sleep about an hour and a half hour later. She checked the clock next to her bed and saw that it was almost two o'clock in the afternoon. *Who could that be,* she wondered, while struggling to unwrap herself from the comforter. Monique entered the room just as Cadence finally swung her legs over the edge of the bed.

"Merry Christmas!" Monique announced as she presented Cadence with two gift bags, a large red one and a small baby-blue one.

Cadence just responded with a glazed stare.

"Come on, I know you're feeling miserable, so these will make you feel better," announced Monique as she sat Cadence on the bed. "I already found mine in the front closet. Thanks for the sunglasses! Now, this one's from me, so open it first."

Cadence complied and took the red bag. She pulled out tissue paper, then the square box buried underneath. Inside was a beautiful, dark purple blouse made of delicate, soft silk. Cadence still felt like crap, but the beautiful gift did make her smile.

"Thank-you," she told Monique, then gave her a hug.

"You're welcome. And this one was just dropped off by one of your neighbors," explained Monique as she handed over the smaller present. "If I'm not mistaken, that's a Tiffany bag. Either you have a really, really nice neighbor, or there is something going on that you haven't told me!"

Cadence ignored her. She pulled out a small card and a box from the gift bag, then read the note silently. There were four simple words: *I miss you. Adam.*

She read the card several more times.

"Who dropped this off?" Cadence finally asked Monique.

"The woman from across the street. She asked for you, but when I told her you weren't feeling well, she said to give this to you. Aren't you going to open the box?"

Cadence refolded the note before setting it aside and picking up the box. She removed the lid and found a beautiful silver link bracelet inside. It had a heart-shaped charm attached, engraved with the famous and classic Tiffany & Co. logo.

"Oh, sis, it's beautiful! Who's it from?"

"Adam," she stated quietly, closing the box with the jewelry still inside.

Monique snatched it out of her hand to look at it more closely.

"He has great taste. Aren't you going to put it on?"

"Monique, I can't accept that! I broke up with him right after you left last week. He is a liar and a sleazy pervert, you know that! He fired you because you didn't sleep with him. I don't want anything to do with him ever again!"

"That's not exactly true," her sister replied.

It took a few seconds for Monique's words to sink in.

"What's not true?"

"I tried to explain this earlier but . . ." Monique took a long breath while still looking at Adam's gift, then she started again. "Adam did fire me, but not because I didn't sleep with him. My manager, the controller, accused me of trying to steal money from the company. But it was a lie! I tried to explain that, but no one would believe me. They said they had proof, so Adam let me go."

Cadence could only look at her with disbelief.

"I was angry and embarrassed, so I told you the story about not sleeping with the owner. How was I to know you would start dating Adam Jackson, of all people?"

"Monique, why didn't you just tell me the truth?"

"I don't know. I was really mad. I liked my job and it hurt that the people I worked with thought I was a thief. It also made me worried that you wouldn't believe me, either."

"Oh, Monique, of course I would have believed you!"

"I know. I've wanted to talk to you about it all week. The story seemed harmless at the time, but I'm really sorry if I've come between you and Adam. He's actually a really good guy despite what happened. I felt bad for him after I had calmed down."

"Why? I don't understand?" Cadence interjected.

"Well, there was definitely something going on there, and I think someone *was* stealing money. They just blamed the wrong person."

"How do you know that?"

Monique shrugged.

"They had hired me to help set up their accounts payable for a new automated accounting system. Everything went fine, but about two months after the set-up was completed, I noticed that there was a withdrawal from the bank account that didn't show up in the reports. Funny enough, I was going to talk to my manager, Peter, about it, when Adam called me into his office to fire me."

"Did you tell them what you had found?" Cadence asked.

"No. I was too shocked by what was happening. And I didn't really think about the banking issue again until a few weeks later."

Both women sat in their own thoughts for a couple of minutes.

"What are you going to do about Adam?" Monique finally asked.

"I don't know. I said some pretty nasty things to him. He tried to defend himself regarding you, but

I just told him to leave. I even threatened to call the police."

Monique grimaced with guilt.

"I'm really sorry, sis."

"It's not all your fault. Adam also conveniently forgot to tell me that he was a wealthy real-estate developer instead of the humble construction worker I was led to believe," explained Cadence in a weary voice.

"Why would he do that?"

"I have no idea."

"Well, now you're going to have to let him explain."

"I guess," agreed Cadence. She then curled up in the bed and pulled the covers over herself.

"When you do talk to him, can you tell him I'm sorry? I really didn't tell you that stuff to hurt him in any way."

"I know, Monique."

They spoke for a few more minutes until it was time for Monique to get going. She and Andre were going to his parents' house for dinner. Before she left, Monique left Cadence a supply of bottled water and painkillers on the night stand. They then hugged and wished each other Merry Christmas again. Cadence was half asleep again within minutes.

Cadence barely left her bed for the next few days. She slept most of the time, but also did a lot of thinking. She listened to Adam's voice-mail message from Christmas Eve, and even made a move to call Adam twice, but put down the phone before dialing the number. What would she say? Part of her wanted to apologize for her accusations and Monique's lies, but the rebellious side of her didn't want to make it that easy for him. If Adam hadn't lied about what he did, she would have been less ready to convict him about firing Monique.

Why had he chosen to let her believe he was a just a general laborer? The more Cadence thought about it, the odder it seemed. From what Monique and Beverley said, his business was very successful. Most of the men she knew would embellish their wealth and accomplishments, hoping to score with easily impressed women. None of them would be hiding their money, or living in a simple apartment and driving a well-used truck.

By Wednesday, Cadence felt well enough to be up for the whole day. She first went to her doctor for a checkup, then stopped at the grocery store. She had just gotten back home when the doorbell rang. It was Yvonne.

Cadence let her in and the women shared polite conversation about their Christmases as they sat down in the living room.

"How are you feeling?" Yvonne asked, then elaborated, when Cadence looked surprised. "Your sister told me you weren't feeling well when I dropped off the gift for you on Sunday. You got it, right?"

Cadence nodded.

"Yes, I did. It was the flu, actually, but I went to the doctor this morning and the worst seems to be over."

"Good. It's definitely going around. I know of at least three people who've come down with it in the last week alone."

They were silent for a moment, and Yvonne cleared her throat before she went into the real reason for her visit.

"Adam stopped by my house on Christmas Eve and asked me to give you the present. He also told me that you weren't talking to him because he hadn't been completely honest with you about his life."

"Look, Yvonne . . ." Cadence started to protest.

"I'm not trying to be nosy," Yvonne cut in. "I understand how you feel. I just wanted to let you know that there is a good reason why Adam did what he did, and he really did not intend to hurt you in any way."

Cadence looked away from her while absorbing the information. She wasn't sure what to say in return.

"Have you spoken to him?" Yvonne asked.

"No, not yet."

"Well, he also wanted me to tell you that he is up at the house near Leesburg, and that he would be there for the week."

Cadence nodded.

"Well, I have to get going. You probably still need some rest," said Yvonne said politely.

They stood up and walked back to the front door. They had said good-bye, but before she walked away, Yvonne turned back to Cadence.

"I've know Adam for a long time and I know he is a really good guy. But I don't remember him ever being as happy or as comfortable as he has been in the last few weeks. Give him a chance to explain things to you."

With that, she smiled and walked back across the street.

Cadence closed the door and leaned against it for several seconds. She didn't know what to do. In her heart, she wanted to run to the phone and call Adam right away. She missed him. But her head said to slow down and give it some more time. Just because his friend spoke highly of him did not mean what he did was easily forgivable.

Eventually, her heart won out. She went into her bedroom and dialed his cell phone number. He didn't answer, so she left a message.

"Hi Adam, it's me. I just wanted to say thank you for the beautiful gift, and I hope you had a nice Christmas. It's Wednesday afternoon and I'm at home. Speak to you soon."

After she hung up, Cadence went back to her cleaning and tried to focus on other things. When she got to the kitchen, she once again saw the bag with Adam's Christmas gift. After staring at it for a few seconds, she took it out of the bag and got to work wrapping it with some leftover Christmas wrapping paper. She then put it up in the closet.

The phone did not ring until almost six o'clock that evening. She recognized Adam's phone number right away.

"Hi, I just got your message," he told her. "How are you?"

"I'm okay," Cadence replied. "And you? Yvonne mentioned you went up to Fruitland Park for the week. How's it going?"

"It's okay," he replied, but there was a hesitation in his voice. "I had hoped you would be here with me, though."

Cadence bit her bottom lip. She really had not expected him to go directly to the issue so quickly.

"Cadence, can I see you? Can we talk about what happened?" he continued.

"Okay," she replied, trying hard to control her rising excitement.

"Okay. Do you want me to come back to Orlando? Or do you want to come up here? I can be there in about an hour or so."

She looked around her place, trying to decide what to do.

"Actually, why don't I go up there?" she offered. "I can't come tonight, but I can be there in the morning."

"That's perfect," Adam replied. "I was planning to be here until Sunday, so feel free to bring enough to stay as long as you like. And don't forget your bathing suit."

Cadence could hear the smile in his voice and it made her grin also.

"How was your Christmas?" he asked.

"Not great," she replied, laughing. "I got the flu over the weekend and was in bed the whole time. This is my first day up, actually."

"Oh no! Are you okay? Have you gone to the doctor?"

"Yeah, I went this morning. I'm fine now, just a little tired and light-headed."

"You should rest some more. Forget driving up here. I'll come get you in the morning," he insisted.

"Adam, that's not necessary. I'll be fine."

"Nonsense! I'll be there for around ten o'clock."

Cadence shrugged her shoulders. He didn't sound like it was open for discussion any more.

"Okay," she replied finally.

They talked a few more minutes about Adam's activities over the last couple of days. Before they hung up, Cadence remembered the present he had left for her.

"Adam, thank-you for the bracelet. It's beautiful."

"You're welcome. I meant what I said; I miss you."

Chapter 22

"He's going to be here any minute," Cadence told her sister over the phone on Thursday morning. "I'll probably stay with him until sometime on the weekend, but I'll be back by New Year's Eve."

"That's good. I'm sure you guys will have a good time once you have a chance to talk," replied Monique.

She had called Cadence a few minutes before to see how she was feeling, and Cadence took the opportunity to update her on the situation with Adam. Monique sounded genuinely happy and relieved.

"Listen, can I ask you a favor? Can I stop by your place on Friday night? Andre is working nights, and Michael wants to take me out again. I will only let him pick me up there, that's all."

"Monique . . ." Cadence was about to go into her typical lecture, but stopped herself and took a deep breath. "All right."

"Thanks, sis!"

The doorbell rang.

"Okay, I have to go," Cadence told her. "I'll call you over the weekend. Be careful, okay?"

She added the last request in a soft, pleading voice.

"I will," Monique promised before they hung up.

Cadence ran to the door and opened it for Adam. They exchanged "hellos," then both stood looking at each other awkwardly, unsure of how to act. Finally, she walked into the house, babbling about getting her bag, and Adam followed her silently. They packed her things in the truck while exchanging polite comments about how Cadence was feeling and how the drive in had been for Adam. It was about fifteen minutes into the drive before Cadence broached the subject that was on both their minds.

"I spoke with Monique a few days ago, and she told me everything," she told Adam.

He looked at her briefly, but didn't add anything. Cadence then went into the background of the situation so that Adam could understand her reaction. She explained that her sister had told her months ago that she had been fired from her job because the owner of the building company had wanted to sleep with her, but she had turned him down.

"Wait a minute! That is a complete lie!" Adam protested.

"I know that now, Adam. But, for months, that is what I believed. I even pressured her to file a lawsuit, but she wouldn't. So, when I found out that you were that same man who I thought had victimized my sister, I saw red."

Adam nodded.

"Anyway, Monique finally told me what really

happened. That her manager accused her of taking money and fired her because of it."

"She admitted what she did?" he asked, clearly surprised.

"No, she completely denies that."

"And you believe her?"

His irony was obvious.

"Yes, I believe her. I understand why she told me what she did. It's not like she did it maliciously. What were the chances that you and I would ever meet?"

Adam shrugged.

"Anyway, she wanted me to say sorry to you."

"So all is forgiven?" asked Adam after a small, silent pause.

"No!" Cadence fired back. "I'm just explaining the misunderstanding regarding my sister. It doesn't explain your behavior at all."

"You're still mad at me," he stated, sounding disappointed.

"No, I'm not angry anymore. But I'm hurt and confused. You told me that you felt comfortable with me and that I brought out a side of you that other women hadn't. But that was such a lie. You were just pretending to be someone else. Why?"

"Cadence, I wasn't lying or pretending to be anything but myself."

"Yes you were!"

"No I wasn't," he replied, deliberately keeping his voice as calm as possible.

Adam knew he had no right to be angry or defensive. He owed Cadence an explanation for his behavior, and he could not blame her for thinking the worst.

"I spent twelve years of my life lying about who I was, then trying to live up to that lie. That was what I meant when I said you brought out a side of me that I didn't recognize," he explained. "Yes, I own a successful business and I have some money in the bank, but that's not who I am. That's who I thought I had to be to live in the world my wife came from."

"Because your wife's family was rich?" Cadence asked.

He looked at her with surprise.

"Apparently, I'm the only one in the dark about you," she added with biting irony.

"Yes, her family was wealthy. And of course they couldn't understand how their precious only child could fall for a middle-class kid like myself. My family wasn't poor or anything, but just average, and certainly not from the 'society' hers was. For the longest time, I couldn't understand what she saw in me, either, but at eighteen, I had vowed to do anything to keep her love. I was just too young to see that it wasn't love at all, just rebellion against her parents. Then, it was too late. She was pregnant and we ran away and got married."

Cadence looked at him with her mouth hanging open.

"What happened?" she finally asked.

"Well, we told her parents about the marriage and they flipped. They threatened everything under the sun, and vowed to disown her. But we didn't tell them about the baby. Rose was too ashamed. It was probably for the best, because she had a miscarriage before three months. So, we spent the first two years of our marriage living in a small apartment living on my income in construction. I think it was the only time we were happy."

He glanced at Cadence, but his expression was blank.

"Anyway, there was something inside me that said that Rose would never be content living like that for long. I committed myself to providing her with everything she could possibly want and earning the respect of her family."

"Did it ever happen?" she asked.

Adam laughed bitterly.

"What a joke. Eventually, her father let her back into the family but he couldn't stand the embarrassment of his daughter being married to a grubby blue-collar worker. They pretended to embrace me and even tried to groom me into a tennis-playing son-in-law. Then came the pressure to work for her father's company. It became disastrous when I refused to give up what I was doing. That was when I finally saw Rose clearly. She told me point-blank that she was tired of living in my world and it was time to go back to hers."

"Meaning what?"

"Meaning, she wanted to go back to the society life. She started spending more time at her parent's house, doing the things other rich wives did, and spending our money like I made millions. Like an idiot, I stayed focused on making more money, convinced that she would continue to love me if I could give her what her father did.

"The funny thing is that the money did come. Rose spent it as quickly as I made it, so I just made more. I even let her turn me into that guy I had refused to be. We bought a big house a street away from her father's, and she threw lavish parties that I was forced to host. On the outside, we seemed like the perfect power couple. I didn't even recognize who I was, and I just worked more so I didn't have to think about it. The truth was, she and her family never let me forget that I was beneath them."

Adam finally paused and glanced over to see Cadence's reaction. She was looking out at the road in front of them. He couldn't read what she was thinking.

"In the end, Rose started seeing one of her father's business associates. Last I heard, they were engaged to get married."

"Oh, Adam!" Cadence said as she finally looked at him.

He laughed.

"I've never been so grateful for anything in my life," he told her. "Who knows how long I would have stayed committed to her and that life. Anyway, it's not completely her fault. The irony is that I had turned into a complete workaholic in order to feed her insatiable greed, and she got bored with me because I was never around."

She just looked at him, clearly amazed and confused by the story.

"Honestly, Adam, I don't even know what to say," she finally stated. "I would never have imagined you like that at all."

He nodded, smiling at her in agreement.

"It really feels like someone else's life, to be honest with you. It took me months after the separation to come to terms with what was driving me to work twenty-four, seven. Once I realized that I was missing out on life, it still took a lot of effort to change my behavior. I'm still a workaholic, but I can honestly say I do it because I'm proud of my company and I enjoy what I do. The money is a bonus, but it doesn't define my success anymore."

Adam turned off the highway and onto the main street in Fruitland Park. They were occupied with their thoughts for a few minutes.

"Long story short," Adam finally added. "I let you believe I was a construction worker because it felt good knowing that you liked me for me, not what I had to offer. It was selfish, and I'm sorry for it. I knew deep down that it wouldn't matter to you, but I didn't want it to matter to me."

Cadence blew out a deep breath and looked away from him and out the passenger window.

"To be honest with you, Adam, I think it would have made a difference to me if I had known up front," she told him in a sad voice. "I was attracted to the idea that you were hardworking, simple, and reliable. You worked with your hands and you had a kind heart. If I had known that you had money, I don't think I would have given you the time of day."

"Wow," he finally replied. "So, it' actually a good thing that I let you get to know me before you could judge me, huh?"

"Hah!" protested Cadence. "That doesn't excuse your behavior!"

"That's okay. You'll come to see the wisdom of my actions eventually. You're just being stubborn right now."

"See, you're one of those arrogant rich people! I knew it."

Adam laughed good-naturedly. He could tell she hadn't completely forgiven him, but at least she understood where he was coming from. It was enough for now.

At the house, Adam took Cadence's bag upstairs and put it in one of the guest rooms. There was still some distance between them, and he didn't want to assume that she would share his room or his bed again, yet. It was going to be hard to wait, but he vowed to be patient and give her as much time as she needed.

She was looking out the back window when he returned downstairs.

"I guess this house is yours, too," she said when he reached her side.

"Technically, it belongs to the company, but I think I'll transfer it to my name soon. My lease on the apartment is coming up and I have to make some decisions."

Cadence nodded.

"You would live up here permanently?" she asked.

"I would love to, but I don't know if it will be practical. It's only an hour away, but I don't think I can spend two hours commuting every day. I thought about continuing to rent in the city and using this house for weekends and stuff. But I've also been looking for something like this property, but closer to Orlando. Something I can build my own house on."

"That sounds nice."

Adam nodded. It was nice to share these thoughts with her, finally.

"Okay, so what do you want to do today? Are you feeling up to going for a walk? Or maybe you want to just rest by the water?" he asked.

"I would love to get some fresh air. I feel like I've been inside forever."

"There is a great park just down the road. We'll drive over and pick a short hiking trail. I'll put some water and stuff in a bag to take with us."

Cadence agreed. They spent the early part of the afternoon in the park, then drove into Leesburg for a late lunch. It was a small city, but they managed to find a nice steak house that also had good seafood.

"How are you feeling?" Adam asked after their meal.

"I'm a little tired," Cadence admitted. "I might have overdone it."

"Well, how about this: We'll go back to the house and I draw you a hot bath. Then, while you soak, I'll pick us up a couple of movies. We can spend the rest of the evening relaxing on the couch."

"Sounds good to me. But don't be surprised if I don't make it out of the tub before I fall asleep," she replied with a slight grimace.

Adam helped her upstairs when they got back to the house. He led her to the spare bedroom where he had put her bags earlier.

"I'll fill the tub in my room, it's bigger than the one in the main bathroom," he told her while she looked around at the space.

"Okay. Thank-you, Adam," Cadence told him when she finally looked into his eyes.

He knew she was referring to more than the bath.

"No problem," he said dismissively, then left the room.

The bath was half full when Cadence joined him

wrapped in a silky red robe. She looked tiny and vulnerable, but sexy as hell. Adam looked away, trying not to focus on the naked body he knew was under the flimsy wrap.

"Okay, it's almost ready. There's a towel on the counter. Take your time and soak as long as you want. I should be back in about an hour."

She nodded, and seemed almost shy as she stepped around him and closer to the bathtub. Adam nodded also and took his leave, closing the bathroom door behind him. He stood in the bedroom for a couple of minutes until he finally went into the other bathroom and took a long, cold shower.

Chapter 23

Adam and Cadence spent the next few days relaxing and doing activities around Fruitland Park. She was feeling much better on Friday, so Adam took her out onto Lake Griffin in his motorized canoe. On Saturday, they played around in the pool in the afternoon, then went back into Leesburg for dinner and a movie.

By Sunday, as they drove back to Orlando, Cadence was starting to feel as though they had recaptured most of what they had before that disastrous Saturday. They had talked openly about Adam's marriage, and she had also revealed some truths about her past relationships. In a lot of ways, she felt even closer to him. But, she still slept in the spare room and he didn't question her actions.

Adam dropped Cadence off at her house just after one o'clock in the afternoon. He had been invited to a New Year's party at a hotel downtown, and asked Cadence to go with him. Since it was very close to his apartment, she insisted on meeting him at his apartment, despite his protests. As soon as he left, she got ready to go to the mall and find something suitable to wear.

She was just coming out of the garage, when she saw Erica and her boys pulling up into the driveway.

"Hey, neighbor," Erica said as she walked up to Cadence's car. "Were you away for a few days?"

"Yeah, I was staying at a friend's house," she explained.

"Okay. I saw a woman go into the house a couple of times, so I was a little worried."

"Oh," Cadence said with a smile. "It was my sister, Monique."

Erica giggled with relief.

"I thought she looked a bit like you, but, still, you never know!"

"Well, thanks for looking out, anyway," Cadence told her.

"No problem, any time. See you at yoga!"

Erica waved good-bye and headed into her house. Cadence shook her head and smiled to herself again as she drove off. Maybe it wasn't a bad thing to have nosy neighbors, she thought to herself. You always knew what was going on at your house when you were not there.

The mall was extremely busy with last-minute party shoppers. At first, Cadence had no clue what she was looking for. It had been a couple of years since she had gone to a large New Year's Eve party, and even then, she had just worn something from her closet. After going into a couple of stores, she decided on something simple and elegant.

Cadence eventually found the perfect cocktail dress, then spent the next hour buying the right shoes and accessories. When she got back home, she spent some time calling a few people to wish them Happy New Year. The last was her mother, who had just gotten back from vacation with Ellis the day before. They spoke for over thirty minutes. Cadence was thrilled by how happy and energetic her mom sounded, and promised to drive down to Fort Lauderdale for a visit soon.

When she finally arrived at Adam's apartment, it was a few minutes to ten o'clock, almost thirty minutes later than she was expected. She had called him a few minutes earlier, so he was waiting for her downstairs when she pulled into the parking lot. Even in the dark, she could tell he looked fantastic in a dark suit and and light blue shirt.

"Sorry I'm late," she said immediately as she stepped out of her car.

"No worries, I'm sure it was worth the wait," replied Adam with a teasing smile. "You look beautiful, as usual."

Cadence laughed and returned the compliment.

"Are we taking your car or mine?" she asked.

"Neither," he told her, then took her hand and led her across the parking lot.

They stopped in front of a gleaming black sedan. She couldn't tell what make it was, but it looked powerful and expensive. Adam unlocked the doors and opened the passenger door for her. She slid onto soft grey leather seats.

"I didn't think either of our cars was appropriate for celebrating the New Year, so I rented this one for a couple days," explained Adam as he entered the car on the driver side.

"It's beautiful," Cadence told him, looking around at the chrome accents.

"I know, and it drives great. It makes me want to give up my pickup truck."

He was right. It glided on the road and they arrived at the hotel without feeling a single bump or pothole.

They parked underground, so when they stepped out of the car, Cadence took off the small wrap she wore over her dress and left it on the seat. Adam saw her fully for the first time, and stopped in his tracks to admire her. She was wearing a strapless satin dress the color of dark chocolate, and with a narrow skirt that ended a couple of inches above her knees. The rich brown made her caramel skin glow, and the bustier-style bodice showed off the tops of her round breasts. Dark copper sling-back shoes completed the outfit.

Cadence could feel the warmth of Adam's eyes as they traveled down her body and back up again. Goose bumps rose over her arms and they exchanged a look that said everything. He reached out and took her hand.

"Come, let's go have a good time."

The party was in full swing when they reached the banquet room. The DJ was playing the latest R&B, and at least two hundred were people on the dance floor. There was also a buffet table with a variety of finger foods and snacks. Adam immediately got her a glass of wine and a beer for himself. They also got a couple of plates of food, then stood at the back of the room to enjoy the music.

About an hour later, they were ready to dance. Midnight was just around the corner, and the crowd had swelled to well over four hundred. Adam and Cadence stayed at the entrance, where it was coolest.

Soon, glasses of champagne were being handed out, along with whistles and other sound makers. Then, the music stopped and the countdown to the New Year started. When the clock struck midnight, the whole room exploded with horns blowing and people cheering. The DJ dropped the needle on a classic R Kelly song, and everyone went back to serious dancing.

"Are you ready to go?" Adam asked Cadence when they had been standing watching the crowd for a few minutes.

She checked her watch, and was surprised that it was already after one o'clock in the morning. The night had flown by.

"Okay," she told him. "I just have to go to the bathroom."

They left the ballroom, and started walking down the hall. Just as Cadence went through the doors of the ladie's room, Adam saw Alexa walking toward him with two other women he didn't know. It was very easy to see that she was well into her drinks.

"Adam Jackson," she said loudly, even though she was almost right in front of him. "Where have you been?"

"Hi Alexa," he said, then nodded politely to her friends.

She laughed, her mouth wide and loose.

"Adam, I thought we were doing so well. You're exactly the kind of man I've been looking for. But you disappeared!"

One of her girlfriends took her arm and tried to continue their way to the party. She was clearly embarrassed by Alexa's behavior. But Alexa pulled her arm away and leaned close the Adam. He could smell the liquor on her breath.

"Call me when you get tired of your little dread girl."

She continued laughing as her friend finally pulled her away, stumbling on her feet.

Adam wanted to wipe the smell of her off the side of his face. Instead, he just shook his head and thanked the Lord he had dodged that bullet. If Cadence hadn't come back into his life, he might still be talking to that bitch.

They left the hotel as soon as Cadence came out of the bathroom. When they reached his apartment, Cadence told him she had something for him in her car. Adam walked her to the vehicle, and was surprised when she handed him a large package wrapped in shiny holiday paper.

"It's your Christmas gift," she told him simply.

"You didn't have to do that," he told her.

"I had bought it a while ago, but I didn't get a chance to give it to you before Christmas."

Adam nodded, understanding exactly what she was trying to explain.

"Okay. Well, come upstairs so I can open it."

In his apartment, Cadence removed her wrap and sat on the couch holding his gift while Adam went into the kitchen to get them something to drink. He came back, minus his suit jacket, and with a bottle of chilled champagne in an ice bucket and a couple of glass flutes.

"I was hoping we would have a chance to celebrate the New Year in private," he told her as he popped the cork on the bottle almost effortlessly.

Adam handed her a filled glass and poured the

second for himself. He then sat beside her and turned so they were facing each other.

"So, what are we going to toast to?" Cadence asked.

"A new beginning," he told her after a second of thought.

They tapped glasses and both took a sip of cold, bubbly wine.

"How about to honesty at all costs?" she suggested with a wink.

Adam laughed and they toasted each other again.

When they finally put down the glasses, Cadence handed him the gift again. Adam tore into the paper like a little boy until he revealed the red toolbox underneath. His surprise was very evident. He just looked at her and smiled.

"Cadence, this is great. You have no idea how old my toolbox is. It's even starting to rust!"

"Look inside," she told him.

He complied, and withdrew the drill, then all the attachments.

"This is great!"

"I know you probably have no use for it, but . . ."

"Are you kidding me? This is wicked! How did you know what to get? It has everything in here."

She shrugged, but Adam put aside the toolbox and pulled her into a hug before she could respond.

"Thank you, it's perfect," he said. "I know you're probably still wondering if you really know me. But only you would give me a gift like that. You know me better than anyone."

They remained in a light embrace while drinking champagne. When their glasses were empty, Adam refilled them and turned on the stereo so they could listen to lover's rock reggae. It could have been the music, the alcohol, or just that fact they had been at arm's length for so many days, but cuddling on the couch swiftly turned into stroking and kissing. They spent a long time just nibbling each other's lips and entangling their tongues. Then, they moved to biting and licking around at the neck and shoulders. Eventually, they both craved more.

Adam eased Cadence up until she stood in front of him. His breathing was harsh and labored as he took in every inch of her image. Her mass of hair was wild around her face, and her lips were full and bruised from their kisses. The beautiful satin dress was crushed and riding high on her thighs, revealing her flawless legs.

"I want to remove your clothes," he told her.

Cadence lifted her left arm, revealing the zipper that ran along the side of her dress. Adam sat at the edge of the couch and slowly undid the fastening. He then peeled the fabric from her body and helped her step out of it. She was left in a strapless lace bra and matching panties. He pulled her close so he could run his mouth over her stomach. Cadence shivered and let out a soft moan.

"I've missed you so much, Cadence," he told her, then dipped his wet tongue into the dip of her navel.

"Oh, Adam! I've missed you, too," she replied, and ran her fingers over his head and down to his shoulders.

Adam continued to lick and nibble her skin while he undid her bra, then tossed it aside. Beautiful, firm breasts hung free, their dusky nipples hard and thick. He took one into his mouth, first sucking hard, then licking with feathery softness, then switched to the twin peak. She tasted so good and smelled so sweet. Every brush of his tongue and scrape of his teeth caused her body to shudder. His own body responded, getting harder and harder until the pressure seemed unbearable.

Without lifting his mouth, Adam eased off her underwear, then sat back slightly to look at her complete nakedness. As always, Cadence took his breath away. She gazed back at him with unabashed arousal, licking her lips in anticipation of his touch. He slowly ran his hands up her body, starting at her knees, pausing at the junction of her thighs, then over her bottom, and ending with her quivering breasts in his hand. She closed her eyes and let her head roll back.

Adam picked up an ice cube from the ice bucket, and slipped it into his mouth, warming it up and re-moving any sharp edges. When he touched it to her upper abdomen, Cadence jumped in surprise, and shivered from the chill. Her eyes were now wide open, watching his actions. The ice against her warm skin created a droplet of water. Adam imme-diately licked up the trickle of cold moisture with his hot tongue. She shivered again. He then ran the ice up between her breasts, his tongue wiping away the trail of water it left behind. When he ran it over her nipples, Cadence moaned out loud.

"Oh, God. Adam!"

After each stroke with the ice, he bathed the quiv-ering nub with his tongue until she moaned again and again. Her fingers dug into the flesh of his shoulders.

"Do you want me to stop?" he asked huskily.

She shook her head, no, so Adam made a path

down her body until he reached the soft curve of her lower stomach. He swirled the slippery cube around her navel until it dripped water down to the sweet folds of her feminine lips. He dipped his head to lick up the moisture. Cadence sucked in her breath, then held it in anticipation, and squealed as he brushed the ice against the bud of her arousal.

Adam tossed the cube back in the bucket, then went to his knees on the floor and pushed aside his coffee table. He lay Cadence down on the rug that covered his floor. Her body immediately opened to him and he kissed his way up her thighs until he reached the apex and covered it with his mouth. Both of her hands entwined in his as Adam worshipped her with his lips and tongue. He couldn't get enough of her, and felt invincible with every moan from her lips and arch of her body. Then she was frantic, begging him to give her more, and finally she came apart for him in the way she always did, freely and fully.

She was still shuddering from the aftershocks when Adam pulled her into his lap while sitting on the floor, his back against the couch. He rubbed her back and kissed her forehead.

"Are you cold?" he asked after a few minutes.

"No," Cadence replied. "Aren't you hot?"

Adam laughed.

"Very!" he told her, and they both giggled at the joke.

"Let me help you," she offered.

They were both kneeling as Cadence quickly helped him remove his clothes. Adam took out a condom from his wallet, but she took it from him and rolled it on with teasing slowness. He was rock hard and breathless by the time she was done. It took him a few seconds to lay her on the floor again, then her legs were hanging over his shoulders and he was deep inside her.

Adam tried to use every ounce of his control and prolong their lovemaking, but each stroke into her wetness brought him closer to completion. She encased him so tightly and moved with him so perfectly that he could not hold on. Finally, the climax crashed down on him with shattering force, robbing him of his ability to breathe or think.

When awareness returned, he and Cadence were wrapped in each other's arms and covered with a light coat of sweat. Eventually, they went to his bedroom, but not to sleep. Instead, they made slow, lazy love until the sun started to peek above the horizon.

Chapter 24

Adam was in shock. He could not believe the evidence before him, but it was irrefutable.

It was Friday afternoon, the day before the last weekend in January. Sandra Evans had just left his office, and had left behind evidence of some sort of embezzlement within his company.

He had asked Sandra to meet with him not only to set up the investment accounts they had discussed before Christmas, but also to get some direction on his personal funds. He had found lakefront property just outside Orlando and was considering purchasing it, and finally building that custom home for himself. In preparation for the meeting, Sandra had brought the company's monthly bank statements for the previous year. Highlighted was a series of fund transfers dating back almost nine months. None of them had been authorized by Adam and he had no clue what account the money had been sent to.

The interesting thing was that, while several hundred thousand dollars were transferred out each time, that exact amount was redeposited within two to three months. There were only four transfers in total, the last of which was for five hundred thousand dollars even, and that one was still missing.

Once Adam confessed to Sandra that he had no knowledge of the transfers, she told him she had seen it before. It appeared that someone at Iris Custom Homes was misappropriating funds for quick, high-gain investments, then returning the principal amounts undetected, but keeping the profits for themselves. She asked Adam how many people had the necessary access to the accounts to do something like this, and he could only come up with one name: Peter Tulic.

Adam looked at the bank statements again, and compared them to the financial reports created by their internal system. Everything was identical, as far as he could see, except for those four fund transfers and three deposits. He picked up the phone and called Peter's extension, then told Peter to be in his office as soon as possible. He then called Tamara and asked her to have Michael Donovan, their systems consultant, come into the office on Monday morning.

Peter stepped into Adam's office a few minutes later.

"What's up, Adam?" he asked in his usual friendly, manner.

"Sit down, Peter," Adam instructed him.

He then handed Peter the bank statements that Sandra had left with him.

"Have a look at these and tell me what is going on."

Peter took the stack of papers and started to study them. His shrewd eyes told Adam that he knew something was wrong, but was more confused than worried. It took him a few minutes to scan the details of the first few months. Then his finger stopped on what Adam knew to be the first large transfer back in May. Peter then continued scanning until he got to early July and saw the redeposit. He looked up at Adam for an explanation.

"What was that two hundred thousand for?" he asked. "I don't remember it in the reports."

"That's what I'm asking you, Peter."

Peter shook his head, and Adam could actually believe he was clueless.

"Was it a bank error? Why didn't it show up in our system?" asked Peter.

Adam sat back in his chair and continued to examine the expression on his controller's face.

"Peter, I have all of the bank statements there for last year, and there are four bank transfers highlighted. I need you to explain to me where the funds went and why."

His face went red from the implied accusation, but Peter didn't say anything in response. He just kept shaking his head as though still confused.

"Peter," Adam stated again, this time more forcefully. "There are only two people in the company with the access to transfer money out of the accounts: You and me. So it's time you tell me what the hell is going on."

Peter stood up suddenly.

"Adam, my God! You think I've taken this money? Come on! That's crazy! It must be a mistake, a bank error, or something," he sputtered in defense.

"Just stop it! It's not a bank error. There are four withdrawals totaling almost two million dollars. All of it has been redeposited excepted for the five hundred thousand dollars taken out in November. What are you doing with the money, Peter?"

"You are really accusing me of this?"

"Cut the shit, Peter!" Adam yelled in exasperation.

He hated having the conversation, hated looking at a man he trusted and respected and believing he was capable of such deceit. But there was no other explanation. Adam turned away and looked out his back window.

"Look, just tell me what has been going on, and return the rest of the money. I won't call the police," he demanded when he faced Peter again.

"I don't know anything about this, Adam, I swear!"

"Today is your last day, Peter. Leave your keys with Tamara and I'll have Tony walk you out. You have two weeks to come clean, otherwise I'm turning this information over to the police."

Peter seemed frozen while Adam did as he said and called Tony to remove him from the premises without explanation. Adam then called Tony and Tamara into his office and told them that Peter no longer worked there for reasons he was not able to discuss. A locksmith was called in to change the office locks immediately, including on the door to Peter's office.

Adam then sent out a brief e-mail to the rest of his employees, and requested that the accounting clerk under Peter report directly to Adam on Monday morning. Afterward, he closed his door and spent the next couple hours going over every aspect of his accounting with a fine-tooth comb, including changing all passwords and access codes.

Finally, he left the office for the weekend. It was only four-thirty, but he was unable to bear the walls around him any longer.

Normally, he would head straight to Cadence's house on a Friday evening. As usual, they had plans for dinner and he was meeting her at six o'clock. But on this evening, Adam used the extra time to go home and take a shower. He also needed to calm down and collect his thoughts.

How could he have let something like this happen? Vince had been right all along. Adam had been too lax in this management of the company and had given too much autonomy and power to his employees.

It wasn't the missing money that infuriated him at that point. Thank God they had already closed the latest property deal and the missing five hundred thousand dollars would not affect his immediate financial position. It was the betrayal by someone Adam considered a friend and partner that really cut deep. He still wanted to believe that Peter was innocent, but his common sense said it was impossible.

When Adam reached Cadence's house that evening, he was still preoccupied, but had managed to come to terms with things a little more. He just wanted to have a nice evening with her, so he chose not to ruin their time by getting into what had happened at the office. They were halfway through dinner when she finally confronted him about his quiet mood.

"It's nothing," he told her, trying hard to smile and be sincere.

"Adam, please. It's obvious that something is wrong. You've barely said two sentences all evening, and you're not eating. What is it? What happened?"

He gave her a long look. It was obvious that she was really concerned, and if he kept his troubles to himself, it would only upset her further. Adam gave in and told her a succinct version of what had happened. She covered her mouth with one hand and reached out to him with the other.

"Oh, Adam. That's horrible!"

He nodded and took a long drink of his beer.

"How long has he worked for you?"

"About four years," he stated.

There was a pause as Adam went back into his thoughts.

"Oh, God!" Cadence exclaimed, but her voice was barely above a whisper.

"What?" he asked.

"Oh, no, Adam! I have to tell you something. I should have told you sooner but, I just forgot about it."

"What?" he asked again.

"You said the withdrawals went back as far as last May, right? Wasn't my sister working for you then?" she asked.

"I think so. She started when we began using the new reporting system. Around April, I think. Why?"

"Adam, Monique told me that she had found an error in the reports. There was money missing in the bank statements that wasn't showing up in the new reports. She was going to tell her boss, but she was fired before she got the chance."

Adam looked at her hard, his brain working through the details.

"Peter was her boss, wasn't he?" asked Cadence.

"Damn it!" he swore.

Monique had been telling the truth. It now looked like Peter had lied about her stealing money to hide his own actions. The details were getting more and more sordid and Adam was sickened by it.

"I should have told you back at Christmas, Adam. You could have looked into it sooner," she lamented.

He shook his head.

"It wouldn't have mattered, Cadence. I had no reason to suspect Peter of anything until today. Chances are, I would have just continued to believe that Monique was making up stories to deny her own guilt. It looks like *I'm* the one who owes *her* an apology."

"So, what happens now?"

"I don't know. The missing money doesn't cripple me right now, but it could in the future. If Peter doesn't return it soon, I'll have to get the police involved and have the funds tracked down."

"Are you sure you don't want to involve the authorities right away? What if he runs off and you never hear from him again?"

"I don't know, Cadence. Maybe I'm an idiot, but I just can't believe Peter would do this just for the money. He has a wife and two daughters in college. The only thing that makes sense is that he is in some kind of trouble and tried to fix it without hurting the company. If I report the theft, it will completely ruin his life and his family," he explained. "I told him he has two weeks to return the funds."

Cadence nodded, and squeezed his hand in silent support. They ate quietly for a few minutes until Adam changed the subject.

"How are things coming along for the show in Atlanta?" he asked.

"I'm feeling a little better about it. I have a few

days left, but I'm really happy with the last four pieces. There is one more that I'm trying to finish, but it's not essential."

"Are you still using Malcolm as a model?"

Cadence smiled at the dryness in Adam's tone.

"No. I finished with him last week. You're jealous, aren't you?" she accused him when she saw him grimace.

"Give me a break! Why would I be jealous of that overpumped pretty boy? I'm pretty sure he's gay, anyway."

Cadence laughed out loud, but Adam refused to concede to her point. Instead, he drained his beer bottle and went back to the subject of the art show in Atlanta scheduled for the end of the following week.

"Are you sure you don't want me to come with you?" he asked.

"It would be nice, but it's not necessary. I'll only be there for a couple of days. Plus, this doesn't seem like a good time for you to be away from the office, even for a short period of time."

"You're right. It will be crazy for a while, and I don't know if I can sort it all out by the time you leave."

"I'll be fine, Adam. I'll tell you all about it when I get back, and I'll even give you your own private viewing."

She wiggled her eyebrows suggestively.

"Now, there is something to look forward to. But, can't I have a sneak preview?"

She laughed sweetly, and their discussion went from business to pleasure.

Chapter 25

The next week was so hectic for both Adam and Cadence that they barely saw each other, though they talked often on the phone. Adam spent most of Monday locked in his office with the systems consultant, Michael Donovan. Michael was an independent contractor who had done work for Iris Homes for a couple of years. He initially installed all their computers and basic software, and more recently implemented the automated accounting system.

Adam spent half the time with Michael being re-educated on how to administer the software in the short-term, and the other half trying to understand how Peter had manipulated the reports. Michael could not find any obvious loopholes in the application or hardware that would account for the fraud going undetected, but he took Peter's computer to conduct a full inquiry.

By Tuesday, there was a job listing posted for a new controller, but Adam was buried, between his normal job and covering Peter's responsibilities. He managed to spend Wednesday night with Cadence, then drop her at the airport on Thursday morning. The event in Atlanta was Thursday and Friday evenings and she was flying back home Saturday afternoon.

Cadence spent the days before her trip in a rush to finish the last painting and get everything shipped to the gallery without delay or incident. She also managed to pick up a new illustration contract with Edison Publishing for a series of children's books. It was guaranteed to keep her busy through the spring and summer.

By the time Cadence kissed Adam good-bye and boarded the plane to Atlanta, she was looking forward to the rest she could catch up on while she was away for two days. Even the hour-and-a-half flight gave her time to relax and think about all the things going on in her life. So much had changed in the last few months, yet the important things had stayed the same, maybe even gotten better. She still felt focused on her art career and had plenty of time to commit to the creative process and the business initiative. Adam was content to work within her schedule, even if it meant she wanted to paint at three o'clock in the morning. Other men had always found it insulting or unfathomable that she would prefer to be in her studio than be with them. They didn't understand her need to work whenever the urge came to her.

There were other parts of her life that had gone through drastic changes. Adam was like the best friend she never had. He listened to her, supported her, and respected her, but he never made demands on her time or had expectations that she could not meet. Cadence only hoped that he felt the same way about her. She was trying as hard as possible to be supportive through his crisis at work.

The other change in her life was the relationship with her sister, Monique. The two women had always talked and spent some time together, particularly since Monique had moved to Orlando from Fort Lauderdale the year before. But, ever since Christmas, when they started to talk more about their relationships, and since Monique had told her the truth about her job with Adam's company, there was a closeness that had never been there before. The sisters now talked a few days a week, and Cadence felt they had more of a friendship than ever before.

She still didn't approve of how Monique was handling her relationship with Andre or with the other man, Michael. Cadence was very concerned that things would come to a head, and either man would harm her sister if he ever found out about the other. But she kept her opinion to herself unless asked, and tried to respect that it was Monique's life. Based on their last discussion from a couple of nights ago, Monique was ready to leave Andre and was planning on telling him soon. She would stay with Cadence until she found a job and decided what to do next.

They were going to talk about it further when Cadence got back home on Saturday. Now that Adam was certain that Monique had been falsely accused of theft, he had offered her another job with the company. Cadence was hoping the two could talk about it more over the upcoming weekend. It might be the incentive Monique needed to finally end things with Andre.

The days in Atlanta sped by. The art gallery events were exciting and successful, and left Cadence feeling fulfilled and energized. A couple of nights of good rest also helped. On Saturday, she landed at the Orlando airport in the early afternoon and Adam's truck was waiting for her on the arrivals level. He immediately took her carry-on with one hand, and pulled her into a hug with the other. Their kiss lasted so long that the people around them started to stare.

"Welcome back," he said after letting her go.

"It's good to be back," she replied.

Adam helped her into the passenger seat, then put her luggage in the cabin behind her. They were driving into the city a few moments later.

"How are things going at work?" she asked. "Any luck with the interviews so far?"

"Not really. I met with a couple of people yesterday, but they don't have any relevant industry experience. There are a few more people I plan to meet next week. Other than that, everything is the same. I haven't heard from Peter, and there is still no evidence of how he was able to manipulate the accounts," Adam explained. "Actually, I have to go back to the building site after I drop you off. I just got a call that one of the plasterers didn't show up this morning. I'm going to lend a hand to keep the house on schedule."

"No problem, take your time. Monique was going to stop by the house, anyway. Give me a call when you're done?"

"Sure."

Adam dropped her off about fifteen minutes later and carried her travel bag inside. They hugged and kissed again, then he was off.

Cadence was unpacking her things when her home phone rang.

"You're back," Monique said. "I'm about to leave, so I just wanted to make sure."

"Yeah. Adam dropped me off about twenty minutes ago.

"Cool. I'll be there in a few minutes."

"Okay. Do you mind if we go out and do a few errands? I need to pick up some art supplies," Cadence asked.

"No problem."

By the time Monique arrived, Cadence had put away her things and changed into jeans and a light sweater.

"Where are we headed?" Monique asked as Cadence locked up the house.

"There's a store on Lee Road, before you get to the I-4. We can take Silver Star across the city. It's usually pretty fast. Do you want me to drive?"

"No, I'm okay," replied Monique.

Her car was a blue Toyota Corolla, and pretty much as old as Cadence's Honda. As the women drove through the north end of the city, they talked about several different things, including the possible job opportunity with Adam's company. Monique was looking at it as an opportunity to start working again and was looking forward to discussing the position with Adam. She also admitted to Cadence that she had spoken with Michael about it the day before.

"He thought it was a good idea. Of course, I had never told him why I had left to begin with."

"Ummm," Cadence replied, noncommittally. "How are things going with him?"

"Okay," Monique replied, but something in her tone hinted at reservations. "We've been talking on and off for months, but it's been a little weird lately. He seems really preoccupied and unavailable. So I don't know. To be honest, Cadence, I'm starting to wonder if I didn't make a big mistake pushing Andre away."

"What do you mean? You and Andre were having problems even before you met Michael, weren't you?"

Monique took so long to answer the question that Cadence looked at her questioningly. But Monique's eyes were fixed on the rearview mirror and there was a frown on her face.

"What's wrong?" asked Cadence. "What is it?"

Monique finally put her eyes back on the road in front of them.

"Nothing. What were you saying?"

Cadence repeated the question about how things had been with Andre before Michael came into the picture.

"There were issues, but now I'm starting to think that they could have been worked out. Andre has been trying so hard, and I can't say the same for myself. I mean how many men would be okay with me off work for so many months? He's been willing to take care of all the bills and he gives me money to buy whatever I need."

"But Monique, that could also be to control you, right?"

"Maybe . . . Oh my God!"

Before Cadence could respond to Monique's scream of sheer terror, they were both thrown forward in their seats, and then jerked violently to the left as the car veered sharply to the right. Monique somehow managed to pull the car back onto the road.

"What the hell happened?" shouted Cadence.

"I don't know! I think we were hit from behind!"

They had just entered a section of Silver Star

Road that looked rural and fairly deserted. Cadence looked around frantically, still shocked and confused. She finally turned around in her seat and saw the truck behind them. Her eyes widened as the front grills zoomed right up into the rear window of Monique's sedan and rammed mercilessly into them.

Adam ended up working much later than he had planned, but, with the crew on-site, they had made up for the lost man-hours and were back on schedule. He stood outside the house they had been working on, dusty and sweaty, and called Cadence at home. It went to her voice mail.

"Hey, sweetheart. It's almost eight o'clock and I've just finished working. Give me a call back when you get this message. I'm going to run home and grab a shower."

Adam waited until he was cleaned up and dressed in jeans and a shirt before he tried to call Cadence again. She still didn't answer at home so he called her cell phone instead. It was now almost nine-fifteen in the evening and he wondered where she was. The phone rang four times, and Adam was about to disconnect when a woman answered the phone. It was not Cadence's voice.

"Hello?"

"Hello, I'm calling for Cadence Carter?" Adam inquired. "Who is this?"

"It's her sister, Monique," the woman said in a voice that sounded shaky and flustered. "Who is this?"

"Oh, Monique. It's Adam Jackson here. Is Cadence around?"

There was no response, so at first he thought she was handing the phone over to her sister. About fifteen seconds went by before Adam realized he was hearing what sounded like stifled crying.

"Hello? Monique? Are you still there?"

The whimpering grew louder and was followed by several sniffles.

"I'm here," Monique finally told him.

"What's going on? Where is Cadence?" He got more crying. "Monique! What's going on?"

"Adam . . . Cadence is in the hospital."

"What? Did you say the hospital? Monique!"

The crying was earnest now, filling the phone with deep sounds of sorrow.

"Oh my God, Monique! Did you say she's in the hospital?"

Adam could barely make out the string of words that were thrown out between sobs and hiccups.

". . . then the car crashed . . . she won't wake up . . . took us to emergency . . ."

He closed his eyes tight, fighting the urge to start screaming for her to stop blabbering and talk to him.

"Which hospital?" he asked as calmly as possible. "Just tell me which hospital and I'll be there in a few minutes."

"Florida Hospital in Orlando . . ."

Adam hung up without another word. He grabbed his keys and was out the door in seconds.

Chapter 26

For Adam, the next twelve hours were some of the worst of his life.

He arrived at the emergency department of the hospital within fifteen minutes of speaking to Monique, but it took an additional half an hour before they would let him in to see Cadence. In the end, they probably allowed him through just to shut him up. When he reached her cubicle, it was to find her lying completely still, and with a large bandage over her left eye. There were monitors and tubes all around the bed. Adam felt his knees go weak. He slowly walked forward until he was standing over her motionless form.

"Cadence?" he said softly, but there was no response.

He held his breath, hoping, praying, her eyes would at least flutter. But there was nothing.

"She's sleeping," a tiny voice said from behind him.

Adam swung around and found Monique sitting in a chair in the corner of the area. He hadn't seen her when he walked in, but he immediately noticed that she also had a bandage over her forehead.

"She was awake a few minutes ago, but they gave her some more painkillers."

He nodded, and looked back at Cadence. She seemed so small and frail. He picked up the hand next to his and laced his fingers through hers.

Several minutes later, her doctor and an emergency nurse stepped in and asked Adam and Monique to leave the room while they did an examination. The two walked toward the cafeteria to get some coffee. There were a few moments of silence before Adam felt ready to hear the details from Monique. Her voice was still shaky, but she was no longer crying.

"We were driving to an art supply store that Cadence wanted to go to. For whatever reason, I noticed this black truck that was behind us. At first I didn't really pay attention because we were driving along Silver Star for a while. Then, it was tailing us really close. It backed off for a while, so I thought everything was fine. All of a sudden, it rammed into us, twice! I tried to hold on to the wheel but I couldn't . . ." Her voice broke, and she took a few seconds to swallow and regain control. "Anyway, we swerved off into a field and ended up hitting a tree."

Monique touched the spot on her forehead covered by the gauze bandage.

"My air bag went off, and I think that's how I got the cut on my head. When I looked over at Cadence, her head was bleeding a lot! And she wouldn't wake up."

She squeezed her eyes shut, but two tears slipped down her face. Adam reached out and put a reassuring hand over her arm. She let out a deep breath, then continued with the story.

"Cadence did open her eyes for a while but she seemed confused and unfocused. I don't know how long we sat there, but it wasn't very long, maybe ten minutes. Someone must have seen what happened because I could hear the sirens coming. They took us here by ambulance."

Adam digested the information, but couldn't think of what to say. His mind was blank, and running in a million directions at the same time. Did someone really run them off the road? Or was it just a traffic accident? *What was wrong with Cadence?*

"When did it happen? How long have you guys been here?" he asked.

He wasn't ready to deal with the more difficult questions yet. He was petrified of the answers.

"I don't know. Since three o'clock, maybe."

He gripped her arm and then forced himself to let go. That was almost seven hours ago! *What was wrong with Cadence?*

"What did the doctors say?" he finally asked.

"It's just a superficial cut, probably cause by the air bag. I might have some whiplash, but I just feel a little stiff. But Cadence . . ."

Her eyes welled up with tears again, and Adam bowed his head with helplessness.

"She has a concussion and they're going to keep her here overnight for observation. They don't know how bad it is yet. They're still waiting for the results of the MRI. But the cut over her eye wasn't too deep. She got a few stitches, but it should be fine, " Monique finally told him.

"When are the results due back?" he asked when he was able to look at her again.

"I don't know. They did the test a couple of hours ago."

"Okay, okay."

He let out a deep breath.

"She was awake for quite a while earlier. We talked, but she couldn't really remember what happened. The doctor said it's pretty common with the type of head injury she may have had. The headache is normal, too, they told me."

Adam nodded.

"We should head back," he told her.

When they reached her cubicle, only the nurse was still there. Adam took the opportunity to ask some questions, but it was pretty much as Monique had told him. The results of the MRI would be in soon, but they felt Cadence was doing well based on her responsiveness. They had given her a sedative for the headache and it was causing her to sleep now. Overall, her prognosis was good and she was likely to be released in the morning.

The MRI results came back about thirty minutes later. Thankfully, there were no obvious signs of swelling or bruising, but they still wanted to keep her overnight in the ER just in case. Adam and Monique decided to stay at the hospital rather than go home for the night. By midnight, they agreed to take turns sleeping in case Cadence woke up.

Adam was awake when she opened her eyes at around three-thirty in the morning.

"Adam?" she said.

He was sitting in a chair right next to the bed. The sound was so faint and weak that he thought it was his imagination. He didn't sit up until he felt her fingers brush his arm.

"Cadence? I'm here, sweetheart."

Her eyes fluttered open, and it was the most beautiful thing he had ever seen.

"Hi," she said.

Her lips quivered as she tried to smile. The sight made him want to weep like a baby.

"Hi yourself. How are you feeling? Are you in pain?"

She shook her head to say "no." Adam took her hand in his and brushed a gentle hand over her forehead.

"That's good."

"What time is it? How long have you been here?"

"It's late, after three o'clock in the morning. I've been here since last night."

"I'm sorry," she whispered.

"Shhhh. What are you sorry for?"

"I don't know. You're here in the middle of the night . . ."

"Cadence, the only thing that matters is that you're okay."

Adam pressed a kiss on her forehead, and he closed her eyes. For a few seconds, he thought she had gone back to sleep.

"Monique said we had a car accident, but I can't remember anything. It's so weird," she told him.

"It's okay, the doctor said it's normal," he told her.

Cadence nodded.

"I'm so glad you're here."

"I wouldn't be anywhere else," he replied, but her breathing changed and he knew for sure she had drifted off again.

Eventually, her grip on his hand weakened, and Adam sat back down to wait for morning.

The police came to the hospital just after nine o'clock in the morning. Adam had just returned from a quick trip to Cadence's house to get her some clothes for the trip home. They had just approached Monique in the hallway when Adam joined them.

"Good morning, Miss Rutherford, how are you feeling today?" asked the taller of the two uniformed officers.

"Much better, thank-you."

"How is your sister doing?" he then asked.

"She should be released this morning, thank God."

"Good, good."

The other officer gave Adam a look up and down, so he felt it was prudent to introduce himself as Cadence's boyfriend.

The policemen nodded, then gave an update on the case.

"Well, we located the truck that hit you. It was found late last night abandoned on the east side of the city. It turns out it had been stolen early yesterday. Normally, I would say it looked like a simple traffic accident, and the perp didn't stop because of the stolen vehicle. But we're concerned by your statements, and those from a couple of other witnesses. It would appear that you and your sister may have been run off the road deliberately. Now, why would anyone want to do that?"

Monique looked shocked and confused. She could only shake her head and shrug her shoulders.

"Mr. Jackson, do you know of any reason why they would be targeted in this fashion."

"Sorry, officer, I can't think of anyone who would want to harm Cadence."

"And where were you at around two-thirty yesterday afternoon, Mr. Jackson?" asked the shorter cop.

"I was at a construction site in Altamonte Springs

from about one-thirty until after eight o'clock in the evening," he replied.

"Is there anyone who can vouch for your whereabouts?"

"There were about eight other guys working with me," Adam explained without hesitation.

He pulled out his wallet and withdrew one of his business cards.

"Here is the number to my office. Please call if you need to and I will put you in touch with everyone who was there."

"Thank you. We will do that."

Adam nodded, respecting the fact that they should be checking every possible angle if there was a chance that this was a deliberate act against either Cadence or Monique.

The police asked Monique a few more questions, but she could not tell them any more than she had the day before. They promised to be in touch over the next few days to give her an update on the progress of the case. When they left, Adam could not help notice that Monique looked agitated and scared. She was chewing on her fingernail, and would repeatedly look over her shoulder as though expecting someone to be watching her.

"Are you okay?" he asked at one point, but she only nodded and tried to put on a smile.

As the doctors predicted, Cadence was cleared to go home. They gave her a list of signs to watch out for in case she had symptoms of postconcussion syndrome. They also suggested she see her doctor about a week later just to make sure there were no complications.

While Cadence took a shower and got dressed, Adam asked Monique where she lived so he could give her a ride home. Her eyes opened like saucers and she seemed surprised by the question.

"Umm, I think I should stay with Cadence for a few days. It's probably best that she's not alone."

"Okay," he replied, but was concerned by her reaction. "I will be staying with her too, but it can't hurt to have us both there."

Monique nodded and went back to chewing her finger.

Finally, they were ready to leave. They stopped to grab some take-out food, but were at Cadence's house by noon. Monique took a couple of painkillers and went to get some sleep, while Adam helped Cadence into bed. He was getting her into pajamas when he noticed her empty suitcase at the foot of the bed. It was so hard to believe it was less than twenty-four hours since he had picked her up at the airport.

Once Cadence was settled comfortably under the covers, he turned on the television and sat beside her. Adam put an arm over her shoulder and pulled her close. She hadn't said very much since they left the hospital and he looked at her with concern.

"Are you okay?" he asked.

She looked up at him and nodded.

"I'm just tired, that's all. It feels like every joint in my body aches."

"Do you want to take one of the pills the doctor gave you? It will help you to relax."

"No, I'll take it later. I feel like I've been sleeping forever."

He pulled her closer. They watched television for several minutes, then Adam was fast asleep before he knew what hit him.

When he finally woke up, the sun was setting and Cadence was also asleep beside him. Careful not to disturb her, Adam got off the bed and went to the kitchen to heat some of the food they had picked up earlier. There was no sign of Monique, so he fixed two plates on a tray. Cadence walked toward the kitchen just as he was going to bring the food to her. Her steps were slow and deliberate, but she didn't seem to be in pain.

"Hey, I was just bringing you some food. What are you doing up?"

"I was starting to feel that if I lay down any longer, rigor mortis would set in," she replied with a grimace.

Adam smiled at her humor.

"Okay. Have a seat in the living room," he told her.

She followed his instructions and they sat together on the couch to eat. He was glad to see that her appetite was healthy.

"Where's Monique?" Cadence asked eventually.

"Still sleeping, I think."

Adam paused, trying to think of the best way to bring up the information from the officers. He didn't want to upset Cadence, but if there was someone who might want to hurt her or Monique, the police needed to know as soon as possible.

He put down his plate and turned toward her.

"Listen, Cadence. Two officers came by the hospital this morning, and they are concerned about the accident. Based on what Monique and other witnesses told them, it doesn't look like an accident."

"What? What do you mean?"

"Well, they found the truck involved and it was stolen. And the people who saw the accident said it looked like you guys were deliberately run off the road," he told her. "Monique specifically remembers seeing the truck behind you guys for a while before the accident. Anyway, the police wanted to know if there was anyone who might want to hurt you or Monique."

"Why would anyone want to hurt me? I don't have any enemies. None that I know of, anyway," she protested.

"I know, and I told them that. But what about Monique?" Adam probed. "Your sister said 'no' to the police, but I have to tell you, she's looked pretty scared ever since. Is there anyone you can think of who may have gone after her?"

Cadence looked down at her hands, then back into Adam's eyes.

"Oh, my God! Andre! Her boyfriend Andre! He wouldn't do something like this, would he?"

"What's going on, Cadence? Why would you think of him?"

She covered her mouth with both hands as though trying to decide how much to tell him.

"Monique lives with him, but she started dating another guy behind his back a few months ago. I told her that it was trouble, but she wouldn't listen. She said she could handle it. But Andre's been violent with her before," she sputtered with wild eyes. "Oh, my God, Adam! What if he found out that Monique's been cheating?"

He pulled her into his arms and ran a reassuring hand over her back.

"It's okay. We'll tell the police right away and they'll look into it. Monique is here with us so she's safe."

Cadence was about to say more, but the doorbell rang, interrupting their discussion.

Chapter 27

Adam left Cadence in the living room while he went to answer the door. Her mind was swirling with what he told her, and she felt a slight headache returning.

Would Andre really try to run them off the road like that? She really couldn't say. Though Monique had been with the man for a while, and lived with him for almost a year now, Cadence had never met him. She only knew what her sister told her, and after the incident where he hit Monique, Cadence didn't really want to know any more.

She was pulled from her speculation by loud voices at the door.

"Hey, man, you just can't barge in here," she heard Adam say.

"I know she's here, so get the hell out of my way," replied another louder voice.

Cadence could also hear sounds of a physical struggle. She stood up in alarm and started walking toward the front entrance.

"Monique!" the other man yelled. "Monique, where are you? The police told me about the accident!"

Monique must have also heard the commotion because she opened the door to the spare bedroom. Her eyes were wide and fixed.

"Andre?" she questioned looking at Cadence. "What is he doing here?"

"I don't know. Stay in the room. Let Adam handle this."

Monique looked indecisive, but finally retreated and closed the door.

There was more shouting and struggles between the men. When Cadence finally crept her way to the foyer, she found Adam holding another man up against the wall, his forearm pressed against the guy's throat, forcing him up onto his tiptoes.

"Just calm down and tell me who you are," Adam demanded.

"Andre?" Cadence asked, drawing startled looks from both men.

The man pressed against the wall tried to nod his head, but Adam's arm limited his movement too much. Adam relaxed his hold and Andre stumbled down onto flat feet.

"Are you Monique's sister? Where is she? Is she okay?"

"Whoa!" Adam demanded while grabbing Andre's elbow to prevent him from approaching Cadence. "I said calm down!"

"All right, all right," responded Andre. He was several inches shorter than Adam and had a very slight build. There was no way for him to overpower the hold that Adam had on his arm.

"Look," Andre said in a much calmer voice. "I

just want to make sure she's okay, that's all. She didn't come home last night and she didn't answer her phone. Then the police came by the house this afternoon talking about her being run off the road. Is she here?"

"She's fine, Andre. We were both in her car when it was hit from behind," Cadence told him, but held back from confirming that Monique was in the house.

Adam tugged on Andre's arm so the men faced each other.

"It turns out the car was deliberately run off the road, *Andre*. You wouldn't know anything about that, would you?" he asked in a slow voice.

"What! Why would I know anything?" he demanded, until he saw Adam raise his eyebrows. "You think I had something to do with this? I would never hurt Monique!"

He looked pleadingly between Cadence and Adam, but neither showed any sign of sympathy or understanding.

"All right! Like I told the police, I was at work all afternoon. I clocked in at eleven in the morning, and I didn't finish my shift until seven in the evening."

Andre looked back and forth at them again, but Adam didn't let go of his grip until Monique stepped into the foyer.

"I'm okay, Andre," she said.

Cadence saw the look of absolute relief on Andre's face before he ran forward and pulled Monique into a hug. She went to stand by Adam while the couple spoke in quiet tones, and Andre brushed gentle hands over her arms. Cadence looked at Adam, and his eyes said he saw the same thing she did. Andre did not look like he had just tried to kill his girlfriend because she was seeing someone else. He looked genuinely worried about the accident and confused by the accusations.

"Look, I'm sorry I barged in here like that," Andre stated after he finished talking to Monique. "I was a little out of my head, I guess."

Cadence held up a hand to dismiss his apology.

"It's too bad we're meeting like this, Cadence," he continued. "I've been telling Monique for months now that we should have you over, but she tells me you're really busy with your painting."

Monique looked down at the floor, avoiding her sister's eyes.

"It is a shame, but it's good to finally meet you, anyway," Cadence told him politely.

After a few minutes, Adam and Cadence went into the bedroom to give the other couple some privacy. In the end, Monique decided to go back home. Cadence was still a little apprehensive about Monique's safety, but Adam was right. If Andre was crazy enough to want to hurt Monique out of jealousy, it was more likely that he would have done it himself rather than arrange for someone else to do it. And, if he was at all involved in the accident, the police would discover it.

For her own peace of mind, Cadence made it a habit to speak with her sister twice a day for the next few days. Adam continued to stay at her house to keep an eye on her condition. He kept a small supply of clothes there, but occasionally went back to his apartment to restock.

By Wednesday, Cadence was almost feeling back

to normal. She was still a little stiff, but there were no more headaches or dizziness. The police had let them know that there were no other leads in the case and were now more convinced that it was just a hit-and-run. Other than helping Monique through some of the insurance issues, they all tried to put the incident behind them.

Adam, on the other hand, was still trying to manage his business while understaffed. He had finally interviewed a strong accountant who had the type of experience needed. If an offer was presented quickly, the candidate could start within two weeks. Everything else in the office seemed to be running smoothly. The clerk who previously reported to Peter was very good at her job and didn't need much supervision, so Adam did not need to spend a lot of time hand-holding her. Tony was very much on top of the fourteen homes still being built on the Altamonte Springs site, and there were no problems anticipated over the next few months. That left Adam free to start working with the architect on their newest building site in the northwest end of the city.

The only outstanding issue was Peter. Adam had not heard from him since he was fired over a week ago. Adam fully intended to go through with his word, and contact the police if Peter didn't return the missing money by the end of the week. He really hoped it didn't come to that, but he would have no choice.

It was late Wednesday afternoon when the call finally did come. Adam was still in the office and was surprised to see Peter's home number on his cell phone.

"Adam, it's Peter."

"Peter. I've been expecting your call."

"I know, but I didn't have anything to tell you before now," explained Peter.

"Okay, well why don't you come into the office tomorrow morning . . ."

"No, I need to see you tonight. But not in the office. There's a small coffee shop about a block from my house. It's called Kathy's Koffee and Treats. Can you meet me there at six o'clock tonight?"

Adam looked at his watch. That was in about fifty minutes.

"All right, Peter. I'll meet you there at six," Adam confirmed before they disconnected.

Adam started packing up his work right away and left the office fifteen minutes later. As he drove toward Peter's house, he felt both satisfaction and anxiety. He was really looking forward to putting this whole episode behind him, particularly if they could resolve it without involving the authorities. On the other hand, it was still hard for Adam not to think of Peter as a friend, and he wondered what would drive such a hardworking and otherwise reliable man to this kind of criminal act.

He reached the restaurant Peter had specified about five minutes early. Adam used the time to call Cadence and let her know he probably wouldn't be home for another hour or two. They talked for a few minutes, and he was glad to hear that she had gotten some illustration work done. It was a sign that she was almost back to normal.

It was precisely six o'clock when Adam walked into the shop and ordered a large coffee before sitting at a table near the window. Ten minutes later, he had finished the drink, and started reading an abandoned newspaper from the table beside him. He occasionally checked his watch, but continued to wait.

By quarter after seven it was clear that Peter wasn't going to show up. Adam was more than a little annoyed. He had tried to call Peter's house number about half an hour before, but there was no answer. There was also no answer on his cell phone. After several minutes of thinking, Adam decided to go to Peter's house. If Peter wasn't there, then maybe his wife would be and could at least provide some information on his whereabouts.

The walk from the coffee shop only took a few minutes. The Tulics lived in an older residential area that was well manicured and quiet. When Adam approached the house and rang the doorbell, everything seemed fine. There was no answer right away, so he pressed the bell again. It was then that he noticed that the lever handle on the front door seemed to be hanging loosely, and the wood near the lock looked frayed and damaged. Adam pushed the door with his foot and it swung open eerily.

He stood in the doorway and peered into the house. Several lights were on, including the one in the front hall. Adam then looked around the dark street. There were no neighbors around.

"Hello?" he yelled into the house. "Peter? Is anyone home?"

Finally, Adam took a couple of steps inside, then a few more.

"Hello?" he yelled again, but was only greeted with silence.

Adam headed to where he thought the kitchen would be, but stopped in his tracks when he passed the first room of the house. It looked like the dining room, but it had been totally ransacked. Chairs were turned over, and all the doors to the china hutch were thrown open, with dishes and cups tossed everywhere, some broken on the floor.

Adam's heart started racing. *What the hell had happened here?* He ran to the next room and found the living room in worse condition. Next was the kitchen, and that's where he saw the shoe-covered feet on the floor, sticking out from behind the counter. He rushed to look who was there, and found Peter spread out on the floor with blood pooled under an injury to the right side of his chest. Every cupboard in the room had been thrown open and searched, and their contents littered the floor and counters.

Careful not to touch anything, Adam walked up to Peter and checked his wrist for a pulse. It was there, but faint. He immediately pulled out his cell phone and called 911.

Chapter 28

Adam was still next to Peter when the police and paramedics arrived. Peter's injuries were examined and treated before they took him away to the hospital, and Adam was led outside to be questioned by two investigators. He told them everything that had happened that day from the time Peter called him to that point. Adam added that Peter had recently been fired for suspected embezzlement and explained the other facts surrounding the situation. The officers questioned him for over an hour.

They were still outside when Peter's wife, Edna, arrived home. She recognized Adam, but was led away by additional officers. Finally, Adam was allowed to go home. He reached Cadence's house at around ten o'clock and found her asleep on the couch. Trying not to wake her up, Adam carried her into the bed. He took a long, hot shower, then called the hospital where Peter had been taken. The nurse on call told him that Peter was in critical but stable condition.

Adam then crawled under the covers and took

Cadence into his arms before he also fell asleep.
The next morning, Adam was up early and out of
the house before she awoke.

The situation with Peter had now blossomed into
a nightmare, and Adam had no idea what to make
of it. He spent the next couple of hours in his office
thinking through everything that had happened
since he had confronted Peter. It was definitely
time to turn everything over to the police and he
would do it immediately. He would then go by the
hospital to check on Peter's progress.

Adam was still pulling together every piece of evidence he could think of when Tamara let him
know there were two officers there to see him. The
two investigators from the night before walked into
the office and Adam invited them to take a seat.
They introduced themselves as Detectives Cooper
and Gomes, and went right to the point.

"Mr. Jackson," asked Detective Cooper, the older
of the two men. "We're concerned about a couple
of things. First, why did you not report the money
stolen from your company to the police when you
discovered it?"

Adam took a deep breath.

"Like I explained last night, Peter was a friend.
All of the money, except for five hundred thousand
dollars, had been returned within a couple of
months, so I gave him the option of returning the
money by the end of this week. I didn't want to
completely ruin his life."

The officers both looked at him hard, then at
each other. Detective Gomes spoke next.

"We understand that your girlfriend and her
sister were in a suspicious car accident over the

weekend. Now, four days later, your accountant is found stabbed in his house. It seems like an unlikely coincidence, don't you think? Can you think of any reason why these two things may be related?"

"I have no idea," Adam replied honestly. "My girlfriend has never met Peter, or anyone else in the office, for that matter."

"What about her sister? We understand that her boyfriend, a Mr. Andre Anderson, was investigated, but dismissed as a suspect."

Adam looked at them dumbfounded for a moment. He had spent the last couple of hours looking at the situation from every possible angle. Why had he not thought of Monique?

He immediately told the officers everything he knew about the three months in which Monique had worked for the company, including the fact that she had been fired for suspected theft, and had been accused by Peter. Adam also went into details about the software they used for their banking transactions, and how the money had been transferred undetected to and from an unknown account over the months. He handed over all the documents he had put together regarding the embezzlement.

"Can we speak with your systems administrator?" one of the detectives asked.

"Sure," replied Adam. "His name is Michael Donovan. He works on contract with us, but handles everything."

Adam wrote out Michael's contact information on a sticky note and gave it to them.

"Are there any leads on who may have done this to Peter?" he asked as the men stood up to leave.

He saw the cryptic look that passed between

them before they answered. Adam got the feeling they thought he might also be involved.

"We found some evidence that we're looking into, but we're going to consider every angle. We'll keep in touch, Mr. Jackson, and it would be in your best interest not to leave the city until the investigation is complete," Detective Cooper told him.

With that statement, they walked out of the office.

Adam immediately called Tamara and Tony into the office and told them what had happened to Peter last night. He also told them about Cadence and Monique, and the accident over the weekend. He then asked them what they remembered about the time when Monique Rutherford worked for the company. Tony had only been there for a couple of weeks when she left, so he didn't know much, but Tamara remembered her well.

"She seemed nice and friendly. She was always on time and worked hard. I know Peter was really happy with her. Frankly, I was really surprised when you guys let her go."

"I had no choice at the time," Adam told her. "Peter said she had stolen some money."

"How?" asked Tamara.

"Something about her creating a fake contractor and transferring a payment to them. He said they caught it in time and were able to reverse the transfer."

Both Tamara and Tony nodded.

"Anyway," continued Adam. "The police are now doing a complete investigation, so give them whatever information they want, and feel free to be completely honest."

"How is Peter doing?" Tony asked.

"As of last night, he was hanging in there. I'm going over to the hospital in a little bit."

The meeting ended, but Adam called Tamra back just as she was about to leave his office.

"Have you heard from Michael?" he asked.

"Not since last week when he was here. Why?"

"The police want to speak to him and I gave them his information. He was also supposed to let me know if he found anything more on Peter's computer. Do me a favor, give him a call and let him know that he should give the officers access to everything."

"Sure," she replied before returning to her desk.

Adam wasn't able to leave the office until after noon. He stopped at a local restaurant for lunch, and called Cadence while he was eating.

"Hey, I didn't hear you come in last night," she stated.

"I know. It was late and you were already sleeping. How are you feeling?"

"Pretty good. I did some more work this morning, and I'm going to a yoga class a little later."

"Are you sure you're up to it?" he asked. "Maybe you should wait until after you see the doctor tomorrow."

"I'll be fine, Adam. It will be good for me, and I doubt I'm going to hit my head while stretching." He heard the humor in her voice and smiled at his own protectiveness. "I'll be going with my neighbor, Erica, so she can keep an eye on me. How is your day going?"

"All right. There are some things going on, but I can fill you in tonight," he replied evasively.

Adam didn't want to stress her unnecessarily.

There was no proof yet of a connection between Peter being attacked and the weekend car accident.

"Okay, I'll see you tonight, then," Cadence said cheerfully before they said good-bye.

Once he finished his meal, Adam headed to the hospital to see Peter. He was told that Peter had been transferred from emergency to a room in intensive care. His condition had improved and it was fairly certain he would recover. When Adam looked at Peter lying in the hospital bed, the events of the past week hit him all over again. He just prayed that the police would get to the bottom of things, and that the craziness and violence were now over.

Peter must have sensed his presence because he soon opened his eyes. Adam walked closer until he was standing beside the bed. The two men looked at each other, both wondering what to say.

"How are you feeling?" Adam finally asked.

Peter nodded. He tried to speak but the only sound that came out was a croak.

"The nurse told me you're going to be fine," Adam continued. "You'll be up and around in no time. Tamara and Tony sent their best."

Peter coughed, trying to clear his throat.

". . . Found something . . ." he said in a rough voice.

"It's okay, Peter. We can talk about it another time. Just take some time to rest."

Adam poured a cup of water from a pitcher on the night stand. Peter drank it quickly.

"I found something, Adam," Peter repeated in a clearer, stronger voice. "I know what happened."

"What do you mean?"

"Do you remember when we fired that clerk,

Monique Rutherford, back in June of last year? It was Michael Donovan who had told me to check out one of the vendors she had created in the system. He said it wasn't on the approved list, and that there had been a payment wired to the company for two thousand dollars."

Adam nodded, remembering the information that Peter had given him back in the summer.

"Sure enough, I looked at the reports and called the company. They didn't exist, and I immediately cancelled the fund transfer. We fired Monique the next day."

"That's right. You wanted to call the police, but I disagreed, since there was no permanent loss. We just tightened security and only allowed you or me to create new payable accounts."

"Adam," Peter continued earnestly. "The fund transfer never happened."

Adam looked at him with furrowed brows, clearly not understanding the point.

"The two thousand dollars was never transferred. I looked over the bank account records you gave me, again and again. It never happened."

"But you said you saw the proof in the reports and cancelled the transaction."

"That's what I'm telling you. The reports from the system are wrong, Adam, and someone has been modifying them all along."

Peter closed his eyes and let out a long breath. It was as though he had used all his energy to convey the information he had been holding since yesterday afternoon. Adam patted his hand.

"I called Michael right after I called you," continued Peter after a short rest. "I told him that his system wasn't secure from the beginning and that he better be prepared to explain how it happened. They broke into the house less than an hour later."

Adam just looked at him and his heart started to race. The evidence now led in only one direction. He felt relieved, but also angry and impotent.

"Don't worry about it anymore, Peter. I handed everything over to the police this morning. I'll call them right away and it will be over soon."

Peter closed his eyes again and nodded.

"Listen, I have to apologize for the way things went down," Adam told him, his voice was heavy with regret. "I didn't want to believe that you were involved, but I had no choice."

"It was my fault, Adam. I talked you into the system and I allowed the theft in my department. You only did what you had to," Peter replied.

The two men talked for a few more minutes until Peter started to doze off. Before he left, Adam promised to visit again the following day. The minute he was outside the hospital, he called the police station and asked for one of the detectives he had met with that morning. He ended up leaving a message for Detective Cooper, saying he had additional information and needed a call back right away.

Once Adam got to the building site, he sat in the truck for a while. It now seemed so clear that Michael had been manipulating them all for months. Peter may have accepted the blame, but Adam was ultimately the one responsible. Iris Custom Homes was his company and his dream, but he had fallen asleep at the wheel. He had been so consumed with keeping busy and making money that he had lost touch with the basic operations of the business. Vince had been right all along.

He slammed his fist against the steering wheel.

Eventually, Adam left the truck and immersed himself in work for the rest of the afternoon. Cadence called him after her yoga class just to assure him she was fine and was on her way home. He let her know he would be home by six and would pick up dinner from her favorite Italian restaurant.

When he arrived at the house, the first thing Adam noticed was that there were no lights on. Cadence should have been home a couple of hours ago, but he wasn't concerned at first, thinking she was probably locked up in the studio. He rang the doorbell, then rang it again when there was no answer. After the third try, he acknowledged that she was clearly not home.

Adam was about to call her cell phone when the next-door-neighbor walked out from between the two houses. She stopped in her tracks when she saw him, then gave a tight smile. Adam nodded back.

The woman was about to go through her front door when Adam called out to her.

"Excuse me," he yelled as he walked across Cadence's driveway. "I'm Adam, Cadence's boyfriend."

His hand was outstretched, and she shook it with a smile.

"Hi there, I'm Erica. I've seen you around a bit."

"Listen, Cadence called me earlier to say she was on her way home from her yoga class. Was she with you?"

"Yeah, we got back a while ago," Erica confirmed. "But, she went back out right after that."

"Really? Did she say where she was going?"

"No, but she left with someone else. I don't know who he is, but I've seen him come by the house a couple of times. He drove up just as she was about to go inside, then she left with him. I was in the garage, but I could tell she was upset. I could see her face as they drove away,"

Adam had no clue who Erica could be referring to. Andre maybe? Or one of her models?

"Thank you, Erica. Can you describe this person?"

"Hmmm . . . not really. He's never really gotten out of his car. But I remember the vehicle. It has this really weird paint color that's halfway between blue and purple, and there are lights around the license plate."

Adam swore viciously under his breath. Erica had just described Michael Donovan's car.

Chapter 29

"Michael, where is Monique now? Is she okay?" Cadence asked frantically. "What happened?"

They had just pulled away from her house. Michael Donovan had called out to her from his car just as she was about to go inside. She didn't know who he was at first, but he introduced himself and told her that Monique was hurt and in trouble. Cadence had jumped into his car right away, throwing her gym bag into the back seat.

"I'm taking you to her right now," he replied.

"Oh my God. I can't believe this is happening. Why didn't she call me?"

"She couldn't."

"Why? I don't understand!"

Cadence fired off more questions, but Michael kept giving her short responses that didn't really provide answers. Finally, he stopped responding to her except to say they were almost there.

Eventually, she gave up, completely baffled and overwhelmed with worry for her sister. It was about fifteen minutes before they turned into a small strip plaza in one of the rougher parts of town. Cadence looked at him hard as they drove to the back of the building. His expression was unreadable, and she knew immediately that what was happening didn't make sense. If something was wrong with Monique, why would she send Michael? And why was he being so evasive?

The car stopped in front of a cargo bay, and Michael stepped out of the car, and she jumped out after him.

"Okay," she demanded. "I want to know what's going on right now!"

He walked up to her and grabbed her arm by the elbow with a tight grip.

"What're you doing? Let go of me! I said; let go of me!"

But Michael just continued toward the back entrance of one of the stores, dragging her along with him despite her struggles. They took rickety stairs up to the second floor and ended up in an empty but filthy room. He shoved her into a chair, then pulled her hands behind her and tied them with something that felt like rope.

"This is a mistake," she told him in a more reasonable voice. "I don't know what's going on, but you've made a mistake."

"Look," Michael finally stated. "There is no mistake. I'm not going to hurt you, so just calm down and be quiet. Everything is going to be fine."

He then pulled a roll of duct tape out of his pocket and plastered a large piece over her mouth.

* * *

Adam practically ran to his car, leaving the neighbor staring after him with confusion. He dialed Cadence's cell phone, but of course there was no answer. He was leaving a second message for the detective when another car pulled up beside him in the driveway. It was Monique in a rental vehicle. Adam immediately jumped out of his car.

"Have you spoken with Cadence? Do you know where she is?" he demanded without even saying hello.

"We talked this morning. I thought she was at home. She's not here?" Monique asked, clearly taken aback by his tone.

"No!" he told her in a harsh voice.

"Well, let's go inside. I'm sure she'll be home soon," she started walking to the house and Adam followed her. "Actually, I'm glad to see you. I've been looking forward to talking about a position with your company. I hope it's still possible. I was talking to Michael about it last week, and . . ."

"Michael? Michael who?" Adam demanded, grabbing her arm to stop her.

Monique seemed completely confused by his sharp tone and gently pulled her arm out of his grasp.

"Michael Donovan. We kind of stayed friends after I left the company. Why?"

"Damn! Damn!"

"Adam, what's wrong? What's going on?"

He looked at her, blowing deep breaths through his nose, his chest rising rapidly like he had been running.

"Monique, Michael has been embezzling money from my company for months now. He was the one who told Peter Tulic you had tried to steal money from the account," he told her. "Peter figured it out, and was stabbed last night in his house."

"What?" she cried, looking completely stunned.

"Listen! He took Cadence, Monique. He came here tonight and Cadence got into his car. Do you know where he would have taken her?"

"Adam, you must be wrong! Michael would never hurt anyone. He and I have been . . . kind of dating. Maybe Cadence just got a ride from him or something."

"Monique, listen to me! He stole half a million dollars from me, and the police are still looking into your accident, okay! There is no telling what Michael is capable of. Now, tell me where he's taken Cadence!"

"I don't know," she shouted back, visibly shaken by Adam's anger and what she had just been told. "I don't know!"

Adam tried to calm down. Clearly, Monique was an innocent victim, and yelling at her wasn't going to get them anywhere.

"Okay. Let's go inside and maybe you'll remember something. I've left a message for one of the detectives who is investigating Peter's attack, but if he doesn't call back in ten minutes, I'm going to call 911."

Monique nodded and they entered the house, using Monique's key. Adam's cell phone rang a few minutes later. He didn't recognize the number.

"Hello," he demanded harshly.

"Adam, it's Michael Donovan."

Adam looked at Monique and mouthed Michael's name. Her eyes flew open.

"Your money has been returned."

The statement was so simple that Adam thought he had heard wrong.

"What?"

"You have your money back," Michael repeated. "You can now tell the police it was an error and there was no theft, after all."

"Why would I want to do that?"

"You don't understand! You need to call off the cops or I'm a dead man."

"What are you talking about? I can't do that. It's not just about the money. People have been seriously hurt, Michael."

"I didn't have anything to do with anyone getting hurt, okay! But the people I work with are serious! They don't play and they will shut me up before the police get to me. Do you understand what I'm saying?"

Adam let out a long breath.

"Michael, what've you gotten into? Why did you take the money?" There was a long silence where Adam could only hear heavy breathing. "You have to tell me what's going on if you want my help."

"It was so simple. I just borrowed the funds for a few weeks. The money was always returned and no one would ever know."

"What were you doing with the money?" Adam demanded.

"Let's just say it was invested with a lucrative return."

"And you kept the profits," finished Adam. "So what went wrong, Michael? How did it go from a simple plan to attempted murder?"

"I told you! I had nothing to do with anyone getting hurt, but it was out of my hands. But these people don't like questions, particularly from the police. Do you understand what I'm saying? Now they know that the police are looking for me. I need the heat off my ass, now!"

Adam understood completely. Michael had made quick money off people who weren't afraid to get their hands dirty. If there was a chance that he could lead the police to their door, they would simply remove him. Now Cadence was caught in the middle.

"Michael, I'm not doing anything for you until you tell me where Cadence is," stated Adam with a calmness that he didn't feel.

"She's fine," he replied briefly.

"Look, let's not play games! You said you had nothing to do with the car accident or the attack on Peter, but you've snatched my girlfriend, Michael! Kidnapping is not something that I can stop the police from prosecuting. So, either you tell me where she is, or no deal."

"I didn't kidnap her! She came with me willingly. I just needed you to know that I was serious. She'll be home soon."

"Really? And how will you know if I keep my promise?"

"Put it this way, the police won't find any evidence in your systems or computers. The only evidence they will have on me is what you and Peter think you know. Without your accusations, the case disappears right now. But, if the investigation continues, I won't be alive when it's dismissed. And I won't be alive to tell you where she is. Do you understand what I'm saying?"

"Let me talk to her, and I promise that I'll speak with the police tonight."

There was a long pause in which Adam heard footsteps and shuffling.

"Hello?" It was Cadence's voice.

Adam closed his eyes and gave a short prayer of thanks.

"Cadence, it's Adam. Are you okay?"

"I'm okay, Adam. What's going on?"

Michael was back on the phone before Adam could reply to her. His instructions were brief.

"I'm going to call you again in one hour and tell you were you can find her. And tell Monique that I never meant for her to get hurt."

The phone went dead.

Chapter 30

Adam almost threw the cell phone across the room. Instead, he clenched it tight in his hand and took deep breaths. *She's okay*, he repeated to himself in a desperate attempt not to lose control. *She's okay.*

"Adam? What did he say? Where's Cadence?" asked Monique.

He couldn't answer her. His mind was too focused on the disaster created by his business, and that Cadence was paying the price. He should have just forgotten about the money. Whether it was Peter who took it or Michael, he should have just let it go. Then at least she would be here with him now, not alone somewhere in the city, and at the mercy of a desperate criminal with his life at stake.

"Adam?" Monique called sharply.

He looked at her, not remembering what she had said earlier.

"Where's Cadence?" she asked again.

"I don't know," he replied gravely. "He says he'll

call us back in an hour and tell me where to pick her up."

Monique looked around, clearly still shocked and confused.

"What should we do? Just wait until he calls back? By then, he'll be long gone!" she asked.

"I don't know. Cadence could be anywhere in the city."

She started pacing and chewing on her finger.

"I just can't believe this. I can't believe that he would do this to me. I was going to leave Andre for him!"

"Monique, Michael said that he had nothing to do with the car accident or Peter's attack. He's obviously been involved with some very dangerous people, but I think he was just in it for the money."

"What about the fact that he got me fired?" she shot back. "I trusted him, and I went to him when I saw the errors in the reports. He told me it was no big deal, just a glitch in the software. The next day, I'm accused of being a thief!"

Adam was silent. He felt partly responsible for what had happened and didn't know what to say to her to make it up.

"He asked me to tell you that he didn't mean to hurt you," he finally told her.

She snorted with disgust, then stomped off to the bathroom.

Adam's cell phone rang again. This time it was Detective Cooper.

"I got your message, Mr. Jackson. You have some information for me?"

"I just finished talking to Michael Donovan," Adam stated in a calm and casual voice. "He let me know that he figured out the problem with our system and fixed it."

"Really," the officer replied. It was obvious that he was skeptical.

"Yup. It looks like the money had just been transferred out by accident, not stolen, after all."

"That's very interesting, Mr. Jackson. Are you sure about that? Because my people couldn't find any sign of wrongdoing in your computers or on the network, but we did look into the banking trail. The monies had gone to an offshore account in the Caymen Islands and were then withdrawn from there."

"Well, I don't know anything about that. My money has been recovered, so I'm satisfied that it's all been a mistake."

"What about the attack on Peter Tulic, Mr. Jackson. And the car accident that almost killed your girlfriend and her sister?"

"I'm sure the police will do a full investigation and find whoever may be responsible," Adam replied smoothly.

There was silence on the other end of the phone, and Adam squeezed his eyes, praying that the detectives would not probe further.

"Okay, Mr. Jackson. We'll let you know if we have any more questions about last night's attack."

By the time they hung up, Adam's heart was beating thunderously.

"What did you just do?" Monique demanded.

He swung around and found her standing behind him with her mouth hanging open.

"You're letting him get away? Are you crazy?"

"It was the only way for me to ensure Cadence's

safety, Monique. If Michael gets stopped by the police within the next hour and before he calls me back, I don't know what would happen to her."

"And you believe him? He's a liar! How do you even know if he's returned the money?"

"I have no choice! And I don't give a damn about the money! I just want to get her back," the last sentence came out raw with anguish. "Look, I've got to get out of here. Stay here and I'll call you the minute I hear from him."

Adam strode out of the house before Monique could respond.

The next forty-five minutes went by painfully slowly. Adam spent the time driving around Orlando hoping he would somehow find Cadence somewhere. It was ridiculous, but he just couldn't stand doing nothing.

He also did a lot of thinking, questioning his decision. Had he made the right move or should he have told the police the truth? What if Michael hurt Cadence? What if he never called Adam back? The thoughts kept swimming around in his head, over and over again.

Finally the cell phone rang. Adam was driving down a small side street, so he pulled the car over to the shoulder to take the call.

"It's Michael."

"Where is she?" Adam immediately demanded.

"Adam, she's fine, man, I promise. Maybe a little pissed, but she's fine. Did you take care of the cops?"

"I told them the money had been recovered and it had all been a mistake. I'm sure they'll still investigate the assaults, but the embezzlement seems to be handled."

"All right, all right."

"Where is Cadence, Michael?" Adam repeated.

The instructions were simple.

"There's a plaza at the corner of Hiawassee and Old Winter Garden. Go around to the cargo bay in the back and up the stairs to unit 8B. She's in that unit."

"This is over now, Michael, and I assume you are as far away as possible from Orlando right now. Stay away or I will have you hauled to jail in a minute," Adam stated in a cold, deadly voice. "But let me make it clear, if Cadence is hurt in any way, there is nowhere on earth you will be able to hide from me."

Adam hung up the phone without waiting for a response, then did a sharp U-turn when it was safe. He knew exactly where the plaza was located and he planned to get there at twice the speed limit. The truck was barely parked before he was running up the back stairs two at a time. He burst into the room that Michael had specified, but it was empty except for a dusty chair lying on its side. Adam looked wildly around the dark room, but there was no sign of Cadence.

His worst nightmare had come true and Adam could only stand there, dumbfounded and devastated.

After letting Cadence speak to Adam on the phone, Michael had re-covered her mouth, and he said very little to her. She watched him leave the room for about ten minutes, but could still hear him outside as he spoke on the cell phone. When he came back in, she watched him dig around in the far corner of the room, then swing a large knapsack over his shoulder.

"Everything's going to be fine," Michael told her. "Just relax and you'll be out of here soon."

Then he was gone.

Cadence sat in that chair with her hands tied and mouth covered for what seemed like hours. Occasionally, she heard voices and footsteps outside, but there was no telling how far away they were. Finally, she got tired of being patient and tried to find a way out of her situation.

Eventually, she managed to tip over the chair until it fell onto its side, taking her with it. Cadence felt the impact hard on her shoulder, and was frozen by the pain for a couple of minutes. She then took a deep breath and started to wiggle around, trying to slip her bound arms out over the back of the chair. It was awkward and uncomfortable, but she finally managed to get free.

Cadence rolled over until she was able to get on her feet. She than ran over to the wall just beside the door. If anyone came into the room, she didn't want them to see her. Her hands were still bound behind her and her mouth still taped, so she knew she would need every advantage on her side.

She stayed there, poised and alert, for another stretch of time, but nothing happened and no one came. At one point, Cadence considered leaving the room, but the idea of wandering around that neighborhood in her condition seemed more dangerous than staying where she was. Finally, fear replaced her anger, and she slumped to the floor, then curled herself up as tight as possible. *Adam, please find me*, she pleaded silently.

Fear eventually turned to desolation, then the tears started to flow.

"Cadence." Adam uttered her name in a voice just above a whisper. His head hung and he bit his bottom lip hard, trying not to give in to crippling panic.

He looked around the room one more time, then swung around to leave. As he stepped toward the door, he heard a small noise coming from somewhere on his right. Adam stopped in his tracks and listened again. There was only silence, but something made Adam step back and swing the door closed.

He could barely make out the shape of someone lying on the floor with their knees bent into their chest.

"Cadence?"

She opened her eyes and they were glazed.

"Oh God, Cadence!"

Adam dropped to the floor and pulled her into his arms.

Chapter 31

It was after eleven o'clock that night before Cadence fell asleep. They were both in bed and Adam was lying beside her with his arms holding her tight. His hand slowly and softly brushed over her forehead. The late-night news was playing on the television in the background.

After Adam had found Cadence and confirmed that she was all right, he carried her out to his truck. He called Monique on the drive back to the house to let her know everything was okay. The three of them spent most of the evening talking about what had happened and trying to come to terms with Michael's actions.

Adam also spoke to Peter to see how he was doing and give him an update. It went without saying that he would be welcomed back to Iris Custom Homes as the controller, and both men agreed that it wasn't worth the risk to tell anyone else about Michael's actions.

Now, as Adam relaxed in bed, he was too wired to fall asleep. Cadence was right beside him and he was touching her, but there was a part of him that was afraid he would wake up and she would be gone. While standing in that dark, dingy room and thinking that he had lost her forever, Adam would have given anything to get her back—his business, his money, his life. It was a sobering realization.

He knew he was in love with her, though he had yet to tell her that, but he had not realized the depth of that love until today. He wasn't even sure he understood it.

He thought he had been in love with his ex-wife for most of his adult life, and it had always meant making more money, buying more stuff, and being more indulgent in order to be good enough for her. Once he stopped trying, the relationship had fallen apart. Yet with Cadence, he truly felt worthy of her love because he would gladly go back to being dirt poor as long as she was in his life.

Cadence shifted in the bed and snuggled closer to him. He kissed the top her head and whispered the words he had been bursting to share.

"I love you, Cadence Carter."

She didn't wake up, but Adam thought he saw the hint of a smile on her face. He closed his eyes and finally drifted to sleep.

Somewhere in his subconscious, Adam heard the details of the news broadcast.

"The police say the victim was shot at least three times in the chest. They don't know the motive of the attack, but suspect it was drug-related. Again, a male victim, identified as Michael Donovan of Orlando, has been found shot to death in his car near an exit of the I-75 just south of Saint Petersburg . . ."